MORTAL HEART

AN ALICE WORTH WORLD NOVEL

LISA EDMONDS

CITY OWL
PRESS

MORTAL HEART
Alice Worth World, Book 1

CITY OWL PRESS
www.cityowlpress.com

Cover Design by Artscandare Book Cover Design. All stock photos licensed appropriately.

Edited by Heather McCorkle.

For information on subsidiary rights, please contact the publisher at info@cityowlpress.com.

Print Edition ISBN: 978-1-64898-252-1

Digital Edition ISBN: 978-1-64898-253-8

Printed in the United States of America

This book is dedicated to my mother, Shirley Connell Edmonds (1943-2022) and to my second mother, Jacqueline Kitchen Longino (1953-2022). You are both forever and always in my heart.

PRAISE FOR LISA EDMONDS

"Edmonds's prose is energetic...Alice is both spunky and self-deprecating, with incredibly advanced magical powers...There is promise in Edmonds's melding of the supernatural and the everyday."
- *Publishers Weekly*

"Alice is a pretty badass heroine who has potential to be one of my favorite in the genre. She takes a beating, heals herself, and goes back into the fray. The plot is fast-paced and revolves around an excellent magical mystery with earth shattering consequences should something go askew. I loved Alice's backstory and learning how this world works. I look forward to seeing what is in store for Alice in the next book."
- *All Things Urban Fantasy*

"Edmonds's suspenseful second urban fantasy novel is just as action-packed and entertaining as the first... Edmonds has an eye for both detail and entertaining characters, and her story is fun and energetic... Readers will enjoy this installment and look forward to more in the continuing saga of Alice Worth."
- *Publishers Weekly*

"What a cracking read...ages since I read a new fantasy story that's gripped me like this, that I so enjoyed. It's up there with my favourite reads and I hope Lisa is hard at work with the next book."
- *Jeannie Zelos Book Reviews*

"There is NOTHING better than finding a fantastic new paranormal series. *Lisa Edmonds* has started a series that grabbed and held my attention...Heart of Malice successfully shows me the new world as it's experienced. With a little info here...and a little info there, I wasn't bombarded all at once and I got to see it all live and in action."
- *Stacey is Sassy*

"Add everything together, great writing, great characters, interesting pasts, and great plotting, I can't wait to read more! Highly recommend!"
- *Librarian, Penny Noble*

"A nice mystery wrapped up in suspense and a few hotties to top it off! A perfect way to describe Heart of Fire—a paranormal romance with a set of characters that pull the reader into the story."
- *InD'tale, Jacey Lee*

"Lisa Edmonds has made an instant fan of me. I look forward to reading the next case that requires Alice's special set of skills."
- *The Reading Cafe*

"The Alice Worth series quickly turned into a must-read series for me. As soon as you think you have a handle on what she can do, another level of power is revealed. She truly is a bad-ass and it's amazing to witness what she can do. As with book one, I didn't want to stop reading when the book ended. I look forward to seeing what book three will bring to the table."
- *Urban Fantasy Investigations*

"Ancient evils threaten Edmonds's magical PI heroine in this fun fifth Alice Worth urban fantasy... The tangled threads and shifting supernatural alliances make for a gripping mystery...Return to Edmonds's delightfully imaginative world."
- *Publishers Weekly*

"Alice is the type of Heroine I live to read about and scour the net looking for others of her ilk. Tough, no-nonsense, a bit damaged, yet so real and full of compassion and needing love yet afraid of it when it finds them. Edmonds can't get book three out fast enough as far as I am concerned."
- *Boundless Book Reviews*

"10 New Urban Fantasy Series You Need to Read: Alice Worth is a

Mage Private Investigator with a ghost sidekick and some really cool magic. She can conjure a cold fire whip! There are vampires and werewolves and all our favorite old school UF elements. I wish more people were talking about this series."
- *Vampire Book Club*

"Edmonds's imaginative description of the underworld is as fun as it is fascinating, and the twists and turns along the way will keep readers hooked. Series fans will be pleased to find it's still going strong."
- *Publishers Weekly*

"Edmonds is at her best, fusing supernatural suspense with down-to-earth family drama. This is a treat for series fans."
- Publisher's Weekly

ALSO BY LISA EDMONDS

AUTHOR'S NOTE

This book, as with all other titles in this series, contains scenes that depict violence, death, sex, and some topics that may be disturbing to some readers.

A complete list of content notes can be found on my website at https://www.lisaedmonds.com/contentnotes

From the moment the stars formed and the universe began, the archangel Michael had wielded his blade like an artist.

Even in battle, as angelic armies under his command clashed with the most powerful forces of evil in the primordial darkness of Chaos and Old Night, Michael moved with a deliberate grace that awed allies and enemies alike. Every cut was as precise as a surgeon's and just as clinical. Never a single wasted sword-stroke, false start, or wrong step. Michael was perfection given form.

Michael pronounced judgement in much the same way as he fought: meticulously, unhurriedly, perfectly...and without mercy.

PROLOGUE

RONAN

RONAN, THE FALLEN ARCHANGEL ONCE KNOWN AS REMIEL, THE Thunder of God, held himself still by sheer force of will as Michael cut into his flesh without sympathy or emotion. If he moved and a cut went wrong, Michael would heal him and start over. He'd be damned if he'd give the archangel of archangels the satisfaction of prolonging his torment.

The words Michael sliced into the skin over Ronan's ribcage recorded the three phases of his trial, written in the language of angels. Each cut pulsed with angelic magic. The cuts would never fully heal. For all his days, he wouldn't be able to escape the reminder of his failures as an archangel *and* a man—as if his bound wings and mortal body weren't punishment enough.

Anger and hate, bitter as poison and heavy as lead, settled in Ronan's stomach. The white-hot glare of celestial power glinting on Michael's bladed wings hurt his eyes, but he refused to close them or pass out to spare himself pain. He was certainly many things, but a coward wasn't one of them.

Finally, after what felt like a century, Michael finished carving and loomed silently over Ronan's prone and bloody body, his sword at his side. The archangel of archangels and the man stared at each other, neither willing to look away or even blink.

Before Michael could command him to rise, Ronan managed to get to his hands and knees. A hundred years of imprisonment and torment had taken a brutal toll. His hands slipped in his own blood. The words in his side burned mercilessly. His angelic sword hung heavy on his back. He'd never noticed its weight before, but now it seemed a burden of a thousand pounds.

"This is your sentence," Michael said very formally. His voice came from all directions, like hundreds of voices speaking all at once. That was how angelic voices sounded to mortals. After eons of speaking in the angelic language, Ronan doubted he'd ever become accustomed to the near-deafening noise.

"You will live a mortal life among the true humans, in a body as close to human as we can make you," Michael continued. "You may not take your own life, either by action or inaction. You may not use your wings or your celestial sword, under penalty of eternal damnation. Once your mortal life ends, you will be judged once more. If you have lived a righteous life in accordance with our laws, you may regain your angelic form. If not, I will cast your soul into Nothingness. Do you understand these rules as I have listed them?"

"Yes." It was the first word Ronan had spoken in a very long time. Blood bubbled up and ran down his chin. His entire body hurt. Other than the words Michael had cut into him, he had no sense of where one pain ended and another began. Still, he'd had quite enough of Michael towering over him.

With a Herculean effort, Ronan staggered to his feet. He was tall, but Michael was taller, even without spreading his razor-edged wings... which he did as soon as Ronan rose, just to make a point, Ronan thought.

"Always you are prideful." Michael's voice remained toneless, though Ronan saw anger in his glacier-blue eyes. "You believe yourself to be as great and mighty as the greatest of us and able to break angelic law whenever it suits you. You believe you are right, when we, in all our eternal wisdom, are wrong."

"I'm not delusional. I never thought myself as mighty as you."

Ronan wiped blood from his mouth with the back of his hand. "And I never broke angelic law without good reason."

"There are no good reasons to break angelic law."

"I wanted to spare my sister Freya from great suffering."

"You were granted neither the power nor the right to spare anyone from suffering." Michael remained implacable. "Nor did I grant you leave to wield your celestial sword in any battle outside my command. You have always known these laws and the consequences of breaking them."

Ronan clenched his fists. He could have reminded Michael that if he hadn't raised his sword against the Titan Typhon in the Underworld, Typhon and the goddess Ammit, Devourer of Hearts, would have killed him and his companions. Then they would have ascended to the human world to slaughter thousands—or millions—but that argument would fall as much on deaf ears today as it ever had before. Michael did not care about Ronan's motives and never would. Angelic law could not be broken. Full stop.

"I don't apologize for raising my sword against Typhon," Ronan said, straightening with difficulty. "Nor do I apologize for trying to save Freya's daughter."

"And so you suffer."

"I can never fully atone for the hurt I caused Freya by promising and then failing to prevent her daughter's death. No punishment you can conceive can heal her pain." Ronan gestured at the words cut into his side. "Not even this."

"Perhaps not." Michael gave him a grave nod and fluttered his bladed wings. "But you broke angelic law without remorse. Justice was called for, and justice was done."

Ronan gave him a bloody, bitter half-smile. "Was it?"

As he'd expected, his tormentor ignored his question. "Where do you wish to be taken to begin your sentence?" Michael asked.

Of all the worlds and realms Ronan knew, there was only one place he *could* go now, and only one person he could trust to care for him until his mortal body healed.

"The same place I was when you took me away for my torment and trial," he said. "The home of my sister-in-arms, Alice Worth."

With one precise movement, Michael used his sword to cut through the boundary between the realm of the angels and the human world. "Then go to her. This realm is now closed to you."

It's been closed to me for a very, very long time, Ronan thought.

Before he had a chance to tell Michael that—not that it would have mattered anyway—the floor gave way beneath Ronan's feet, and he was gone.

1

RONAN

The two skinny scumbags sitting at the other end of the bar put themselves on Ronan's shit list when he walked past and caught a strong whiff of sulfur mixed in with their body odor. Human minions of some low-level demon, he figured. They hadn't even bothered to shower off the telltale rotten-egg stench of their master. If there was anything he hated more than demon trash, it was *lazy* demon trash.

The men moved themselves higher on the list by loudly mocking his all-black attire and then catcalling every woman in the bar. So he went out to the Rusty Pelican's gravel parking lot, figured out which two-tone shitbox was theirs, and strategically punctured its tires in such a way that they'd probably make it at least a couple of miles from the bar before they ended up stranded on the side of the road.

And since he was getting paid by the bartender Mireille's daddy to make sure she got home safely, and *not* to break the skulls of these two idiots, he would have let it go at four flat tires if he hadn't discovered they had a terrified young woman locked in the trunk of their car.

Now he had a problem. A big, annoying problem that required very serious consideration and another shot of tequila, or three.

No, make that *two* big, annoying problems...and a tantalizing little mystery.

Problem one: René Richards had paid him a ridiculous amount of money to babysit his youngest daughter and make sure her abusive boyfriend came nowhere near her, plus a hefty bonus if Ronan delivered the boyfriend to René personally for what René referred to as *disposal*.

Problem two: Thanks to his still-acute hearing, Ronan had overheard enough of the demon-minions' conversation to figure out they planned to sell the young woman in the trunk to a contact they called Ace. That meant he'd stumbled upon not just a kidnapping but a trafficking ring. In his centuries as a bounty hunter, he'd learned to recognize the signs.

The only good trafficker was a dead trafficker, as far as he was concerned. Simply freeing the woman wouldn't be enough; the whole ring had to be dismantled and its victims freed. At the moment his only leads were the minions and the girl in the trunk. If Mireille's boyfriend showed up, Ronan would have to choose between his paying gig and following the minions to their contact.

Those problems made the tantalizing little mystery of the blonde woman in the corner booth feel relatively unimportant...and yet even the equally pleasant thoughts of René's ten-grand bonus and stomping the skulls of the minions, Ace, Ace's boss, Ace's boss's boss, and everyone else in the trafficking ring couldn't make him ignore her.

In the Broken World, where thousands of species of supernatural beings roamed the land, air, and sea thanks to fractured boundaries between realms, he would have assumed the blonde was a Valkyrie on Earth hunting prey for pay or sport. This world had relatively few such beings, however, so she was likely human.

At any other time in his very long existence, that would have probably been the end of his interest. But he was human now too, more or less, and that meant he noticed how sweet her mouth looked as she sipped the same brand of tequila as the bottle in front of him. And he imagined how she'd feel beneath him—or on top of him—with her fingernails digging into his shoulders and her body writhing at his touch.

Maybe she wasn't human after all. The way she made his skin tingle and blood rush could mean she was the daughter of an incubus or succubus. That would certainly explain his reaction.

She seemed to be watching him without watching him. He recognized that skill immediately as one he used himself on a regular basis. She was a hunter, a warrior. He liked the taste of warrior women more than the finest tequila.

Ronan scowled, shifted his weight on his creaky barstool, and downed the rest of his drink. He had work to do. He couldn't afford to think with his dick—especially when he had to figure out what the hell to do about the girl in the trunk. Thanks to his enhanced senses, he could tell she was relatively unharmed and could breathe normally. As much as he disliked the idea, for now she had to stay where she was so he could follow the minions to their contact. That seemed like the best and probably only way to find out more about the traffickers. As soon as he'd ascertained the next link in the chain, he'd find out what she knew and then get her to safety.

Meanwhile, Mireille Richards pulled pints, poured shots, and glanced at the door every few minutes, waiting for the man she loved, who'd given her the bruise she'd covered so carefully with makeup.

Oblivious to why Ronan had sat at the bar for the entirety of every shift she'd worked since Tuesday, Mireille used a towel to wipe the scuffed bartop and leaned toward him, her arms folded under her cleavage. Ronan kept his gaze on her face and didn't let it stray to her neckline. She was a lonely kid with a violent bookie father, desperately in love with an abusive punk, and he wasn't some drunken predator cruising the bar for tail.

"Hey, Johnny." She called him that because he wouldn't tell her his name and he wore all black. "You're quiet tonight."

"I'm quiet every night," he said, his voice gruff.

"Oh, he talks!" She giggled and tucked some stray hair behind her ear. "What do you do, Johnny?"

I put people like your boyfriend in dumpsters with the rest of the trash, he wanted to say, but didn't. Telling her she deserved better than abuse would fall on deaf ears. Even disposing of the boyfriend wouldn't solve the problem, since she'd likely find a replacement soon enough, but he'd settle for what he could get.

"I'm between jobs at the moment," he said finally.

"You and everybody else here. I'm lucky to have this job." She lowered her voice. "If you need some money, I could probably get Carl to give you some work. He needs someone to watch the door, haul kegs, that kind of thing. You look like you could do that." She reached for his bicep, probably intending to give it a playful squeeze.

He moved out of reach. "I'm not looking for that kind of job." Or flirtations from a vulnerable twenty-one-year-old woman he'd been hired to protect.

Her smile vanished. "Fine. Never mind. Don't know why I bother trying to be nice. Everyone's an asshole. Even you, Johnny."

His conscience pricked him. More than once, Alice had called him an asshole, and he'd certainly deserved it every time. He'd left her house fifteen days ago and hadn't checked in to let her know he was all right. No doubt she understood why he'd left, but he also knew he was an asshole for leaving, and doubly so for not at least calling her.

Mireille had genuinely tried to help him, and he'd all but slapped her hand for trying. She was the first person to do something nice for him since he'd walked out of Alice and Sean's house.

"Thanks for the offer," he said before Mireille could storm away. "I've got something lined up."

"Oh." She put her hands on her hips. "You could have just said that, you know."

"What can I say?" He sipped his tequila. "I'm an asshole."

Her lips twitched. Before she could reply, her attention went to something going on behind him.

Ronan turned just in time to see a burly, bearded man take a swing at a shorter, dark-haired man holding an empty mug that had probably contained the beer now soaking the burly man's clothing. The shorter man backpedaled to avoid the punch and crashed into a table, spilling the drinks of the three other men sitting there. The men at the table jumped to their feet and started swinging.

Several patrons sitting at the bar burst out laughing. Others jeered or egged the fighters on. Mireille swore and ran for the back office, presumably to get Carl, the bar owner.

Ronan sighed and turned back to his drink. As he did, he caught sight of the blonde woman watching the scuffle, her chin in her hand. He interpreted her expression as the mild interest of someone who'd seen lots of better fights but figured they might as well watch this one for lack of other, more interesting entertainment.

One of the brawlers took an impressive uppercut to the chin and stumbled back toward the blonde woman's booth. Just before he collided with her table, she raised her right foot, planted the sole of her boot right in his lower back, and sent him sprawling. Ronan got the distinct impression that was a move she'd used a number of times before. His interest ratcheted up another couple of notches.

She glanced up and caught Ronan's eye before her sharp blue gaze flicked to something going on behind him. The back of his neck prickled.

He half-turned and caught a badly thrown bottle less than a second before it smashed into the side of his head. The man who'd thrown it blinked at him, stupefied. Even as drunk as he was, the bottle-thrower seemed to realize Ronan shouldn't have been able to catch that bottle, much less sense it coming. The bottle-thrower backpedaled into another man who'd picked up a chair, probably intending to use it as a weapon. Both men went down in a tangle.

Ronan spotted the demon minions get up from the bar and head for the back door. They probably figured they could duck out during the fight and avoid paying their bar tab. *Nice.* Just when he thought his opinion of them couldn't possibly get any lower.

Carl, Mireille, and a man Ronan didn't recognize finally emerged from the back office. Carl and the other man carried baseball bats that looked like they'd seen their share of action.

"Cut this shit out!" Carl shouted at the brawlers, brandishing his bat. "What's going on, Gerald? Logan? You assholes forget you were on your last warning?" He and his male companion started breaking up the fight, applying judicious whacks of their bats to the brawlers who were too drunk or defiant to stand down immediately. Many patrons seemed as entertained by this part of the proceedings as the fight itself.

Meanwhile, Ronan stuck some cash under his glass and ambled to the front door as if he'd simply had enough for one night. Mireille already had a broom and dustpan in hand. She'd be busy with cleanup at least long enough for him to follow the minions out to the parking lot. After he got some answers out of them, he'd have to choose whether to continue babysitting duty or go bust some heads.

Just before he went outside, he glanced at the corner booth. The blonde had vanished like smoke. The only signs of her presence were an empty glass, cash on the table, and the man she'd kicked, who sat slumped in a chair massaging his back. Dirt in the shape of a boot print marked his T-shirt in the area of his left kidney.

The moment he'd locked gazes with the blonde, Ronan had figured out two things. The first was that she knew who he was, somehow, though strangely he had no recollection of ever meeting her. That raised the disturbing possibility that he'd suffered some kind of memory loss during his imprisonment. *Yet another reason to hate Michael*, he thought.

His second—and much more pleasant—realization was the blonde's interest in him wasn't entirely professional. She'd tried to hide it, but he knew that hungry look. He'd seen it often enough over the millennia in the faces of human women and men he'd encountered, and in the mirror during the centuries since his Fall. And despite his anger, bitterness, and hollowness, his body responded in a primal way.

Michael had always mocked humans' desires for food and sex as pathetic pleasures of the flesh, but long ago Ronan had figured out the truth behind Michael's sneering. It was the concepts of *needing* and *wanting* anything that the archangel of archangels dismissed as beneath contempt for one as great as himself. Such a being desired nothing, or so Michael wanted others to believe. The truth was, Michael needed and wanted many things—most especially the obedience and devotion of all angels.

Twice Ronan had disobeyed Michael's laws, and for all his faithful service he'd never shown true devotion. In either punishment or retribution, Michael had sentenced him to live a long mortal life, subject to pain, hunger, grief, want, and need.

Ronan wanted the blonde, and that was as much a part of Michael's punishment as his bound wings and unusable celestial sword. And with that thought, Ronan's desire shriveled on the vine.

He still needed to find out how she knew him, so he could ascertain whether he'd lost memories. Once he had that answer, he had no more use for her.

"Wait, Johnny!" Mireille called.

Ignoring her, Ronan shoved the door open and went outside, letting it slam closed behind him.

2

ARKADY

ARKADY WOODALL, FORMER PSYOPS SPECIAL FORCES SOLDIER turned private investigator, sat cross-legged on the hood of a two-tone rust bucket in the parking lot of the Rusty Pelican. She took a swig from a bottle of mid-range tequila and smiled in the way her business partner Alice Worth called "predatory." Generally that smile made people with even the slightest sense of self-preservation run in the opposite direction.

She didn't want her prey to run, though, so she switched to a much friendlier expression, let her hair down from her ponytail, and waited.

As for the names of the driver and passenger of this car, she'd taken a page from Alice's book of standard operating procedures and given them nicknames: Ren and Stimpy. Really she supposed it was insulting to the cartoon characters they were named after, but it was the first pair of names that popped into her head when she spotted them and it had stuck in her brain.

Fortunately, she didn't have to wait long for the dipshits to appear. They'd snuck out the bar's rear door without paying their tab and then gone into the trees out back to take a piss and hide long enough to make sure the coast was clear. That had given her plenty of time to get situated before they appeared in the parking lot.

Ren, the driver, stood five-ten, looked to be about thirty, and had shaved his head to disguise a receding hairline. Stimpy seemed a few years younger, about six-two and wiry, with long hair that would benefit from a cut and some conditioner.

When they saw her, they both licked their lips without seeming the least bit apprehensive about her presence, or angry that her ass had dented their car's hood. She supposed they'd probably stolen the car. She'd also taken off her shirt and sat drinking tequila straight from the bottle in tight jeans and her second-best bra. She had it on good authority she looked really fucking fantastic in this bra. In her experience, men's brains ceased to function when they saw a fine pair of tits.

The dipshits didn't seem to have a whole lot of brains to begin with. They grinned from ear to ear as they approached. So far, so good.

"Hey," she said in a breathy voice.

"Hey yourself, sugar." Ren punched his buddy's bicep and chuckled. "Looks like we've got some company for the evening."

Stimpy had a laugh like a braying donkey. "Yeah, man, and it's my turn to go first."

Arkady swayed and giggled, feigning extreme drunkenness. "M'sorry...is this your car?" She hiccupped loudly and added, "I thought it was mine."

The breeze shifted. Her nose twitched. The odor of sulfur wafted from the dipshits' skin and clothes.

A thrill of anticipation ran down her spine. The evening was *definitely* looking up. First a halfway decent bar fight to watch, and now she'd get to kick the asses of two demon servants. She had to tighten her grip on the tequila bottle to keep from rubbing her hands in glee.

But right at that moment—damn it all to hell and back—Ronan, Alice's mysterious runaway houseguest, came storming out the front door of the Rusty Pelican like a tall, dark, and gorgeous jackass and ruined her entire plan.

Ronan took in the scene with the same quick, highly trained appraisal she'd noted earlier. Once he'd assessed the demon-servant dipshits, his gaze raked over her. His expression remained impassive, but she thought she saw something like disgust in his eyes. Only minutes before, when their gazes met in the bar, he'd looked at her with interest. Now, even in her second-best bra and tight jeans, she might as well have been a bug.

Her eyes narrowed. *Asshole.*

Cold and silent, Ronan's stare fixed on the demon servants. Ren and Stimpy pulled guns and took cover behind their car. Apparently they had a little bit of common sense after all.

No sense getting shot in the crossfire. Arkady rolled across the hood and landed in the gravel on Ronan's side of the car. The tequila bottle broke on impact, spraying her with shards of glass and wasted booze. To make matters worse, sharp-edged rocks cut into her bare arms and torso. She gritted her teeth and stayed down, out of the line of fire.

Footsteps crunched in the gravel on the other side of the car as one of the demon servants moved to the back of the vehicle. "Get lost, whoever the hell you are," the driver, Ren, warned Ronan. "Or I put two holes in the bitch we got in the trunk and six more in you."

Shit, shit, shit, Arkady thought. This was not the first time she'd had a good plan, only to have it go to hell in the proverbial handbasket thanks to the not-so-timely interference of a guy who assumed his "help" was required. But despite his big entrance, Ronan didn't respond to Ren's threats—nor did he move. What was he waiting for, a trumpet fanfare?

The dipshits, on the other hand, had plenty to say. "Is this your bitch?" Stimpy asked, pointing over the hood at Arkady. "Fine piece of ass. If there's anything left when we get done, you can have her back."

Ronan still said nothing. He seemed to be locked in some kind of macho staring contest with Ren. Stimpy took a few steps forward, his gun still pointed at Ronan's chest. She wanted to yell, *Are you assholes going to fight, or is this some kind of foreplay?*

She'd never been one to wait for anyone else to throw the first punch anyway. Slowly, she reached into her boot and soundlessly slid a knife from its hidden sheath.

Ronan hadn't looked at her, but she still felt certain he'd seen her pull the knife. Glancing at her would have tipped the others off that she was up to something besides lying drunk in the gravel. It took a lot of training and practice to be able to resist reflexively looking at movement, especially in a tense, potentially deadly situation. He might be an arrogant prick, but he knew what he was doing.

Without looking at each other, it was damn near impossible to coordinate their attack, but Arkady knew her target had to be Ren. He was a hair's-breadth away from shooting the poor girl in the trunk, while Stimpy had his gun on Ronan. Only their first move would take the dipshits by surprise and she was the only one with the drop on both of them. She was willing to bet Ronan's thoughts had mirrored her own.

"Look, you asshole, I *said* to get—" Ren began.

Before he could finish the sentence, Arkady rolled to her feet and threw her knife in one smooth motion. The blade, matte black, nearly invisible in the darkness, and sharpened until it could cut through bone like butter, buried itself in the center of Ren's heart. He was dead before he had a chance to grunt or fire a shot. His body dropped like a sack of dog food.

Bullseye, Arkady thought with satisfaction as she hit the gravel again. The pain barely registered this time. The rush of adrenaline, on the other hand, felt really damn good.

Gravel crunched beside her. It had to be the other dipshit, since Ronan was a good twenty feet away. She reached for another knife, in case Stimpy didn't go down easy.

A heavy boot connected to a denim-clad leg crushed her right arm into the gravel. Now *that* she felt. Stimpy had moved much faster than she'd anticipated. Sometimes demons made their servants drink vamp blood to make them stronger and faster.

With a furious curse, she twisted and used her other hand to pull her spare knife. Before she could stab him, however, he hit her wrist with the side of his hand in a lightning-quick move that made her vision go white with pain. Her fingers went numb. For the first time in many years, Arkady Woodall dropped her knife.

Her attacker grabbed the blade, turned, and threw it faster than even she could have managed on her best day. She heard a gurgle and the sound of a body hitting the ground. *Ronan. Oh no.*

She drew back her left fist and punched the leg pinning her right arm with all the force she could muster. Her fist connected with solid muscle. She might as well have punched a steel plate. It sure as hell hurt like she had.

She looked up. Ronan towered over her. Well, he wasn't dead, but how the hell had he gotten to her so quickly, and more importantly, why was he grinding her arm into the gravel?

When their stares met, Arkady couldn't help but notice even the vamps hadn't looked down their noses at her as much as Ronan did at this moment.

So he might be gorgeous and highly trained and *almost* as good at knife-throwing as herself, and smell like leather and have eyes as perfectly blue as ancient glacier ice, and Lord almighty that ass—

She lost her train of thought for a moment.

Okay, he was obviously some kind of supernatural badass. But did she want anything to do with someone *even more* conceited and arrogant than a vamp?

Abso-fucking-lutely not.

Moving like lightning, she wrapped her legs around his and twisted, knocking him over. As he fell, she flipped to her feet and dove at him, knife in hand, intending to land with her knee and all her weight right in his gut—or lower.

Sky, cars, and gravel whirled around her, and one blink later she was on her back, pinned in place. His eyes, edged with the tiniest glint of silver, were less than six inches from her own. What the hell did the silver mean? No time to wonder about it right now.

She twisted and bucked, trying to use his weight and body position to throw him off her, but his balance was perfect and all she managed to do was grind her back deeper into the sharp gravel. So she stuck the tip of her knife through the denim of his jeans and into his skin right at his groin, just deep enough to draw blood but without severing anything important. Yet.

Ronan grabbed her wrist and squeezed in the exact spot that caused maximum pain. She tried to head-butt him and break his nose. Somehow he jerked back just in time. She felt the crown of her head brush his bristly chin. He squeezed her wrist even tighter, but she stubbornly held onto her knife. The price was numb fingers and white-hot agony that ran all the way up her arm.

They stared at each other. Her chest heaved, but the bastard wasn't even breathing hard. "Get the fuck off me," Arkady said. "Or you're a dead man."

"I know your voice, but not your face." Ronan's eyes darkened. "Who are you? How do you know me?"

His voice was deeper and rougher than she'd expected. And if she wasn't mistaken, the roughness wasn't just a result of disuse. His entire body felt taut, like a volcano about to explode. Alarm bells went off in her head. She recognized that kind of tension—she'd seen it often enough in soldiers and Vamp Court enforcers under so much pressure they were on the verge of breaking. And when they snapped, they had a tendency to take others with them.

This time when she tried to buck him off, she managed to throw him off-balance just enough to free one hand. She went for what should have been a solid right hook to his jaw.

Instead, Ronan caught her fist in his much-larger hand and squeezed. "I asked who you are," he said coldly. "Talk."

The Pelican's front door flew open and bounced off the outside wall. Angry male voices drifted across the lot, along with the sounds of feet scuffing in the gravel and fists striking flesh. Several of the combatants had apparently decided to take their dispute outside.

Arkady glanced in their direction, then up at Ronan. "Company's coming," she said in her most annoying sing-song voice. "We're either gonna have to hide these bodies or start killing witnesses. Thoughts?"

3

RONAN

THE BLONDE WOMAN RAISED HER EYEBROWS AT RONAN, AS IF daring him to keep her pinned until the brawlers spotted them.

This woman was made of solid brass, Ronan decided. Highly trained, unflappable, and undaunted even now. She'd stabbed him, but just deep enough to make her point and no farther. She'd given him the choice to back off and live, or push his luck and end up with a sliced femoral artery.

He liked it. All of it. Even the pain. Maybe especially the pain.

This desire could all be part of Michael's plan, but with his body against hers, Ronan had a hard time remembering that. And up close he could tell she was entirely human. Not one drop of demon blood or anything else that could explain why the sight, touch, and smell of her burned in his blood like a drug.

She was right, though—they couldn't stay where they were. Even the Pelican's shifty patrons wouldn't ignore a man pinning a partially clothed woman on the ground. The last thing he needed was to be attacked by a drunken mob.

Ignoring the twinge in his upper thigh where she'd stabbed him, he let go of her hands and rolled off her body. He crouched next to the dead minions' car, out of sight of the men fighting near the bar's front

door. She did the same, still holding her blade. Its point dripped blood
—*his* blood. Her wrist had already begun to darken and swell where
he'd squeezed it, and her arms, side, and back bled where the gravel
had cut and embedded itself into her bare skin.

With a muttered curse, she picked broken glass out of her arms and
flexed her wrist to test its range of motion. "So? Hide the bodies?" she
prodded. "Or kill the bar patrons one at a time as they head this way?
We'd probably be doing society a favor."

He didn't disagree, but she didn't really mean it, he decided after
studying her expression. "I'll hide the bodies," he said. Staying low, he
made his way around the back of the car, where the older of the two
men had gone down with the blonde's knife in his heart. It had been
one hell of a throw, and not a lucky strike either. He was willing to bet
she could do it nine out of ten times. Possibly ten out of ten.

She retrieved her knife, an exquisite tactical blade he coveted, with
a matte black finish. It took a very sharp blade *and* a powerful throw to
go through a man's sternum. She wiped it on the dead man's shirt and
returned it to her boot.

"You want to stash 'em in the back seat or trunk?" she asked in an
undertone, jerking her head at the body. "Once we make some room in
the trunk, that is."

He kept his expression bland. "What do you think is in the trunk?"

"We both know what's in the trunk." She smiled thinly. "Or should
I say, *who*. The question is, what do we do about her?"

She'd known about the girl even before the car's driver threatened
to shoot into the trunk. Her reaction to his threat had made that clear.
But how? He doubted she was involved in the trafficking ring, but
everything about her was a mystery.

When he didn't immediately respond, she scowled. "Fine. While
you scratch yourself and wonder how I know things, *I'll* put the bodies
in the back seat before someone sees them." She glanced at the second
dead man and made a face. "You got him in the eye. That was a lucky
throw."

"No more lucky than yours," he retorted.

"I don't need luck." She smirked and blew on her fingertips. "Not
when I've got these skills."

Once she reclaimed her other knife—with another wrinkle of her nose as she pulled it from the younger man's eye socket—they put both bodies on the floor behind the front seats. Ronan covered them with the threadbare blanket that had doubled as a seat cover for the torn back seat, plus the empty fast food wrappers and other trash from the front seat as extra camouflage.

The blonde located her discarded T-shirt next to the car. It had fallen off the hood, gotten soaked with tequila, and covered with broken glass. She held it at arm's length and sighed. "Damn it, I loved this shirt." She glanced at him. "Be a gentleman and give me your shirt. Or your jacket."

"I'm not a gentleman." He couldn't keep the derision out of his voice. "Not even close."

He'd said that once before, but it took a moment for him to remember when and where. He'd said it to Alice in the so-called Broken World, he recalled, just before he'd brought her back to her own world. He'd said it playfully then, but this time his voice held all the bitterness in his heart.

To his surprise, the blonde woman chuckled softly. "I never thought you *were* a gentleman, sweet pea. I just thought I'd give you a chance to pretend." Before he could formulate a response, she jerked her head at the trunk. "Now, what to do about this girl? Take her somewhere safe?"

"I planned to kick some answers out of the demon minions, use them to find the rest of the trafficking ring, and then drop the lot of them on the cops' doorstep, or in a landfill, whichever turned out more warranted." He scowled. "You managed to destroy my plan."

"You destroyed *my* plan," she shot back. "All you had to do was stay in the damn bar for five more minutes and I would have found out everything those bozos knew, but *no*, you had to come prancing out here and wreck the whole thing."

The fact she'd planned to extract full confessions didn't surprise him in the least—and since he'd seen her in action, he didn't doubt her ability or willingness to do so. But now that the minions were dead and their respective plans had gone up in smoke, how could he find this mysterious contact called "Ace"? And what to do with the victim in the meantime?

And what about Mireille Richards, the reason he was in this damned parking lot in the first place?

His attention went to the bar's front door, where the second and lesser of tonight's drunken fistfights had finally fizzled out. As the half-dozen brawlers stumbled toward their vehicles, the blonde hopped onto the hood of the minions' car, grabbed his belt, and tried to pull him close.

When he resisted, the corners of her mouth turned up in a wry smile. "We don't need anyone getting suspicious about what's going on over here, do we? Play along, Ronan. Pretend you're into me, just for a few minutes. I promise my knives will stay in my boots."

She knew his name. Despite his misgivings, he liked the way she said it, drawing out the vowels. Perhaps sensing his uncertainty, she tugged on his belt again. This time he let her pull him close until his hips nestled against her inner thighs. The pose felt far more comfortable than he had any right to be. Her heat and scent made him painfully aware of how long it had been since he'd enjoyed the warmth between a woman's thighs.

He bent his head and brushed her ear with his lips. "How do you know me?"

"We have a mutual friend," she said softly. Her fingertips traveled over his abdominal muscles, following their hard lines, not as a lover might, but in a way that made him think she was assessing him somehow. Her voice hardened. "We met before you fucked off to find yourself, or whatever it is you're doing in dive bars like this one with lonely little bartenders."

"It's not what you think." He caught her hand before it slid into the waistband of his jeans and held on when she tried to free herself from his grip. "She's my client's daughter. He's paying me to keep an eye out for her abusive boyfriend."

She studied him for a long time. "Fine. I believe you."

With her free hand, she traced a lazy circle on his chest. Her nails were trimmed short—all the better for fighting—but that didn't stop him from imagining how they'd feel on his skin. "I guess you don't remember me. Not surprising." She grabbed his shirt and pulled his head down to hers. "I kept watch over you a few times while you slept," she murmured, her lips millimeters from his. "While the others had to be away."

Now he knew her voice. She'd been at his side while he lay sleeping at Alice's house. She'd talked to him for hours, more than once. He couldn't remember what she'd said—not one word—but he recalled feeling at peace listening to her speak. He also knew Alice would never have left someone alone with him unless she trusted that person entirely. Alice did not trust easily.

"You're a friend of Alice's." He drew back and looked into her eyes. "Tell me your name."

When she laughed, he scowled. "Quit playing games," he snapped. "I can easily find out who you are with one phone call."

"I was just remembering how many times I asked Alice, Sean, and Malcolm to tell me what you are." Her smile vanished. "And you haven't called Alice since you left without saying goodbye, you ungrateful shit. So don't pretend you'd call her now."

He opened his mouth, but she kept talking. "You hurt her deeply, you know. I don't like it when people hurt my friends. Especially half-dead bounty hunters who would have died in a ditch if it weren't for someone else's kindness."

They were once again the only people in the mostly empty lot, so he let go of her hand and took a step back. She didn't fight to hang onto his shirt, which probably meant she'd feigned all her flirtations.

Of course it was all for show, he berated himself. *She's here because I haven't checked in with Alice.* "That's between Alice and me," he said icily. "I owe no one else any explanations, least of all someone who won't tell me their name."

"Fine. I'm Arkady Woodall." She slid off the hood of the car and dusted her hands briskly, as if wiping off his touch. "I'm Alice's new business partner."

A private investigator, after he'd asked Alice not to come looking for him until he was ready. His hands squeezed into fists. "She sent you to find me?"

"No. She was actually pretty clear about *not* wanting me to look for you."

Ronan's shoulders relaxed. So Alice hadn't betrayed him after all. He wasn't surprised that Arkady looked completely unrepentant about going against Alice's wishes. She seemed the type to play by her own rules, like Alice. Interesting they'd decided to become business partners. They must have more in common than a penchant for pissing other people off.

"If that's the case, why did you track me down?" he demanded.

"Couple of reasons, none of which you need to worry your pretty little head about."

He growled under his breath. Another evasion. And here he'd thought *Alice* was difficult to get along with. "How did you find me?"

"I'm a detective. I detect." Arkady put her hands on her hips. "Are you done with the twenty questions? Can we get back to important things now?"

"There is no *we*, Miss Woodall." He headed for the rear of the vehicle, car keys in hand. He'd taken them from the driver's pocket.

She blocked his way and didn't back down when he almost ran into her. "The hell there's not," she hissed. "How do you think that poor girl's going to react if some big, hulking man dressed like the goddamn Grim Reaper opens that trunk?"

He glanced down at himself. That, he reflected, was a fair point.

Grudgingly, he handed her the keys. "Do you have a vehicle? Can you take her somewhere safe?"

"While you do what?"

"Nothing you need to worry your pretty little head about."

Her reaction to him using her own words against her caught him off guard. He'd expected and maybe even wanted an angry response. Instead, she smiled. Not the smirk he'd seen earlier, but a real, genuine smile that made him think he'd somehow just made her whole day. "Oh darlin', you don't want to play that game with someone like me," she said.

Oh, but he *did*. And she wanted him to play, too—her tone and smile made that obvious. He felt caught between anger that she'd somehow already figured out how to manipulate him and intrigued as to what she had in mind.

He should just walk away. Instead, he heard himself ask, "What game?"

He hadn't really expected her to answer—at least, not seriously. But she did. "The game where you devastate me with your superior wit and skill and put me back in my place." Her smile widened. "That's not a game you're going to win, sweet pea."

The way she looked at him indicated she somehow knew this was just the sort of challenge he liked. Or *had* liked, until his imprisonment and sentencing had siphoned away most of his will to exist, much less enjoy that existence.

"I don't have time for this," he said.

"Oh, yeah, I can see you're *swamped* with more interesting offers." She tossed him back the car keys. "Well, when you're done feeling sorry for yourself and decide to grow a pair, you know where to find me." Ruined shirt in hand, she turned on her heel and walked away.

She's Alice's business partner. A private investigator. A hunter. Bad, bad news all around. His brain made it clear what he should do. *Let her go*, it insisted as he watched her stride through the gravel in the direction of a small, dark blue SUV parked near his Harley. *Let her go and get back to the job René Richards is paying you to do, you moron.*

"I'm not feeling sorry for myself," he said.

"Yes, you are," she said over her shoulder. She didn't stop walking, and she didn't turn around. "Somebody kicked you in the balls, so you're going to curl up and cry and let them get away with it. No wonder you ran away from Alice's house. She'd put her boot up your ass for sulking like this. Big fucking baby."

He caught up with her before she finished speaking. He couldn't move nearly as quickly as before his imprisonment, but he still got from Point A to Point B much faster than a human.

"How could someone have kicked me in the balls if I don't have any?" he asked.

"Touché." She turned to him. Her smirk was back. "So maybe you *do* have balls, but they're feeling bruised these days and you're moping about it." She rested the tip of her index finger against his chest—not quite poking him, but making her point nonetheless. "I've taken my share of kicks in the metaphorical balls. We might get knocked down, but we gotta keep getting up, every time. You know why?"

"Why?" To his surprise, he wanted to know her answer.

For the first time, he saw a glint of pain in her hard blue eyes. A blink later, the pain vanished, replaced by the same wry cynicism he'd seen on her face all night. "Because fuck 'em," she said. "That's why."

"Very pithy." Despite his dark mood, he felt his mouth twitch. "Given your penchant for waxing philosophical, I expected something a bit more profound."

"Yeah, well, the longer you think about it, the more profound it gets." She eyed him. "Do you have a line on the people waiting for delivery of that girl in the trunk? Before you ask, I saw Ren knock on the trunk and say something before he and Stimpy went into the bar. And when I walked past, I heard whimpering. I can put two and two together."

He frowned. How did she manage to constantly make him feel three steps behind? "Ren and Stimpy?" he asked.

She shrugged. "Don't know their real names and don't care, but I had to call them something. Well, *do* you have a lead? We're both bored and I don't know about you, but I feel like kicking some asses."

He'd never met a woman like this in all his eons of existence. Suddenly her partnership with Alice made more sense. Alice thrived on new challenges and unexpected twists, and Arkady Woodall seemed the embodiment of both.

When he said nothing, she poked his chest hard and added, "Come on. If you were looking for a sign to quit moping, I'm it."

Irritated, he caught her hand to keep her from poking him again. And that was when it happened. Like a bolt of lightning, the vision seared him from the inside out.

Bloody, battered, and breathing hard, Arkady crouched with her back against the wall, clutching a knife that dripped thick, dark blood. Something had ripped her clothes to shreds and her feet were bare.

The room they were in was dimly lit and smelled of sulfur and rot. The stone floor and walls radiated heat. He gripped the bars of his cage and tried to pull them apart, but they wouldn't budge. He felt weak and lightheaded, and he had no magic and no weapons. No way to defend himself or anyone else.

Someone laughed mockingly—someone he couldn't see, standing in the shadows to his left. "Strange that after all you've been through and seen, you end up dying here," an unfamiliar voice said. "Any last words, my sweetness?"

He thought the voice had addressed him, but Arkady responded instead. She rose, spat out some blood, and wiped her mouth with the back of her hand. "Just the ones I figured would be my last," she said. "Which are, fuck you."

She'd barely finished the sentence when a knife wielded by that unseen tormentor plunged into her heart. Without a sound, she fell.

"No!" He tried to get through the bars of the cage. To his surprise, they gave way easily, as if the cage door had swung open. He flung it aside and charged ahead.

He heard a thud and a grunt at the same moment his brain recognized the smell of cool night air and the sound of his boots crunching on gravel-covered asphalt. No odor of rotten eggs or filth.

Take the curse, he'd shouted at Michael again and again. *Take the damn curse and give it to someone who wants it.*

But of course Michael hadn't taken his curse of foresight, because that would have been a reprieve. Making Ronan keep his unwanted "gift" was yet more punishment, like his bound wings and unusable celestial sword. Just one more burden on a man already struggling to stand under the weight of his sorrows.

To make matters worse, his mortal mind wasn't quite as adept now at distinguishing visions from reality, or adjusting when one ended and another began. In his disorientation, he'd thrown Arkady aside, mistaking her for the door of a cage he wasn't yet imprisoned inside.

She leaned against the side of an old truck, cradling her left elbow as she glared at him. "I'll give you a pass *this time* because obviously you just had a flashback or hallucination of some kind and didn't know what you were doing. But so help me, the next time you put a hand on me in any way I don't like, you're going to wear your left arm as a bowtie. We green?"

"Very green." He felt humbled, both by her fierceness and his own actions. "And I apologize."

She rubbed her elbow and hunched over. He must have hit her in the midsection. For a moment he saw that other version of Arkady superimposed over this one: bloody, wounded, crouching, and clutching her knife. Then that image faded, leaving behind the faint echoes of his own anger and desperation.

He'd been desperate to save her from that unseen, mocking threat. As far as he could recall, he'd never been desperate to save anyone. Wanted to very much, yes, but desperate...never. Desperation was a human emotion, and not one he wanted to experience.

"You were about to tell me about your leads." With a grimace, Arkady straightened and flexed her left elbow. "And now you *owe* me the chance to kick someone else's ass, or it'll be yours."

He didn't want to watch her die. He opened his mouth to tell her they had to go their separate ways, then closed it again. No matter what they did now, his vision said they would end up in that room. The future couldn't be changed.

Except when it came to Alice.

He'd seen a vision of Alice's death while they were in the Broken World. Yet somehow she'd survived being shot by a sniper, thanks to her lover, bound ghost, and mysterious guardian wolf. That fact was as inescapable as his prior belief that once he'd seen events unfold in a vision, they were set in stone. Alice had lived. And if Alice could live, there was a chance Arkady's life wouldn't end with a knife in her heart as he watched helplessly from inside a cage.

Not to mention she'd dared him to accept her challenge. He might be mortal now, but backing away from a challenge wasn't something he'd ever done, willingly or otherwise.

Besides, the idea of kicking a whole lot of asses had never appealed to him quite so much as it did in that moment. He wanted to punch someone so badly, his knuckles itched.

"Well, I *do* have a lead," he told her.

She smiled. Her hunter's smile was back, and it made him feel right at home and ready to track their prey. "What kind of lead?" she asked.

"A name." He gave her his own hunter's smile. "Ace."

4

ARKADY

*A*CE.

Well, it ain't much to go on, but hell, I wanted a challenge, she thought. And not just the challenge of not decking Ronan every time he opened his idiot mouth. At least searching for Ace would distract her from the pain in her back and wrist and the fact now her damn elbow ached from hitting the side of that truck.

In the throes of whatever flashback he'd just experienced, Ronan had thrown her aside as easily as she tossed an apple core out her car window. Earlier he'd moved impossibly fast to catch up with her, and then there was that weird silver glint in his eyes when he got angry. She knew what he *wasn't*—not fae, vamp, shifter, or ghoul—but she was no closer to figuring him out than before. How could she trust him at her back if she didn't know what the hell he was?

And yet despite her natural wariness and all her years of training and experience, her gut told her she *could* trust him the same way she trusted Alice, Malcolm, and Sean. That made no sense, but there it was. That annoyed her, though she wasn't sure why.

"The bartender's father paid me to keep her safe and watch out for her abusive ex-boyfriend," Ronan said in an undertone as they made their way back to the dead men's car. "I'm sure you noticed the bruise on her face. I do not want this ex anywhere near her."

She put her questions about Ronan aside and focused on the task at hand. "I saw it, and he needs to disappear," she said. "But first, we need to get this girl out of the trunk, see what she knows about the traffickers, and get her somewhere safe."

"I agree," he rumbled.

Wonder of wonders, she thought dryly. She'd begun to think he intended to argue every point with her, just because.

But what to do about Mireille? Arkady hummed as she pondered some options. One of them could stay at the bar while the other took the girl in the trunk to safety, but her brain had fixated on the idea of teaming up with Ronan to track Ace down and their quarry might disappear if they took too long to go after him. So they needed a quick way to sort this out and start their hunt.

"Other than an attraction to shitheads, does Mireille have brains?" she asked.

He seemed to consider her question. "Yes," he said finally. "She needs to find her way, but she's smart. And under all that attitude, she has a kind heart."

"Good. So we have one girl who needs a reason to find her strength, and another who needs help." Arkady leaned against the car near the broken passenger mirror. "You thinking what I'm thinking?"

He stared at her. "You're not serious."

"Do you know how a girl who's been beaten down finds her strength?" she countered. "She gets a chance to be the strength for someone who needs it. Two birds, one stone, and we're off to find Ace before that trail goes cold. We'll come back for the ex."

He eyed her.

She sighed. "I don't want your paycheck for watching Mireille or turning over her ex. I'm not hurting for money. I'm between cases and itching for a fight." *And besides, I want to know who and what you are*, she thought. No better way to accomplish that than watching him in action.

"I didn't think you wanted money," he countered. "I was wondering when *you* were the beaten-down girl who needed to find her strength."

His words hit her like a slap. "Fuck you," she said coldly. "I've never been weak."

The moment the words came out of her mouth, she wished she could take them back. She'd just given away way too much because he'd caught her off guard.

"I didn't say you were weak, Miss Woodall. That was your word, not mine." Once again, he tossed her the keys to the dead men's stolen car. "What's your plan?"

He might not be a gentleman or anything close to it, but he'd changed the subject rather than continue to needle her in a sensitive spot. So he was an asshole with at least a shred of decency.

"Mireille has a car?" she asked.

"A little one." He jerked his head toward the Pelican. "Parked around back."

"Good. Go bat your eyelashes and get her to leave work early. I'll get the girl out of the trunk and meet you out back in a few."

Ronan made a rumbly sound. "I do not bat my eyelashes." His tone sounded oddly formal, as if he'd not only been offended, but made some kind of pronouncement from on high.

"I don't care *how* you get her outside, Your Majesty," Arkady said irritably. "Just do it."

"I am to be addressed as *O Great and Mighty One*, but I forgive your ignorance." Now he was mocking her openly. "You give Alice such orders?"

"I don't have to. Alice is smart enough to know what to do without being told."

Chuckling, he strode purposefully toward the bar's front door. She scowled at his back as he walked.

He must have sensed her stare, because he paused about fifteen feet away. "Enjoying the view of my posterior, Miss Woodall?" he asked without turning around.

"Hardly. I've seen lots better." She deliberately turned her back to him and ignored his laugh. *Go to hell, O Great and Mighty One*, she grumbled inwardly.

Once Ronan went back inside the bar, she took out her phone and sent a text to Alice. *Can you send Ghost Boy to me?*

Her phone buzzed about fifteen seconds later. *Alice: Malcolm will be on his way shortly. What's up?*

Arkady: Need his help with something. Your garden hungry?

Alice: My garden is ALWAYS hungry. Delivery or carry-out?

Arkady chuckled. Alice's backyard carnivorous garden certainly came in handy for body disposal. *Carry-out. Malcolm will give you the deets.*

That done, she sent texts to a couple of potential sources offering a cash reward for information on Ace. Ronan might have cultivated some connections in his short time in the city, but he probably didn't have nearly as many as she did. Besides, she wanted to get a lead first, just on principle.

A familiar cold sensation prickled on the back of her neck just before a voice she knew all too well piped up from behind her. "What in the sleazy dive-bar hell happened to you?" Malcolm demanded. Arkady could hear him, since he'd shared magic with her in the past, but only Alice could see him. "And where the heck's your shirt?" he added.

"Over there somewhere, covered in broken glass and tequila." She waved her hand in the general direction of her discarded shirt. "Need your help, Ghost Boy."

He snorted. "Clearly."

"Oh, cram it."

Several cars had come and gone since Ronan went inside, but at the moment Arkady was the only person in the lot. *Time to get that girl out of the trunk*, she thought. *Goodness knows what she thinks has been going on for the past fifteen minutes or so.*

She crouched by the back bumper. "Hi there," she said, making her voice as warm and nonthreatening as possible. "I know you're scared. Can you hear me?"

The girl in the trunk didn't reply. Her kidnappers had probably threatened to hurt her if she made a sound. She might think this was a trick to get her to violate their rules.

"My name is Anna," Arkady continued. No one involved in the situation needed her real name, just in case they didn't sweep up all loose ends. "Anna Whitman" was one of her usual pseudonyms. She'd chosen it in honor of the lead actress from her favorite vampire television show and her second-favorite American poet.

Ronan probably didn't want his real name used either, so she needed to give him a fake name too. Her mouth quirked. "My friend *Johnny* and I are going to get you out of there and make sure you get somewhere safe," she added. "I'm going to unlock the trunk now, but stay put until I make sure the coast is clear."

Still no answer. The girl had no reason to trust Arkady, or anyone else, for that matter.

She slid the key into the lock, turned it, and started to raise the trunk lid. Something knocked the trunk lid out of her hand. In the same moment Arkady realized the girl had kicked it open, a hard metal object came flying out of the trunk and hit her square in the face with enough force to make her stumble. The missile turned out to be an unopened can of cheap beer.

A thin, red-haired teenager in a T-shirt and shorts, her hands cuffed in front of her, tried to get out of the trunk. She lost her balance, fell, and landed in the gravel at Arkady's feet with a muffled yelp. Duct tape covered her mouth and wrapped all the way around her head. She hadn't been able to pull it off, or hadn't had time.

The girl, who looked to be about seventeen, took one look at Arkady's furious, bloody face and started screaming. Thankfully the tape muffled the sound or everyone in a half-mile radius would have heard the racket.

"Well, this is going about as well as I'd imagined it would," Malcolm said.

"Son of a bitch." Arkady spat out blood and kicked the beer can under another car. She found some fast food napkins in the back seat that looked clean, held them to her mouth, and crouched. "Stop hollering," she snapped. "I told you I'm trying to get you out of this mess. I know you don't know who I am, but if I was with the assholes who kidnapped you, I would give you a good whack for hitting me with that beer can instead of helping you."

The girl stopped screaming, but her red-rimmed eyes remained wide and terrified. Her breathing came fast and shallow. She wiped her runny nose with her cuffed hands and sniffled.

Arkady's split lip had already begun to swell. That beer can had done some damage. Her injury would probably bleed for a while, but at least she hadn't ended up with a broken nose. *Small favors*, as Alice would have said. She folded the napkins the other way and put them back to her mouth.

"Good move, by the way," she added, making her tone conversational. "Caught me by surprise. It might have even worked if you'd been able to run instead of just belly-flop out of the car like a carp falling into a rowboat."

The girl let out a half-laugh, half-hiccup, and sniffled again.

"We've already taken care of those two jokers who had you, but we gotta get moving before any of their friends show up. So I'm going to take off that duct tape and we're gonna hustle out of here, okay?"

The girl shook her head and scooted back against the car's rusty bumper. Arkady sighed.

"I know it's not one of your top skills, but you gotta be more sympathetic and less threatening," Malcolm said. The girl couldn't hear *or* see him, which was just as well, Arkady thought, given her mental state.

"I *am* sympathetic," she muttered.

"Well, try not glowering like you're about to turn into an eldritch god and eat her."

She reached behind her back, where the girl couldn't see, and extended her middle finger.

"Yeah, okay." The ghost snorted. "Real mature, Cthulhu."

"Look." Arkady ignored him and tried to look more friendly. "Like I said, I know you have no reason to trust me, but I really am trying to help you. If you don't want to take my word for it, I can show you the bodies of the two men who kidnapped you. My friend Johnny and I made sure they won't mess with you or anyone else ever again."

The girl's eyes widened into saucers.

"Maybe telling her you just killed two people wasn't the best idea," Malcolm said. His cold presence moved closer to her right shoulder. She'd gotten better at sensing where he was when he lurked nearby. "Especially if you want her to trust you. And who the hell is Johnny, and why would you ever hang out with someone named *Johnny*?"

"Shhh," Arkady hissed. She dabbed her bloody lip. "It's okay if you don't trust me. I probably wouldn't either if I was in your shoes. I just want to get you away from this bar to somewhere safe. Do you have someone you trust who could come pick you up?"

The girl shook her head. Her tears streaked the dirt and grime on her cheeks.

"You don't have *anyone* to call?" Arkady prodded.

Another shake of her head.

"Poor girl," Malcolm said. His voice had lost all its mirth. "Let's get her to Alice and Sean. They'll take care of her."

"Okay, here's what you're going to do," Arkady told the girl. "My friend Johnny is inside talking to the real nice girl they've got bartending tonight. She's going to give you a ride to my friend Alice's house. Alice is a private investigator. She'll make sure you're safe, and then she's going to help you get on your feet. And just to make sure you arrive there safely, I'm sending my other best friend, Malcolm, with you. One thing, though: Malcolm's a ghost."

The girl's eyes got huge again.

"You sure about this?" Malcolm asked worriedly. "She might really freak out."

"She'll be fine." Arkady smiled. "Malcolm's here with us now. He thinks you're going to freak out if you know about him. But he's just a sweet little boy, and you're not afraid of sweet little boy ghosts, are you?"

The girl shook her head slowly.

"*Sweet little boy*," Malcolm muttered. "Oh, I'm going to zap you *so hard*."

"Awesome," Arkady said brightly, ignoring him. "So I'll take off that duct tape and get those handcuffs unlocked, and we'll get you on your way, okay?"

The girl nodded reluctantly.

Carefully, Arkady got the duct tape off first. As slowly as she pulled it off, it still left an angry red mark on the girl's face. Getting it out of her long, matted hair proved impossible. Rather than prolong the torture, Arkady used her knife to cut the tape loose. Up close, the girl smelled like she hadn't bathed in days. How the hell long had she been in this trunk? Arkady had the sudden urge to use the dipshits' corpses for target practice before they ended up feeding Alice's garden.

Once the tape was off, Arkady wadded it up and tossed it into the open trunk. "What's your name?" she asked as she studied the girl's handcuffs.

The girl sniffled. "Regan."

"Cool name." Arkady fished a little lock-pick kit from her pocket. "From *King Lear*, right?"

"Yeah." Regan blinked at her. "No one ever gets that. They think Reagan, like that old president."

"People should read more." In a few seconds, Arkady had the handcuffs unlocked. She tossed them in the back too and shut the trunk. They'd make sure the car disappeared once its contents were on their way to Alice's garden.

Regan massaged her bruised wrists. "Thanks."

Arkady stood and held out her hand. Hesitantly, Regan took her hand and Arkady hauled the much-smaller girl to her feet.

"Why'd you help me?" Regan asked. She still sounded suspicious.

"Because I don't like assholes who pick on people who can't defend themselves." She hadn't bothered to hide her anger and disgust, but Regan didn't flinch at her tone this time. Maybe she was starting to believe Arkady really was helping her. And she seemed less skittish and steadier on her feet, so she might be able to answer some questions. "When and where did they grab you?" Arkady asked.

"I don't remember." Regan rubbed her eyes. "They must have given me something. Everything's super blurry."

Dang it, Arkady thought. She'd really counted on getting *something* from Regan. "You can't remember *anything* about how they got you?"

"All I remember is going to sleep where I've been staying lately, in an alley off Sixth Street. I woke up in this trunk." She looked ready to burst into tears again. "I don't even know what these guys looked like. I'm sorry."

"It's okay," Arkady assured her. "We've got other leads. We'll figure out who's involved and we'll make them pay. And maybe something will come back to you."

She sniffled. "Yeah, maybe."

Regan's feet were bare. The cruel dipshits had taken her shoes to make it harder for her to run away, even if she got the chance. Arkady let out a little wolf-like growl. *Too much time around Alice's pack*, she thought wryly. *But how the heck do I get her to Mireille's car? A piggyback ride?* Malcolm would never let her hear the end of that.

A small blue hatchback appeared from behind the bar, ending Arkady's internal debate about how to get Regan safely across the glass-strewn gravel lot. Mireille was behind the wheel. She parked beside them and hopped out. Arkady saw no sign of Ronan, but she had the feeling he was watching them from somewhere close by.

Regan had taken a step back when the car pulled up, but Mireille's sympathetic expression and similar age seemed to ease her fears. "Hey, I'm Mireille," the other girl said, coming around to open the passenger door. "I'm your chauffeur. What's your name?"

"Regan."

"Cool." Mireille's brow furrowed. "Like the president?"

Regan sighed. Arkady pressed the bloody napkins to her busted lip to hide her smile.

"I'm starving, and I bet you're hungry too," Mireille continued. "So first we're going to get some cheeseburgers and like two *huge* orders of fries. And then we're going to this lady Alice's house. She has a really sweet dog and a cat. And a *jacuzzi tub*."

Which of those words were the magic ones, Arkady wasn't sure, but Regan's eyes lit up.

"She needs lots of water," Arkady said and handed Mireille some cash. "Buy her a couple of bottles at a convenience store to go with those cheeseburgers and fries."

"Yes ma'am." Mireille pocketed the money, helped Regan into the passenger seat, and shut the door. "Thanks for trusting me to take care of her. Oh, and thanks for kicking Ricky earlier in the bar too. I've been wanting to do that for months."

"Happy to be of service. Drive safe."

Mireille gave Arkady a quick salute and ran around to the driver's side. As she got into the car, Malcolm spoke from Arkady's left. "You got things under control on this end while I ride with Thelma and Louise Junior out to Alice and Sean's house?"

"Yeah, we got this." Arkady scanned the shadows. Still no sign of Ronan. She thought maybe he didn't want Malcolm to see him, which was interesting. "Just make sure the girls get there safely."

"I guarantee nobody will touch them."

For all his playfulness, when it came to taking care of business, there was no one she'd trust more than Malcolm, except Alice and Sean. It was the only reason she felt comfortable letting the girls drive off.

"Can I tell Alice and Sean that you're going to deal with the people responsible for this?" he asked. "You and *Johnny?*"

She smiled. "You absolutely *can* tell them that."

"I expect a full report on this Johnny too, the next time I see you," Malcolm added. "If you need backup later, let Alice know and I'll be here before you can say *spicy meatball*." And with that, the telltale cold sensation of his presence disappeared as the car pulled away.

Arkady let Alice know they were on their way and stuck her phone in her back pocket. She looked down at herself and muttered a curse. Her T-shirt was unsalvageable, but she couldn't go around in her bra without attracting unwanted attention. She usually had spare clothes in her vehicle, but she'd used them a few days before and forgotten to put new ones in the back. So what to do?

Ronan still hadn't reappeared, but he'd parked his Harley on the edge of the lot, under one of the few working lights. On a whim, she hurried over to it and carefully touched one of its saddlebags. No wards that she could feel. She opened it, rummaged through the contents, and came up with a black T-shirt that looked reasonably clean but had clearly been worn because it smelled rich and earthy, like Ronan's body.

"Beggars can't be choosers," she muttered and put it on.

Even at her height of five-eleven, Ronan's shirt still hung comically almost to her knees like she'd borrowed it from a giant's closet. Grumbling, she used her knife to cut more than a foot from the length and then knotted it at her waist. Good enough.

She didn't hear any footsteps or sense him approach, but she was in no way surprised when Ronan's voice came from behind her. "That was my favorite shirt, Miss Woodall."

"Ah, so that's why you left it filthy and stuffed in your saddlebag for what smells like a week." She turned. Ronan stood about six feet away, arms crossed so his biceps and chest strained the fabric of his shirt. That hint of silver glinted in his eyes again. What the hell *was* he?

Meanwhile, his attention had focused on her injury. "I only left you alone for a few minutes. How'd you get the busted lip?"

"Milwaukee hand grenade." She grimaced and stuffed the napkins in her pocket. She'd picked up Alice's habit of never leaving anything lying around with her blood on it. "Regan was ready for whoever popped the trunk. She wouldn't have gotten far handcuffed and barefoot, but she got a lick in. I liked her style."

He frowned. "A Milwaukee what?"

"You haven't heard of a Milwaukee hand grenade? Take a can of cheap American beer, shake it, and chuck it at your target. Luckily, the one she threw at me didn't explode. A bloody lip is one thing, but I get soaked in shitty beer, I'm out."

His mouth quirked. "It's good to know what your boundaries are."

Her phone buzzed in her back pocket. She checked the screen. "Excellent," she murmured. "It pays to have friends in *really* low places."

"You got a lead on Ace?" He appeared at her side in an inhuman flash of movement. His sudden nearness and aura of power elicited a spike of adrenaline, disgust, and nausea. Instinctively, her hand raised to protect her throat. She forced it to drop to her side and clenched her fist.

And of course he noticed her reaction. She could tell from the way his eyes darkened and his scowl deepened that he'd recognized that flinch for what it was: the reaction of someone who'd been brutally bitten by a vampire against their will.

No one knew about the bite but herself and the vamp in question —not even Alice or Malcolm. Arkady had wanted it to stay that way, at least until she had a chance for revenge. After that, she wouldn't care who knew because the story would end with "...and then she staked them." Or took off their head, whichever way the whole thing played out. She wasn't picky, as long as the vamp ended up as ash under her boots.

As she entertained herself imagining that scene, Ronan did something entirely unexpected: he smiled that hunter's smile that had started to grow on her. "They got you, but you got back up after," he said. "Because fuck 'em. Am I right?"

He understood how hard it was to keep getting back up again and again—that much was clear. And someone had beaten him almost to death and dumped him in Alice's yard not that long ago. She had no idea what other indignities he'd suffered during those beatings, but maybe he empathized with her a little more than most.

"That's right; fuck 'em sideways," she said finally. She waggled her phone. "Back to business. I think I know where we might find this Ace."

He raised his eyebrow and held up his own phone. "I also know where to find Ace."

"But my lead is better."

"How do you know?"

"Because my leads are always the best, especially compared to fly-by-nighters like you. If you've got a lead on *an* Ace, it's probably some jack-hole who has nothing to do with this situation. Now *my* Ace..." She tapped his chest, which rumbled audibly in a way that absolutely did *not* stir any heat in her lady bits. "*My* Ace is *the* Ace."

His smile didn't waver. "If *your* Ace is the manager of a restaurant off Sixth and Maple, your Ace is actually *my* Ace."

"Damn it," she muttered. "Well, I bet *your* source doesn't know where he is right now."

"At Bella's, you mean?"

She crossed her arms and glared.

Her surliness played right into his hands. His smile grew. "And judging by the time stamp on your source's text, my lead came in first."

God, he's insufferable. "Shove it up your ass, Ronan."

"Only if you say pretty please, Miss Woodall." He produced a set of handcuffs from a zippered pocket inside his jacket. "I'm sure you already know how we're going to get in to see Ace, aka Oliver Mora."

With Regan safely on her way to Alice, he'd probably planned some scenario where she'd play a helpless victim and he would try to sell her to Ace to gain entry to the trafficking ring. And there was no way in hell she would have any part of that.

"I surely do." She took the cuffs and twirled them around her finger. "We're going in as *partners* to ask him some very important questions and then decide whether to hand him over to the cops or toss him over the fence into Alice's garden. As for these cuffs..." She peered up at him through her lashes and gave one of the cuffs a playful little lick with the tip of her tongue. It was all a show, of course. She didn't put on cuffs for *anybody*, least of all someone like him. But if she could take off her shirt and feign drunken attraction to the dipshits, she could pretend to be coming on to Ronan if it meant seeing him squirm. "If we have a reason to celebrate later, maybe they'll come in handy," she purred.

He didn't squirm, however—not even close. Instead, he bent his head close to hers and brushed her ear with his lips. "Oh darlin', you don't want to play that game with someone like me," he murmured. "That's not a game you're going to win."

He'd used her own words against her, and she'd be damned if that and the almost intoxicating scent of his leather jacket and hot skin didn't make her want to drag him into the back seat of her SUV and ride him like the stallion she reckoned him to be. No doubt she'd probably regret it later, but she strongly suspected it would be one hell of a ride.

His lips still against her ear, he chuckled. "I like the way you smell when you think about me."

"Oh, get over yourself," she retorted. "I wasn't thinking about you. I was thinking about kicking some answers out of Oliver Mora and feeding those dipshits to Alice's garden, and it got me all hot."

"If you say so." She could hear the smile in his voice. "How about we see about getting you satisfied, then?"

"Gee whiz, I thought you'd never ask." She stalked off toward her SUV without waiting for him to follow.

"We're taking my bike," he said from behind her. "I never leave my lady in the lurch."

Arkady paused mid-step. As a general rule, she preferred to take her own vehicle, but how could she say no to a ride on a Harley? It had been a long, long time. Too long.

"Fine," she said, making her voice sharp so he wouldn't know how much she liked the idea. "I've gotta get my jacket."

"Whenever you're ready, Miss Woodall," he said, his tone mocking. "Your noble steed awaits."

A noble steed. A *stallion*. And now that image of all nearly seven feet of him beneath her was well and truly stuck in her head.

Her face burning, Arkady stomped through the gravel to her car, with Ronan's chuckle following her the whole way.

5

RONAN

THE LAST TIME RONAN HAD RIDDEN A HARLEY WITH A FEMALE passenger, it was in the Broken World and Alice was sitting behind him, her arms around his waist. By then they were more like pack mates. They'd fought side by side, and she'd saved his life at great risk to her own. Riding the Harley with her was comfortable and easy, and their closeness was a friendship or kinship tempered by battle and mutual respect.

Riding with Arkady Woodall, however, felt like something else entirely. His skin tingled wherever her body touched his, even through their clothes.

While only a few weeks had passed in this realm, his captivity in Michael's cell had lasted a hundred years. His suffering was only eclipsed by his loneliness. Even after his return, though, he hadn't seen human women as potential bedmates, not even to break his fast. He didn't need to be a psychiatrist to figure out his aversion to human women was far more about his rejection of his own mortal body than anything else.

All that had changed tonight.

The moment Arkady put on his spare helmet and settled in behind him with her thighs tight against his hips, he couldn't think of anything except how damn *hungry* he was and how good she smelled, especially when she put a leather jacket on over what remained of his favorite shirt. He felt drunker on her scent than on the half a bottle of tequila he'd consumed at the bar. Not even thoughts of Michael could dampen that heady, effervescent sensation.

Arkady poked him hard in the back with her index finger when he didn't start the bike immediately. "Are we gonna blow this popsicle stand or what? Ace ain't coming to us, O Great and Mighty One. Get the lead out."

He flipped down his helmet visor and obeyed.

From the first day he'd adopted it as his preferred method of transportation, the rumble of a Harley's engine had become a balm for his soul. In many ways it reminded him of hunting on horseback. If he let his mind drift, he could still hear the thunder of his horse's hooves galloping across the hard, sunbaked land and feel the steady rhythm of the animal's gait. Then and now, when he let the horse run—or took his Harley out on the open road—all the bullshit faded away to nothing and left him peaceful and free.

Arkady had done her best to hide her excitement, but her eyes lit up at the prospect of riding with him. It didn't occur to him to mind that her eagerness had far more to do with the Harley than him.

As they flew down the two-lane highway toward the city, with the speedometer heading for eighty, she finally gave up playing it cool and whooped. He smiled. He'd smiled more tonight than in the last hundred years. The expression still felt strange, but undeniably good.

"Faster," she urged via the microphone in their helmets. He was only too happy to indulge her.

They made the thirty-minute drive to Bella's in nineteen minutes.

As soon as he parked the Harley in the club's lot, Arkady hopped off the back, stretched, and took off her helmet. She startled him by taking off her leather jacket, removing the T-shirt she'd stolen from his saddlebag, and putting her jacket back on, leaving it unzipped enough to show off her cleavage and bra. Then she released her hair from its ponytail, flipped it over her head, and mussed it with her fingers until it looked like she'd just rolled out of bed. *His* bed.

Good luck getting that *image out of your head*, he thought wryly.

She applied bright red lipstick with the aid of a small compact, stuck the tube and mirror back in her inside jacket pocket, and gave him a brilliant smile. In moments, she'd transformed from Valkyrie to vixen. The lipstick disguised her busted lip.

She put her hand on her hip and struck a pose. "So, would you do me?"

He blinked. Was this some kind of test? And if so, what was the right answer? Both *yes* and *no* seemed like equally dangerous responses.

Apparently she misinterpreted his uncertainty as skepticism. She heaved a sigh. "We have to get to this Ace guy without him figuring out what we're up to. Can you think of a better way to do that than an indecent proposal by a voyeur and his exhibitionist girlfriend? It works every time. I've got the tits, so I'll do all the heavy lifting. You just gotta do *your* part and not be creepy when you pretend you like to watch."

"Who says I'd be pretending?" he asked, just to rile her up.

She didn't rile easily, though. "I figured as much, O Great and Mighty One. You look like the type. Now let's get in there before someone else catches his attention."

"Scared of a little competition?"

"Are you kidding?" She gestured at her body. "I *have* no competition."

He could not have agreed more. Valkyries, even human ones, had no equal.

Chuckling to himself, he rolled his neck and slipped into character with the ease of someone who'd spent centuries playing various roles as part of his bounty-hunting career. He gave Arkady his bedroom smile —in keeping with his role as a voyeur looking for a partner for his frisky lady—and ushered her to the club's front door. "Show me what you've got, Miss Woodall."

She wasted no time doing exactly that. At the door, she unleashed a smile on the bouncer that would have launched a satellite into orbit and slipped her hand into Ronan's back pocket. She didn't grab him or even squeeze, but he rather wished she had, even if it was just part of their ruse. He liked the sensation of her hand on his denim-clad ass very much.

"Howdy," she purred, and looked up at the bouncer through her lashes, as she'd done to Ronan in the parking lot at the Pelican. And despite the fact he worked the door at a strip club and saw more than his fair share of beautiful and sultry women, the bouncer fell right under Arkady's spell.

"No cover charge for the lady," he said, his eyes on Arkady's breasts in her red-and-black lace bra. He finally managed to tear his gaze away to look at Ronan just long enough to add, "Twenty for you and a two-drink minimum. No weapons allowed inside."

"That's fine." Ronan handed over a twenty and allowed the bouncer to pat him down. With most of his attention on Arkady, the bouncer missed all three of Ronan's knives. He didn't bother to search Arkady at all, meaning her weapons made it inside too. *Excellent*, he thought.

Judging by the number of luxury vehicles in the parking lot and its posh booths and tables, Bella's catered to a more upscale clientele than most strip clubs Ronan had visited. Even so, almost everything about its interior, from the loud thumping music to the neon and flashing lights, DJ booth, main stage, dancers, and busy lingerie-clad servers looked virtually the same.

"Hello there, darlings." The hostess, a pretty redhead in an emerald green bustier and panty set, checked their IDs. Her gaze swept over both Arkady and Ronan with equal amounts of appreciation. "Welcome to Bella's. I'm Bunny."

Arkady didn't seem to mind how the hostess's gaze lingered on her curves. "Hello, Bunny," she replied, her tone playful. "I *love* your outfit. That green looks amazing on you."

"Thank you." Bunny's smile revealed cute dimples. "Where would you lovelies like to sit? Main stage area or VIP lounge?"

"Main stage area." Ronan put his arm around Arkady's waist and rested his hand lightly on her hip. They had to play their roles, but she hadn't explicitly told him how much touching she'd allow. For all his teasing, he wasn't one to grab first and ask forgiveness later, and that went double for women as well-armed as Arkady.

"If we see someone in the audience we like, we can invite them to join us in the lounge for a private dance?" he asked.

"Of course. We want everyone to enjoy themselves." Bunny led them to a table with plush chairs and a good view of the stage. Ronan pulled out Arkady's chair for her, then sat in his own. "Cleo will be right with you," Bunny added. "Cherry and Coco are up next on the main stage. Have fun, darlings." With a wink, she headed back to the hostess desk.

As soon as Bunny left, Arkady got up and sat sideways in Ronan's lap. She crossed her legs toward him so she was almost curled up against his chest, and nuzzled his neck. To an observer, they would seem like nothing more than an overly demonstrative couple, but Ronan sensed Arkady was all business now. She could talk to him in an undertone without anyone being able to overhear.

"You see him?" she murmured. Her breath felt warm against his skin. She smelled of mint and tequila. "Second table from the right, next to the main stage."

"Yes." Ronan had spotted Ace—real name Oliver Mora—the moment they'd entered the club.

When he'd first seen Mora's photo, courtesy of a contact he'd made not long after he'd left Alice's house, Ronan had thought Mora an unlikely candidate to be part of a trafficking organization. His appearance seemed average in almost every way. He looked fit but not overly so. In a nondescript blue button-down shirt and khakis, he would blend into any crowd and not attract much attention. Ronan supposed he could be considered moderately handsome in the right light, but again, not in a memorable way.

After several hundred years of operating as a bounty hunter, however, Ronan knew never to judge a target by their appearance. He'd earned a couple of scars while learning that lesson. Often the most uninteresting-looking people proved to be the most dangerous.

When their server, Cleo, came by, they ordered top-shelf tequila for both of them, with a twist of lemon for Arkady. Ronan recalled that at the Pelican, Arkady had purchased a bottle of the same brand he'd been drinking. Coincidence? He suspected it wasn't. She'd wanted him to notice her, or she would have ensured he didn't. He had a couple of theories as to why that would be the case, and he found each possible explanation more intriguing than the last.

Once Cleo left their table, Arkady went back to murmuring into his ear about their target. "Looks about as bland as unseasoned mashed potatoes until you look at his eyes," she said. "He's got shark eyes."

Ronan had noticed Mora's eyes too. Even in the photo his contact sent via text, the eyes were what stood out while the rest of the man looked entirely uninteresting. Both in the photo and in real life, they were hard, dark, and very cold.

Shark eyes, Arkady had said. Not a bad way to describe them.

Ronan nuzzled her hair and pretended it was just for show, and that he didn't enjoy the feeling of her body so close to his.

As if she'd sensed how he felt, she smiled. Not her predator smile or the thousand-watt grin she'd unleashed on the bouncer, but the rare genuine smile he'd grown to really like. "What's your gut feeling about him?" she asked.

Mora sipped his bourbon and watched the performers onstage. He smiled appreciatively as Cherry and Coco twirled and danced and shimmied out of their costumes, but his smile struck Ronan as entirely superficial. His odd detachment stood out even more when Ronan compared it to the body language of everyone else in the audience. He came across less as an enthusiastic patron of the club than a man here on business. And unless Ronan was very much mistaken, women were the business in question. The way Mora looked at the dancers reminded him of a merchant evaluating goods for sale rather than a man here for entertainment purposes.

"I think we've got the right Ace," he said quietly. And since he felt sure Arkady would understand he meant it as an assessment of Mora's character, he added, "I don't like him."

"Me either. He looks like he has cold hands." She chuckled softly. "Maybe I should make *you* seduce him into accepting an invitation to the VIP lounge. I don't really want him to touch me."

"I don't really want him to touch you either. Because you don't want him to," he amended. "Not because I think it's up to me who touches you."

She leaned back to get a good look at his face. "If anyone else said that, I'd think they were full of shit and just trying to impress me. Why is it I believe you, when I *know* how full of shit you are?"

He gave her his own real smile. As far as he could recall, the only other person who'd ever seen it was Alice. "Because you can't resist my easygoing charm and good manners?"

She laughed. *What an amazing sound that is*, he thought. "No, I think it's because when you're bullshitting me, you don't try to hide it," she mused. "You're shockingly honest, especially given your chosen profession and the whole outlaw vibe you've got going on."

"I might say the same of you."

She laughed again, this time more caustically. "Well, there goes my assessment of you as a good judge of character. I'm incredibly dishonest, Ronan. In fact, the more honest I seem to be, the more full of shit I am."

She seemed convincing in her claims of dishonesty, but he felt sure it was an attempt to make him think things he'd noticed about her earlier weren't true.

"I *am* a good judge of character, and my bullshit detector is very finely tuned," he said, his lips close to her ear. "So don't bother trying to bluff me, Miss Woodall."

Her smile turned predatory again. "If it makes you happy to think you've figured me out, go ahead and think it, sweet pea. I don't mind. It just means you'll never see it coming."

Ronan wondered what it was he'd supposedly never see coming.

"I didn't say I have you figured out," he countered. "I'm a long way from that. I *do* know more about you than almost anyone else knows. And what's got you confused is that it doesn't bother you nearly as much as you think it should."

"I'm not confused," she said icily. "And you don't know anything more than I've let you know."

Cleo returned to the table with their drinks. Arkady stayed on Ronan's lap, but he sensed tension and distance between them now. He'd blundered across a boundary with his comment about knowing her better than she'd realized, and he wasn't sure he could repair the damage.

Once they'd sipped their drinks and she seemed to have relaxed a little, Ronan said, "You're not at all thrown off by any of this. Setting a honey trap in a strip club is just another night for you."

"Why shouldn't it be?" Arkady shrugged. "It's business. I'm surprised by how businesslike *you* are."

"Why?"

"Because you're a boy and we're in a strip club." She peered mischievously over the rim of her glass. "Boys usually have a difficult time focusing with so many *luscious* distractions."

"It's been a very, very long time since I was a boy, Miss Woodall."

In fact, he'd never been a child of any sort. Even a newborn archangel was not a child. He remembered the moment he came into being eons ago, already in his angelic form and with the collective wisdom of the ages. Archangels evolved as their experiences shaped them, but he'd never known childhood.

It occurred to him suddenly to wonder why Michael hadn't begun his sentence with human birth, rather than leaving him in the body of an adult man. He supposed whatever the reason was, it was more punishment. Perhaps Michael didn't want him to experience the love of a family or the wonders and simple pleasures of human childhood.

Arkady gasped. "Ronan!"

He'd crushed his glass without realizing it. He looked at his bloody hand with detachment, as if his injury had happened to someone else.

Arkady grabbed their drink napkins and wrapped his hand, using her body to hide his wound from those sitting nearby. "What the hell's wrong with you?" she demanded.

Her anger confused him until he realized he'd startled and scared her. "I'm all right." He caught her hand with his uninjured one and held on. "It was an accident. They use cheap glasses here that break much too easily."

"Ronan." She pulled her hand out of his. "What did I just say about trying to bullshit me? What's wrong?"

What could he tell her that was close enough to the truth to appease her? He considered several options, rejected each of them, and settled on a simple, "Nothing that either of us can fix."

"Are you moping again? Don't make me get tough with you." She glared at him. "And how are we supposed to co-seduce Mora if you look like you stuck your hand in a garbage disposal? Blood isn't sexy.

Well, okay, blood is *sometimes* sexy," she amended. "But not in this context."

He wanted to know in what contexts she found blood sexy and whether they matched his own thoughts on the subject, but as she'd pointed out, they were here for business.

He drew on the healing power Michael had allowed him to keep and let it pulse through his hand. His skin itched as it healed.

"Go get him to bite the hook," he told her. "I'll clean up my hand and join you." When she eyed him distrustfully, he gave her his bedroom smile again and enjoyed her little shiver. "I want to watch you work your magic, don't I, my little exhibitionist? Isn't that part of our game?"

"Call me your little *anything* again and you're going to be real sorry," she muttered. "Fine." She took a deep breath, exhaled, and returned his sultry look with one of her own. "Watch me work if you dare." She slid off his lap, smoothed her jeans over her hips, lowered her jacket zipper another inch, and took her drink with her to Mora's table.

Ronan watched her cross the room. So did almost every man she walked past. Some spoke to her, but she ignored them. She stalked Oliver Mora like a lioness going after prey.

Arkady bent over and touched Mora's shoulder. Mora glanced up and got an eyeful of her cleavage before he managed to tear his gaze away and look up at her smile and fluttering lashes.

In moments, Arkady was seated next to Mora at the table and murmuring into his ear. Thanks to the loud music, Ronan couldn't hear what she said, but she appeared to have one hundred percent of Mora's attention.

The trap was sprung and Mora didn't have a prayer. Ronan almost felt sorry for him. Almost.

As Arkady worked her magic, Ronan unwrapped the napkins from his hand. The cuts had disappeared. He brushed the broken glass into the napkins, told Cleo he'd dropped the glass, and traded the little carefully wrapped bundle of shards and a cash tip for another full glass of tequila.

Drinks in hand, Arkady and Mora rose and moved toward the doorway leading to the VIP lounge. Ronan growled to himself when

Mora rested his hand possessively on Arkady's ass and gave it what looked like a painful squeeze. Somehow she managed to stay in character and even giggled playfully, when Ronan was sure she'd rather have punched Mora in the jaw hard enough that he ended up gargling several teeth.

Still smiling, Arkady murmured in Mora's ear and gestured in Ronan's direction. Mora glanced Ronan's way, his expression one of cool assessment. Ronan kept his focus on Arkady. To Mora and any casual observer, she probably seemed entirely at ease, but Ronan couldn't have missed the cold fury in her eyes as Mora gave her another squeeze. He had a feeling what her opinion would be on whether to toss Mora into Alice's garden once they finished with him.

Meanwhile, whatever Arkady had said and done, Mora wanted her. His body language made that clear. Even the prospect of performing for an audience didn't seem to put him off. Or maybe he thought he'd be able to get Arkady to ditch Ronan for a more private encounter.

Either way, so far, so good. Arkady had done her job. Now Ronan had to play the part of a voyeuristic lover who liked to watch his woman have sex with other men. But the more he thought about Mora's hands on Arkady's body, the more difficult the role seemed. He didn't deserve any say over who touched her and who didn't, but that didn't make the prospect of Mora pawing her any less infuriating.

This is all a ruse, he reminded himself as he made his way toward the lounge. *Mora's hands are going nowhere near her body. Those shark eyes won't see anything more of her than what they see right now. And if I blow this, Arkady will have put up with his groping for nothing.*

Those reminders helped him focus. He took a deep breath and stepped through the curtained doorway into the VIP lounge. The lounge featured low lights, no flashing neon, quieter music, and a dozen semi-private nooks. All but one were occupied by a client and a dancer providing individual attention and bottle service in return for a steep fee and tip.

Arkady and Mora had already settled into a nook to Ronan's right. He wasn't at all surprised to find Arkady had chosen Bunny, the lovely red-haired hostess, for their private dance, or that Mora had ordered a bottle of the most expensive champagne on the menu. Mora might be

many things, but subtle wasn't one of them. The cold smile he gave
Ronan made it clear he saw Arkady as a prize to be won and Ronan as
nothing more than an obstacle.

Arkady wasn't anyone's prize. Ronan felt compelled to emphasize
the point by feeding Mora to Alice's garden feet-first, and very slowly.

Bunny met Ronan just inside the doorway. "Hello again, darling."
With her hand on his arm, she led him to Arkady and Mora's nook. As
he sat opposite the others, she asked, "Is there anything I can do to
make you more comfortable?"

"I'm very comfortable just like this." He handed her a couple of
discreetly folded bills. "I'm here to watch my lady enjoy herself.
Anything she wants, she can have."

Bunny slipped his cash into her bustier and smiled playfully at him.
"What a gentleman."

"Don't let him fool you," Arkady said, her hand resting on Mora's
thigh. Her smile seemed brittle, at least to Ronan. Maybe she wasn't as
blasé about this ruse as she'd wanted him to believe. "He's no
gentleman. I've just trained him well and he knows who he belongs to."
Her voice took on a hard edge. "Don't you?"

"That's right." Ronan draped his arms over the back of their plush
velvet booth. With his gaze locked on Arkady's, he added, "I know
who I belong to, and I wouldn't want it any other way." His words
weren't part of the ruse. He meant what he said. And she knew it,
because he was an honest man.

If she wanted him tonight, he'd say yes and have no second
thoughts about it. For the first time since Michael dumped him in
Alice's yard, he had something he wanted that didn't involve killing bad
guys for money. That felt good.

Judging by the way Mora's eyes narrowed, he hadn't missed
Arkady's reaction to Ronan's unblinking stare. Rather than making him
rethink things, it seemed to double his desire.

Meanwhile, either misreading the animosity in the booth as
shared sexual tension, or recognizing it for what it was and
wanting to distract them, Bunny got down to business. "I like a
man who knows what he likes." She slid her hands down her sides
and over the curve of her hips, her body moving in time with the

music playing in the lounge. "I belong to all of you tonight," she added with a smile. "And I wouldn't want it any other way either."

As Bunny danced, Mora turned to Arkady. "Take off your jacket." His tone seemed polite enough, but his eyes had a cruel look Ronan very much did not like. "Let me see what I'm getting."

Arkady stiffened and moved her hand from his leg. "I think you misunderstood my invitation, Oliver. You're auditioning for *us*, not the other way around. It's a buyer's market, or hadn't you noticed?"

Mora smiled. Ronan liked that smile even less than his previous expression. Mora tipped Arkady's chin up with his fingertips and moved closer. "It *is* a buyer's market, and you came to me. So who's buying, and who's *selling*, my sweetness?"

At that, Arkady's entire body went taut. Ronan was instantly on alert, though he managed to maintain his deliberately casual pose.

Mora took advantage of Arkady's shock and brushed her lips with his own. Ronan stayed in his seat because Arkady could take care of her own business, but he entertained himself imagining new and creative ways to turn Mora into plant food.

"That's what I thought," Mora murmured. With a smirk, he tweaked Arkady's chin. "I knew you'd come around. Now, let's enjoy our private dance and drink our champagne. Then we'll ditch your boyfriend and go somewhere else." His eyes cut over to Ronan. "If you like an audience, I can arrange a much better one than what you've got."

Arkady seemed to shake herself. Whatever Mora had said that upset her, she'd put it aside and refocused on the job at hand.

She gave Mora the same smile Ronan had seen her use on the demon servants—the one that looked like an invitation but was really a promise of suffering. "I think I'm interested in your offer," she told Mora, and beckoned Bunny closer. "But first, you're right...we want to enjoy our dance." She took off her jacket, tossed it to Ronan, and raised her eyebrow. "Make yourself useful, dear, and serve the champagne."

He met her gaze and asked with his eyes if she wanted to keep going. Her smile gave him the answer.

"Your wish is my command," he said, and reached for the bottle of champagne in the bucket of ice beside him.

As Bunny danced on Mora's lap, Arkady watched and toyed with the dancer's hair. Ronan poured two glasses of champagne. He handed one to Arkady, who gave it to Mora and then accepted another for herself.

She'd told Ronan she'd dose Mora with something to make him more agreeable, but he didn't see her slip anything into his glass. Maybe she'd banked on Bunny distracting him and then decided his attention wasn't diverted enough to make it possible for her to drug his drink. They couldn't afford to get caught in the act.

Mora drank his first glass of champagne quickly—much too quickly for such an expensive label. Even Ronan, who tolerated champagne more than enjoyed it, thought it was a waste. Without comment, he poured another and passed it to Arkady. And though Mora seemed focused almost entirely on Bunny, Arkady still didn't put anything in his glass.

Ronan tried to catch her eye to figure out what she planned to do, but she'd curled up next to Mora as if Ronan wasn't even there. On the one hand, that had been part of their plan, but he got the impression Arkady was ignoring him on purpose. Maybe she wanted to goad him into doing something. He already knew she enjoyed keeping him off-balance. Or maybe she wanted to make sure Mora didn't lose interest in her.

Bunny, the other person in the booth besides Mora who had no idea what part she played in their plot, was certainly an excellent dancer. Already Mora's smile seemed far more genuine and relaxed than it had been since they'd met him. His arousal was unmistakable. And if he didn't know better, Ronan would have thought Arkady had forgotten why they were there. She seemed thoroughly focused on enjoying Bunny's dance too. She alternated between playing with Bunny's long hair and running her hand up and down Mora's thigh. Ronan had to concentrate on not imagining how good those languid strokes of her fingertips would feel on his own leg.

Arkady finally seemed to notice the way he was watching her.

"Why don't you go dance for my lover boy?" she murmured to Bunny. "I think he looks a bit lonely, don't you?"

"I think he does." Bunny smiled at Ronan. "Would you like some company?"

He felt certain Arkady had a good reason for sending Bunny his way. "Definitely," he said.

She sashayed over to him and bent to let her long hair brush against his cheek. "You know I don't like to see anyone lonely," she murmured in his ear. She turned her back to him and braced herself with her hands on his thighs as she moved against his lap.

He started to think about cold showers, then decided he might as well enjoy Bunny's attentions. Arkady certainly had. To do otherwise would be rude, after all, and he was nothing if not appreciative of honest, hard work.

Meanwhile, champagne glass in hand, Arkady sat sideways in Mora's lap like she'd done with Ronan earlier. To Ronan's surprise, Mora's eyes now appeared glazed, and his face seemed a little slack. Had Arkady managed to dose him after all? And if so, how?

She spoke into Mora's ear. "I have some questions for you," Arkady murmured. Thanks to his acute hearing, Ronan could hear what she said, but he doubted anyone else, including Bunny, could. "You're going to tell me the truth, right?" she prompted.

Mora nodded jerkily.

"Good boy." She wiggled on Mora's lap and bit his earlobe playfully for the benefit of anyone watching. "Oh, what a *good boy* you are. I knew you just needed a firm hand."

As Bunny danced and the music played, Arkady interrogated their target and Ronan listened in. She didn't waste any time getting to the point. "Were you going to meet two guys tonight to buy a girl from them?"

"Yes," Mora said, his voice toneless and expression blank.

"Where were you meeting them?"

"Parking lot." He rattled off an address. Ronan wasn't familiar enough with the city yet to know where it was, but he figured Arkady would know.

Arkady nuzzled Mora's neck. "And what were you going to do with her?"

"Clean her up and turn her over to a broker."

"Who is the broker?"

"I don't know any names."

Under the influence of whatever drug or spell Arkady had dosed him with, everything Mora said seemed truthful. Ronan made a mental note to find out what she'd used. It certainly seemed efficient.

Bunny straddled Ronan's lap and slowly unhooked the many fasteners on her bustier. In that position, she blocked his view of Arkady and Mora. He watched her and smiled while he listened to what Arkady whispered into Mora's ear and the man's responses.

"How do you contact the broker?" Arkady asked.

"I'm contacted once a week," Mora mumbled. "Always a different number calling. They tell me when and where to meet them."

"Have you ever tried to call that number again?"

"Yes. They never answer."

Bunny had discarded her bustier in favor of a coquettishly draped arm that only nominally obscured her ample breasts. Ronan smiled at her appreciatively, but he grumbled inwardly.

Whoever this broker was, they were extraordinarily careful. Even if Mora got caught, there was little or nothing he could reveal about anyone above his middle-management level in the trafficking organization. That told Ronan a couple of things—not the least of which were that the people at the top had been in this game a long time and they wouldn't hesitate to do whatever was necessary to protect their interests. Good. That just made the prospect of taking them out even sweeter.

"Where do you meet the broker?" Arkady asked Mora.

"In a different place each time."

"How much are you paid per girl?"

"Five hundred to fifteen hundred dollars each, depending on the quality of the merchandise."

Her rapid-fired questioning and deliberate lack of reaction to Mora's answers confirmed his suspicion that she had experience with interrogations. Given her combat skills and ability to quickly and accurately assess the people around her, among other things, he'd pegged her for former military with specialized training. The fact she'd likely been an interrogator did not surprise him at all.

What *did* surprise him was her next question.

"Who did you hear use the phrase *my sweetness?*" she asked Mora.

Ronan recalled her reaction earlier. So it was the term of endearment itself that had upset her. It *was* an odd phrasing, to be sure. And strangely it also rang a distant bell, though he couldn't recall where or when he might have heard it. He was suddenly very curious to hear Mora's answer to Arkady's very pointed question.

Unfortunately, neither of them got an answer to that question—or at least, not in the way they wanted.

Oliver Mora opened his mouth to respond. Then he pitched forward, blood gushing from his nose, mouth, eyes, and ears. He was dead in less than three seconds.

Stunned, Ronan rose. His abrupt movement displaced Bunny. She landed on the carpet with a yelp and stared up at him, wide-eyed with surprise and annoyance.

Covered in blood, Arkady pushed Mora aside and stood. The dead man slid from the booth and flopped on the floor.

"Oh my *God!*" Bunny shrieked. Sobbing hysterically, she scrambled to her feet and ran away from their booth as fast as she could on her platform heels.

The rest of the customers in the lounge finally noticed what had happened. Everyone abandoned their activities, started screaming, and ran for the exits.

"Well, that could have gone better," Ronan said.

"Shit." Arkady reached into her jacket pocket and threw something on the floor. The item turned out to be a small black spell bag.

Ronan's nose twitched at the sharp odor of burned licorice and something rotting. Black magic. What the hell was she doing?

"*Exit!*" Arkady yelled.

The bag exploded, and all the lights went out.

6

ARKADY

WHEN RONAN WAS FURIOUS, HE VIBRATED.

Arkady would have enjoyed that sensation more if she wasn't drenched in Oliver Mora's blood and they didn't both smell like roadkill thanks to witchy black magic.

He'd also gone menacingly silent, which she *did* enjoy because in the first few minutes after witnessing Mora's messy death, she was in no mood for either a lecture or pointed questions.

About ten minutes later, as Ronan tried to put as much distance between them and the chaos at Bella's without driving recklessly enough to attract attention, she finally spoke to him via the microphone in their helmets. "Nobody's following us. We need to go to my house to clean up and change."

He didn't respond, but she sensed he was listening, so she gave him her address and directions. Without a word, he slowed, turned left, and headed for her home, still buzzing with barely suppressed rage.

"We could have just waited there for the cops to arrive, I suppose," she said as they made their way through nearly deserted back streets toward her neighborhood in the southeast part of the city. "I'm assuming you don't mind explaining who you are and what you do to the police, or them getting their hands on a video of us watching a man die. I think they'd be *particularly* interested in the fact you didn't bat an eye as it happened."

With her arms around his waist, she felt his chest rumble.

"That's what I thought," she said. "So the stench is the price we have to pay for a spell that made them forget about us, fried their video recordings, and let us get away."

"How did you know that spell wouldn't affect me?" he grated.

Ah—so *that* was what he was so pissed about, not the black magic or the smell. "Because you're not human," she said.

He didn't say another word until they arrived at her house. Nor did he stop buzzing with anger.

When they pulled into the driveway of her little bungalow, Arkady typed the code for the garage door into the app on her phone. As the door rolled open, she climbed off the back of the Harley, took off her helmet, and shook out her hair. It felt sticky and matted with drying blood.

"Well, I have a new least-favorite experience at a strip club," she said under her breath. "Just when I thought it couldn't get worse than coming in *second* at an amateur strip contest."

She watched Ronan steer the Harley into the garage, turn off the engine, put the kickstand down, and take off his helmet and gloves, all very deliberately. His anger crackled in the air like static. The rigidity of his shoulders made hers ache, but she had way too much blood on her clothes and troubles on her mind to waste time and energy worrying about his feelings.

My sweetness. My sweetness. My sweetness. The words echoed in her head.

Her searching fingertips found the thick scar tissue hidden under her unblemished skin on the side of her throat. The healing spell she'd bought had done its best, but it hadn't been able to repair all the damage. At least it was enough to keep anyone else from knowing what had happened.

My sweetness, Oliver Mora had called her. Then he'd died spurting blood from every orifice.

Like Alice, Arkady didn't believe in coincidences, especially when it came to vampires. Big cities like this one were in reality very small worlds. Mora hadn't hemorrhaged to death because they'd questioned him about the traffickers. He'd died because she'd asked him where he'd heard the phrase *my sweetness* before.

She'd known someday her path would lead her back to the vamp who'd damn near torn out her throat. She just hadn't imagined it would be tonight, and especially not with Alice's runaway houseguest riding shotgun.

First things first, she thought. She needed a very hot shower, a change of clothes, and a drink—and not necessarily in that order.

Before they'd left Bella's, she'd put on the shirt she'd stolen from Ronan under her jacket so the leather didn't end up covered with blood. It was bad enough that her second-best bra was toast. Even if she could clean it, she wouldn't be able to wear it again without remembering whose blood had soaked into it and why he'd died.

She took off her jacket and studied it with a critical eye, then sighed in relief. She'd have to get rid of her bra and jeans, but at least her boots and jacket could be saved with a bit of cleaning. Ronan's shirt, on the other hand, was saturated with drying blood and she had to peel it off.

Jacket in one hand and T-shirt in the other, she opened the door that led to the kitchen. "I'm hitting the shower," she announced. "Shut the garage on your way in. You can wait until it's your turn for the shower or use the sink in the laundry room to clean up. Soap, washcloths, and towels are in the cabinet above the washer."

Heavy footsteps came up behind her. He could have moved silently if he'd wanted to, but he'd let her know exactly where he was so he didn't startle her, despite the fact he was still furious. At any other point in her very eventful life, she would never have allowed someone who harbored so much resentment to lurk behind her.

From the moment they'd stood close to each other in the parking lot at the Pelican, she'd felt she could trust him to have her back. It hadn't made sense then, and it made even less sense now. Maybe that was a clue to what he was, but she didn't know what it meant.

"Can I touch you?" Ronan asked, his voice gruff.

"Why?" She spun around. "Touch me where?"

She stood two steps above him, so now they were face-to-face despite their difference in height. Up close, his eyes were a perfect ice blue. At the moment, she couldn't see any hint of that mysterious silver glint.

"Here." He reached up, his gaze locked on hers.

She watched him warily but held her ground. His surprisingly gentle fingertips touched her neck right where the vamp had bitten her. She couldn't remember ever feeling such a wonderful warmth. She saw no sympathy or pity in his eyes, as if he understood those were the last things she wanted. Still, her stomach knotted.

"Don't." She took an involuntary step back. Her boot heel caught on the threshold of the kitchen doorway.

Lightning fast, he jumped to the top step and set her back on her feet almost before she realized she'd stumbled. His sudden movement left them less than an inch apart. His hands stayed on her bare arms, but he just rested them there without holding onto her. She shivered despite the warmth of his touch.

His gaze moved to her mouth. The way he studied her lips sent a wave of heat straight through her. She'd noticed him watching her throughout the evening, enough to make her think she knew what stirred his drink. Not her ass or tits, though he'd admired those too when he thought she wasn't paying attention. He liked her mouth.

She moistened her lips with the tip of her tongue. The corners of his mouth turned up.

Damn it, they had a case to solve. No time to knock boots, no matter how much her lady bits ached. "I've got blood all over my clothes," she said. Her voice sounded breathless, even to her ears.

"I can see that," he rumbled.

"And I stink like black magic." Now she sounded a bit desperate. That would have annoyed her more if she could think of anything besides that baritone rumble and how good he smelled even over the odor of witch magic and Mora's blood.

Ronan raised his eyebrows. "Do I look like I care?"

"*I* care." She pressed her hands to his chest. When he didn't move, she gave in and moved back. "I told you blood isn't sexy. Black magic stench definitely isn't."

"Then you need to get out of those bloody, stinky clothes." Mercilessly, he closed the distance between them again. "The sooner, the better."

"Yeah, maybe." She didn't retreat, because backing up even once had set her teeth on edge. "But you're in my personal space uninvited, sweet pea. Move back, or I'll move you."

He chuckled. "I'd like to see you try."

Before he finished the sentence, her fist was already in motion. He easily blocked the blow *and* her follow-up left jab with his forearms. *Damn it.* Her attempt to kick the back of his knee and fold him like a lawn chair accomplished exactly nothing. Though she made contact, he barely flinched.

She went into overdrive then with a flurry of right and left hooks, jabs, uppercuts, and body blows. Each connected only with his biceps or forearms, and none caused him to budge an inch, as if his boots were nailed to her kitchen floor. And the smug son of a bitch kept smiling.

Arkady saw red.

She jumped, spun, and unleashed a lightning-speed roundhouse kick that had left previous opponents flat on their backs and seeing stars, if not unconscious.

Instead of his chin, her boot heel hit his hand. He grabbed her ankle and lifted her until she dangled upside down almost three feet from the tile floor.

She let out a furious yell and tried to kick him in the jaw with her other foot, but he caught that one too. From her inverted position, she punched him square in the gut. Her fist struck rock-hard abs. He didn't so much as blink—just kept smiling.

With few options left, she said to hell with fighting clean and swung her elbow straight at his groin with all the momentum she could muster. Before she could make contact, he tossed her right side up, caught her by the waist, and set her back on her feet in front of him where she'd started.

It didn't escape her notice that despite the fact she'd attempted at least a dozen punches and kicks, only two of which had managed to hit their targets, he hadn't done anything more than prevent her from striking him. And of course his feet hadn't moved a millimeter.

"What the hell was that?" She was breathless again, but for an entirely different reason. "You goad me into a fight, and then you just stand there? What are you trying to prove?"

Ronan's reply took her entirely by surprise. "I don't think we have anything to prove to each other." He tucked some loose hair behind her ear. "Do you?"

"Everyone always has *something* to prove." She held her ground, even when he caressed her shoulder. "Don't pretend you don't. All this black leather and riding a Harley and 'I'm a big bad loner' stuff is all about proving how tough you are, right?"

He tilted his head. "Is that what you really think?"

"No," she admitted. "But you *are* trying to prove something to yourself."

He didn't answer her, but she knew by the way his brow furrowed that she'd guessed right.

"The problem is, it's *way* harder to convince yourself of something than it is to convince someone else." She gathered up her jacket and T-shirt from where she'd dropped them on the floor. "So good luck with that."

"But I still say we have nothing to prove to each other." He tipped her chin up with his fingertips and looked into her eyes. "It makes a nice change from people we've been with in the past, don't you think?"

She wanted to tell him to go to hell, that she hadn't had anything to prove to any lover, but she couldn't bring herself to lie to him. Not about this.

In every relationship she'd ever had, no matter how brief, how it began, or how it ended, she'd felt as though she had something to prove. Even her friendship and partnership with Alice had felt that way up until very recently. Alice's neurotic need to protect everyone made Arkady feel as though she had to prove she didn't need protecting.

Her most recent affair, an on-again, off-again fling with former Vampire Court enforcer Matthias Albrecht, had consisted almost entirely of trying to prove to each other how strong, stubborn, and *right* they each were. No wonder they'd been doomed from the start despite their mutual attraction.

Ronan, whatever the hell he was, had just told her they had nothing to prove to each other, and she thought he might be right. And if that was the case, she had no idea how to act around him. She wasn't just in uncharted territory—she was in an entirely different dimension.

His gaze stayed locked on hers. "It's a first for me too," he said, his voice strangely rough. "But I *do* know one thing: how much I want to do this." He bent his head and kissed her.

She was in no way surprised to discover Ronan was one hell of a kisser, or that he tasted of tequila. Strangely, he also tasted like something that reminded her of the ocean. Her busted lip hurt when his kiss became more demanding. She didn't mind a bit of pain, however, not when it came courtesy of a man this bewitchingly attractive.

You have a case, her conscience protested. *No time to knock boots, remember?*

Shut up, she ordered that annoying inner voice. *It's been a long night. I deserve to have some fun.*

With a little moan, she dropped her T-shirt and jacket again and arched against Ronan. He pulled her close, one hand cupping her head and the other at the small of her back. Her hand slid up his thigh and gripped his very firm ass. *Mmm.*

"Like that, do you?" He smiled against her lips. "I had a feeling you might be that sort of woman."

The intensity of her desire made her feel dizzy. "What sort of woman do you mean?"

"The sort who likes to either kick a man's ass or find other ways to entertain herself with it."

She grabbed a handful of his shirt. He let her pin him against the wall next to the kitchen door. "That doesn't scare you off?" she asked. "What I might like to do?"

He trailed his mouth along her jaw. "I've faced some pretty terrifying things. Your kinks in no way scare me...but they *do* intrigue me."

Distracted by what he'd said and the fact she was pretty sure he meant it, it took her a few moments to realize his lips were right where the vamp had bitten her. When she tensed, he kissed her in that same spot and nuzzled her again. She tried not to flinch but failed.

"Your body is your own and no one else's," he told her, raising his head to look into her eyes. "Tell me not to touch you there and I won't. Or let me turn it into something good to think about instead."

She wanted to give him permission to do just that, but she couldn't. Not yet. Not until the vamp who'd bitten her was ash.

"I have a better idea." She took his hand and put it on her belt. "Give me something good to think about by touching me somewhere else."

"Don't you want to shower first?" he teased as he unfastened her belt. The button and zipper of her jeans followed next. "I thought blood and black magic weren't sexy."

Thoughts of his fine ass and other body parts had completely banished her concerns about the blood and roadkill smell. She yanked at his belt impatiently. "Okay, fine, sometimes blood is sexy. I guess I could feel the same way about the magic smell, given a good reason."

His smile widened. "I can do much, *much* better than just a *good* reason, Miss Woodall."

"Ever so modest." She pulled his T-shirt free of his jeans. "Why are you wearing so many clothes?"

His hands caught hers and held them still. Startled, she looked up. His expression had turned grim. She spotted an unexpected glimmer of pain in his eyes before he had a chance to hide it. "What's wrong?" she demanded.

"I have scars." Gently, he pulled her hands away from his shirt and kissed her knuckles. "Bad ones."

Oh, right—the scars. Back at Alice's house, Arkady had glimpsed the symbols someone had cut into Ronan's flesh over his ribs. Though Alice had never revealed the details of what had happened to him, Arkady had gleaned enough to understand the scars were some kind of cruel punishment.

She started to tell him she'd already seen his scars, but stopped. Something about the pain in his eyes told her he wouldn't take the news well. He'd been unconscious and vulnerable when she'd seen them. Better to let him show them to her on his own terms.

"So you've got scars," she countered. "Do I look like I care?"

She'd used his own words on purpose, hoping to elicit a smile and ease the sudden tension, but it didn't work. His expression remained stony, and now he seemed to be pulling back. The frenzied desire that moments ago had them ready to tear off each other's clothes began to evaporate.

"Of course you have scars. So do I." She pointed to a knife scar on her left bicep, another on her forearm, and the semi-circular scar on the left side of her abdomen that had come from a .22 fired at point-blank range. "And those are just the obvious ones. I've been punctured more times than a cheating boyfriend's tires. Your scars won't bother me."

When he still said nothing, she glared at him. "So you're not going to win Mr. Universe with your shirt off. Big fucking deal. I'm no beauty queen myself."

"I beg to differ." He gave her a ghost of a smile. "You are so beautiful that when I first saw you, I thought you must be a Valkyrie come to this realm to hunt for sport."

She blinked. A *Valkyrie?* If anyone else had told her that, she would never have taken them seriously, but Ronan was not a bullshitter. If he said he'd initially mistaken her for some kind of supernatural being or goddess or whatever, then he had.

"Well, thank you," she managed to say. "That's a lot better than what I usually get called. You're pretty hot stuff yourself." She put her hands on her hips. "Now that we're done complimenting each other like a couple of sorority girls, may I point out that you just got done saying we have nothing to prove to each other. Now you pull this, after promising me a good time? The least you could do is follow through, Mister *I never leave my lady in the lurch.*"

"I'll happily follow through." Now his smile turned roguish. "My Harley isn't all I have that'll give you a smooth ride—or a rough ride, if that's what you prefer."

That promise sent a shiver down her spine. Even her jeans felt wet along the seam at this point.

It wasn't the worst offer she'd ever had—far from it, in fact—but she'd hate herself if she accepted, knowing he'd have those scars in the back of his mind, hidden under his shirt.

What *were* those symbols? What sadistic bastard had made them? And why would a man so fierce feel he had to hide them from a willing lover's eyes?

"Ronan," she said carefully, "if the shit really, *really* hits the fan while we try to get to the bottom of this trafficking thing, do you trust me to have your back?"

He didn't hesitate. "Yes."

And damned if that didn't turn her on almost as much as the thought of a rough ride. *Forget firm asses, handcuffs, and all the rest*, she thought wryly. *Turns out trust is my ultimate kink.*

"Glad to hear it." She took his hand and put his palm on her blood-splattered chest over her heart. "If you trust me with your life, you can trust me to see your scars."

His mouth twitched. "Impeccable logic, Miss Woodall." His smile faded. "The heart is not logical. Sometimes pain runs too deep."

Arkady had her own share of pain she didn't talk about. So who the hell was she to push Ronan past his boundaries? He'd respected hers.

"Okay." She leaned forward and kissed his T-shirt where the cuts were hidden. He trembled at her touch. He didn't try to hide it, which made something strange and light stir in her heart. He also didn't seem to notice that she'd known where to kiss him. He'd probably assumed she'd guessed.

"Scars only have power if you let them," she told him as she straightened. "And that's the truth."

"Even yours?"

"Yeah, even mine. I don't pretend I'm an exception to the rule." She touched her throat, then dropped her hand to her side. "I'm going to take that power back, though."

His genuine smile returned. "Because fuck 'em?"

"Yep. So take yours back too."

"Some scars have their own power."

"Even if they do, that doesn't mean you can't take that power and make it your own."

He blinked at her as if that thought had never occurred to him.

"That's what passes for a deep thought tonight." She chuckled. "Stick around—if you're lucky, there'll be more wisdom where that came from." She picked up the shirt and jacket again and hooked her thumb at the door on the other side of the kitchen. "That's the laundry room if you want to clean up. I'm going to shower so we can get back to work."

His brow furrowed. "Where do you propose we go from here? The men we killed at the Pelican were demon servants, but we don't know who they belonged to or whether the demon was part of this trafficking ring. And we didn't get much from Mora to work with."

"Since when has that put us off?" She handed him her jacket. "See if you can get this clean, would you?"

He rumbled. "Do I look like a laundry service?"

"No, but you look like a man who knows how to get blood off leather." She grinned at his scowl. "Oh, and while I'm in the shower, find us a lead to follow. Bet you can't."

He pounced on her words, as she'd known he would. "What's the wager?" he asked.

"*When* you fail to find us a lead, you will make us coffee and dispose of our bloody clothes so they'll never ever be found." She considered. "Then you'll come back and clean my kitchen and buy me a bottle of any tequila I want."

"That's pretty steep," he mused. "Though I've never lost a wager and don't intend to start now. That being the case, what do I get when I win?"

"Oh, something comparable." Arkady smiled. "You like my mouth a lot, don't you?" Her gaze moved to his belt and then lower. His body's reaction to her stare was instantaneous and unmistakable. "So *if* you win—which you *won't*—I'll let you decide what I do with mine."

His brow arched. "I accept the wager, though I wonder if you really know what you'll be in for."

"Oh, I have a pretty good idea." She gave him her most irritating smirk—the one that had historically led to numerous bar fights and one or two messy breakups. "I've faced some pretty terrifying things. Your kinks in no way scare me...but they *do* intrigue me."

For the first time since they'd met, he laughed. He had a good laugh. She turned around so he couldn't see her smirk turn into a smile.

"Laugh all you want, O Great and Mighty One." She tossed her blood-matted hair and headed down the hallway. "You're the one who has no idea what you're in for. I'll want my kitchen to sparkle like a lame-ass vampire whenever we're done with this case."

He was still chuckling when she shut the door to her room.

7

RONAN

FOR THE FIRST FEW MINUTES AFTER SHE DISAPPEARED BEHIND HER bedroom door, Ronan was almost positive Arkady Woodall wanted to lose their wager.

But then again, he reflected as he washed up at the laundry room sink and pulled on a clean black shirt and jeans from his saddlebag, she didn't seem like the type to like to lose—intentionally or otherwise— no matter how intrigued she seemed by what he might want her to do with her mouth.

After all, she'd asked him to clean her jacket *and* find a lead, and he doubted he had very long to accomplish either. Some women might be a half-hour just showering after what they'd been through and then take that much time or more getting ready. He'd bet his Harley she'd be ready to leave again in ten minutes.

Well, seven minutes now.

The shower was still running, but he figured it would shut off at any second. So he sent a couple of text messages to contacts he'd made in town, put her jacket and his clothes in the laundry room sink, tossed in one of the spell crystals he kept in his inside jacket pocket, and invoked it.

With a sizzle of power, the burner spell housed in the crystal flared. White air magic swept over Arkady's jacket and his clothes, turning all the blood on them to fine ash. When the spell finished, it left the faint scent of ozone in the air and no trace of Oliver Mora's lifeblood. He pocketed the spent crystal, shook off the ash and washed it down the sink, and draped her jacket over the washing machine. It was clean, but he thought it could use some leather conditioner.

He found a small bottle of conditioner and an orphan sock obviously dedicated to the purpose in the cabinet over the dryer and took Arkady's jacket to her living room. He settled on the couch just as the shower in the bathroom shut off. Moments later, he heard another door open and footsteps in Arkady's bedroom. Her room must have a door that led directly into the one full bathroom.

As he waited for replies to his messages and rubbed the leather conditioner into the jacket, he glanced around the main living area of Arkady's cottage. He'd noticed when they drove up that it appeared to be a converted guest house that had once belonged to the much-larger home behind it. An economical solution for a single woman living alone. The neighborhood seemed quiet. He imagined she enjoyed some peace after what he assumed had been years of violence and chaos.

At about a thousand square feet, the house was anything but spacious, but the layout made it seem bigger than it was. And as he'd expected, Arkady's tastes ran toward the utilitarian. He smiled at the sight of the square target mounted on the wall opposite the couch. The wood was pockmarked edge to edge from repeated knife hits. She must sit on the couch and practice her throws. The even distribution of the marks indicated she aimed all over the target, not just at its center. He'd never met anyone as precise with a blade as himself until tonight. She might even be better. He was surprised to discover that didn't bother him.

He didn't want to compete with her. He just wanted her.

And he would have had her, and she would have had him, if only Michael hadn't carved him up and made him ashamed of his own body.

To distract himself, he continued looking around Arkady's house. In an odd contradiction to the well-used target, she'd left a cozy blanket folded neatly on the back of the couch, perfect for an evening at home reading, listening to music, or in front of the television.

When had he last spent a quiet evening in front of a television? He frowned at the jacket, trying to remember. Had he *ever*? Surely in all his long years he must have, but so much time had passed that he no longer recalled when or where. His nights tended to involve riding his Harley from one job to the next or sitting on a barstool or at a table in a crowded, noisy bar. For that matter, he doubted he'd enjoy a dull, quiet night watching television.

The door to Arkady's room opened almost exactly ten minutes after she'd closed it. She emerged, her hair wrapped in a towel and a different pair of boots in her hand. Other than the towel and shoes, she'd redressed completely.

"Conditioning my jacket wasn't part of our wager, but I'll accept it as a bonus," Arkady said as she sat cross-legged on the other end of the couch to towel-dry her hair. She smelled of soap, peppermint oil he thought might have been in her shampoo, and minty mouthwash. And of a few swigs of tequila, which she'd tried to cover by using the mouthwash. "Obviously you don't have a lead for us," she added. "So where's my coffee, Ronan?"

He *did* have a lead, though...just not from one of his contacts. But did he want to win their wager, or lose? If he won, there was the promise of Arkady's mouth, and he'd be a liar if he claimed that prospect didn't make him hard.

If he lost, he'd get to return to her home to clean her kitchen until it sparkled and bring her the best bottle of tequila his money could buy. Given the way he'd started to feel about her, which had more promise?

He weighed a couple of factors and made a decision. "I have a lead," he said.

"Right." She snorted. "My ass."

"If only your lovely ass was the lead in question, I would most assuredly investigate it thoroughly," he said dryly. "But alas, that's not what I suggest we investigate next—unless we're giving up to spend the remainder of our night engaged in other activities."

She didn't take the bait, however. "We're not giving up on

anything." She tossed the towel over the back of the couch and combed her damp hair. "So tell me about this supposed lead you've magically gotten in the last ten minutes, O Great and Mighty One."

He settled back into the couch. "First, just to clarify: since I've won our wager, I get to decide what you do with your mouth?"

She raised her eyebrows. "I haven't seen any evidence whatsoever that you've won jack shit, sweet pea."

"But if I have a viable lead, I win, yes?" he persisted.

Now she definitely smelled a rat. Her eyes narrowed. "You wouldn't be trying to trick me into an unearned blowjob, would you?"

"I'm insulted." He wasn't really, but he leaned forward and locked his gaze on hers so she could see how serious he was. "First, I'd never trick you. Second, I assure you that *when* you do that for me, it will be entirely of your own accord, and I will have more than earned it."

She squirmed in a way that made it difficult for him to think about anything besides her mouth on him. "Stop deliberately turning me on when we have work to do," she said crossly. "I know you said you're not a gentleman, and that's fine, but you don't have to be a dick."

He had to fight to keep a straight face. "I shall endeavor not to be a dick."

"Yeah, right. I'll believe it when I see it." She set her comb aside and put her hair in a ponytail. "Fine. What's your lead?"

He figured she'd either go along with him or stab him. Possibly both. There was only one way to find out what her reaction would be. "You," he said.

She stared at him for a few beats before comprehension made her expression go cold and her eyes turn flinty.

"You know where Oliver Mora learned that phrase *my sweetness*." He kept his voice matter-of-fact, knowing sympathy would only anger her more. "And you know as well as I do how and why Mora died."

If he'd thought her expression was cold, that was nothing compared to the deadly chill in her voice. "A *geas*," she said.

"Exactly. Someone spelled him to never say the name of whoever he'd heard use those words, or probably even to describe them."

"But I'd spelled him to speak the truth," she interjected. "And so he tried to tell me the name and promptly croaked. Fucking vampires."

She stuck her right foot into her boot and stomped the floor to put it on, then did the same with her left boot, as if the hardwood beneath her feet was the face of her enemy.

He waited while she tied her boots. At least she hadn't stabbed him yet. Maybe that was a good sign.

"I'm not sorry Mora's dead, but I *am* sorry we didn't get more information out of him." She rested her forearms on her knees. "So I'm supposed to blow you because you picked up on the blatantly obvious?"

He knew she'd said it that way because he'd angered her, and because she very much did not want to talk about the vampire in question. And maybe she wanted him to feel cheap for trying to cash in on their wager.

"You never asked me what I wanted you to do with your mouth," he pointed out. "You keep assuming I want a blowjob."

She gave him an incredulous look. "If you tell me you don't, I'm going to be very insulted. So think real hard about what you say next."

"Miss Woodall, there are few things in all of Creation I want more," he said, very seriously. "But at the moment, what I want you to do with your mouth is tell me about this vampire who called you *my sweetness* and bit you without your permission."

Without a word, she rose and stormed into the kitchen. He heard cabinet doors slamming, a string of curses, and the unmistakable sound of a heavy object smashing in the sink. Then silence.

He set her jacket aside and joined her in the kitchen. The casualty turned out to be a coffee mug. Judging by how far the pieces had flown, she'd thrown it with considerable force.

Now she had her back to him, scooping ground coffee into her coffeemaker. The coffee looked to be from a local shop and smelled good. Something else she had in common with Alice: a love of first-rate, strong coffee.

He reached into the sink, but her sharp voice stopped him. "Leave it," she said without turning around. "It's my fucking mess. I'll clean it up."

"All right." He leaned against the counter while she started the coffeemaker. As it gurgled, she threw the largest pieces of the mug in the trash.

When she picked up a handful of smaller pieces, she sucked in a breath and examined her hand. One of the broken edges had cut her palm.

She stared at the cut as blood trickled down her arm. A surprisingly overt parade of emotions flashed in her eyes: pain, anger, grief, and even some shame. He didn't need to be a mind-reader to know the sight of the blood had conjured up the memory of the vamp's bite. The shame might be a result of the bite, the fact the vamp still walked the earth, or both.

He was at her side before he realized he'd moved and cradled her injured hand. She didn't flinch this time, but he wanted to apologize anyway. "I'm sorry for moving so quickly."

"Never apologize for fast reflexes. They're the only thing that keeps people like us alive." She gave him a crooked smile. "Some Valkyrie. Bloodied by a coffee mug."

"Little-known fact," he said, returning her smile. "Coffee mugs are a Valkyrie's only natural enemy."

She chuckled, but the sound was strained. Ronan covered her hand with his own and summoned his healing power. It didn't take much to heal a superficial wound, but he quickly discovered that healing someone else was much more difficult as a mortal. Before his imprisonment, he'd been able to heal others' near-fatal injuries without too much effort. Now it took all his concentration and an unsettling amount of power to fix a simple cut.

Arkady watched as his soft silver-blue magic pulsed in her hand. His vision had a silver edge, meaning his eyes shone a bit silver. Very few humans knew what the silver signified. When he didn't see any recognition or surprise in her expression, he knew she hadn't recognized the angelic magic for what it was. Just as well. That was not a conversation he was in a hurry to have.

When her hand finished healing, he held on for a few beats before he released her. She studied her unblemished palm. "Thanks," she said finally.

"You're welcome."

"By the way." Her eyes narrowed again. "Blackmailing people into giving up their secrets is being a dick."

"You made the wager," he pointed out.

"Yeah, I know. That'll teach me to think I'm so smart." She returned to the coffeemaker to watch the carafe fill. "What are you?" she asked with her back to him.

He felt torn between wanting to keep his identity a secret and wondering if she could figure it out, and how long it would take until she did. She was observant and smart, and she was no stranger to dealing with nonhumans. He doubted she'd ever encountered any kind of angel before, however, and as such that wasn't likely to be on her list of possibilities. It wasn't any kind of test, because he didn't need her to prove anything, but it *did* feel like a game—one that, strangely, he wanted her to win.

He came up behind her and rested his hand on her hip. "I'm a man."

"Not a *human* man." She leaned against him. "But you're definitely a man."

"The more time I spend with you, the more I think that's not the worst thing to be." He liked the way her body fit against his. He kissed the top of her head and then made his voice stern. "Tell me about the vampire, Miss Woodall."

His tone invited her to recount the story in the form of a report, while his closeness offered support if she chose to tell the tale as a personal story. He certainly wouldn't hold it against her if she gave him the clinical version. He knew as well as anyone how complicated and difficult it was to process personal violence.

"I used to work for the Vampire Court as an investigator," she said. "That's how Alice and I met, in fact. We crossed paths on a case and discovered we have a lot in common."

"I'd noticed," he said dryly. "The words *mule-headed* and *fearless* come immediately to mind."

"Can't argue with you there." She chuckled. "She's even more stubborn and neurotic than me, which is really saying something. She makes up for it by being able to level buildings."

Buildings? Try whole armies, he thought. Ronan recalled watching

Alice use her magic to command lightning in the Underworld to smite the Titan Typhon and destroy hordes of Typhon's monstrous creations. He wondered if Alice had told Arkady about her exploits. Likely not, since at the time Alice had been on a mission for the Vampire Court and the vamps took their non-disclosure agreements deadly seriously. *You probably don't know the half of it, Miss Woodall.*

"Getting back to the Vamp Court, I didn't last nearly as long working for them as I expected." Her voice had lost all its mirth. "I thought I had realistic expectations of what they were capable of and what I'd need to do to stay clear of their fangs. I *did* manage to avoid becoming a meal for any of the Court vamps, even the very bitey ones, during the time I worked for them. They had plenty of better sources of blood on hand, like mages and witches, so they didn't really try all that hard to turn me into a juice box. Plain-Jane human isn't their favorite flavor."

He got the impression she would be any vampire's flavor, but he stayed quiet and just let her talk.

"I hated them anyway, though." She watched the last of the coffee drip into the pot, then shut off the machine. "You can only be around creatures like that for so long before you realize you and the rest of humanity are less than dirt to them. Your value is measured solely by your usefulness."

He pictured Michael's cold gaze and bladed wings. When he tried to stretch his own bound wings, his back muscles twinged painfully. "I'm familiar with that philosophy," he said.

"Yeah, I figured you were." She poured them each a cup of coffee and added whiskey to both. "Somehow, people like us always seem to end up working for people like that."

Mugs in hand, they returned to the living room. She curled up next to him on the couch, her head against his shoulder. He didn't put his arm around her because he sensed that wasn't what she wanted, so he sipped his coffee and waited for her to start talking again.

"I'd wanted to leave the Court for about two months before it happened." Arkady smiled without humor. "I guess it was only a matter of time before one of them got me. If you lie down with dogs, you end up with fleas, as the saying goes. Or in this case, you cross paths with a strung-out vamp, you end up with hidden scars and PTSD."

Ronan frowned. "Strung-out vampire? What do you mean?"

She went quiet and pondered the coffee in her cup. She had a reasonably good poker face, but he couldn't miss the little furrow between her brows. If he had to guess, her internal debate focused on whether to violate the Court's NDA.

And as he'd expected, she decided to tell him the full story. She struck him as the sort who now only gave her loyalty to those who showed loyalty to her.

"The Court sent me after what they called a *rogue vampire*," she told him. "As I'm sure you know, that term can mean a lot of things—a young vamp whose maker has died or cut them loose without oversight, a vamp who's run away from their maker, someone who's broken Court law and is hiding from punishment, et cetera. I'd done several of those cases for them, so I didn't think much of it. The dossier they gave me basically indicated this was a young vamp who had a habit of spending his days outside his master's home and his nights 'carousing with negative influences,' as they called it." She sighed. "I knew vampires were liars, but usually when I got an assignment the information was at least accurate, even if it was heavily redacted. In this case, however, the redacted part turned out to be very, *very* important."

Ronan's anger had built steadily as she spoke. When she paused, he growled quietly. "I was led to believe the Court sent its dhampirs, if not its Hunters, after rogues. Surely mages at least. Not humans—no matter how highly skilled they are."

Dhampirs, also known as half-turned vamps, were still technically human, but fed on so much powerful vampire blood regularly that they had senses, speed, reflexes, and healing power almost equal to that of a newly turned vampire. Most older vampires and all members of the Vampire Court had multiple dhampirs as part of their security details.

Hunters were a form of dhampir. Unlike other half-turned vamps, they were driven to near insanity by cycles of blood intoxication and then starvation until their master controlled them completely. They were the Court's most feared and single-minded trackers. When triggered or released from their master's control, they became merciless killing machines. Many believed Hunters to be a vampire's only true predator, other than creatures like the fae.

"I'd brought in young rogue vamps before. The challenge appealed to me." She eyed him. "Don't tell me you've never gone after something out of your league, just to see if you could take it down."

He smiled. "Touché, Miss Woodall."

"Plus I have a theory about why they sent me and not a dhampir, but let's put a pin in that for now." She sipped her coffee and swirled it in her cup. "The vamp's name is Henry Farrell. He works at Nyx. It's a vamp-owned club here in the city—the kind you have to sign a lot of waivers to get into."

"I'm familiar with Nyx."

"Might have known you'd find time to go there, even though you've only been in town a few weeks." She raised her eyebrows. "Were you there on business or pleasure?"

"Is there a difference?"

"Another shockingly honest answer." She chuckled. "I'm starting to think you can't lie at all."

"Oh, I certainly can. I simply choose not to lie to you."

"Sooner or later, everybody lies. Even you." Her smile faded. "Anyway, Henry Farrell worked at Nyx first under its original owner, Josiah Harrison. Henry became manager of the place after the Court sentenced Harrison to death by sunlight for making rogues and letting them attack humans."

"To what end?"

"It was all apparently a dumb ploy to unseat Valas, who was the head of the Vampire Court at the time." She clinked her mug against his. "May the bitch rot in hell."

"What personal grudge do you bear against Valas?" He tilted his head. "The vampire Charles Vaughan deposed her and she is dead, is she not?"

She glared at him. "If you'd bothered to check in with Alice at any point in the past few weeks, you'd know on New Year's Eve Valas had Alice and Daniel Holiday kidnapped. She tried to force Alice to help her regain her throne. Alice and Daniel almost died."

Stunned, he said, "I didn't know."

"Yeah, well, now you do. You can ask Alice about it if you ever nut up and face her." She set her coffee cup on the side table. "Anyway, it was Henry Farrell who'd gone rogue, the vamps said. So I was supposed to round him up and deliver him to the Court for what they call *correction*. They gave me his dossier, a list of possible haunts, and instructions to deliver him alive and only *reasonably damaged*." She put air quotes around the latter. "Long story short, I found him the next night—or I guess I should say, he found *me*. He got the drop on me, literally. He jumped off a roof and landed right in front of me. I stabbed him with silver, but it didn't even slow him down. He was out of his damn mind."

"You mentioned that before." Ronan rubbed his bristly chin. "I believe you, but as far as I know, vampires are more or less impervious to illicit drugs, whether taken directly or contained in the blood of their victims."

"Yeah, that's the official word. But you know the vamps—they'd walk into the sun before admitting they have any of the same vices as us lowly humans."

Again, he thought of Michael. The archangel of archangels would likely turn Ronan to dust for saying so, but it occurred to him that Michael had much in common with vampires. "So vampires have a drug, or drugs, of choice?"

"Besides power? Of course they do." She snorted. "Have you ever met a species of supe *more* likely than the undead to need an escape from reality? Look past the façade of sophistication and *savoir-faire*, and they're really a bunch of miserable fucks. And where there's a will, there's a way."

In all his time and travels Ronan had never heard of a drug capable of affecting a vampire, but he couldn't argue with either Arkady's logic or eyewitness account. "What is the name of this drug?"

"The vamps who don't take it call it the Scourge. They're so dramatic." She shrugged. "What the addicts themselves call it, I don't know. Farrell was too busy chewing on my neck to say much."

Ronan envisioned his Valkyrie lying in an alley, pinned beneath a drug-crazed vampire as he savaged her beautiful neck, and had a nearly irresistible urge to transform into his full angelic form. He might have done so if he still had that form—his rage was that overwhelming.

And then his thoughts came to a screeching halt. Wait...*his* Valkyrie?

Arkady was so laughably *not* his that he almost scoffed out loud at himself. In any case, he'd better be real damn careful not to say those words out loud anywhere near Arkady or he'd probably lose a body part he'd miss.

"How did you survive this attack?" he asked. He managed to keep his voice calm and even, despite his fury.

"I stabbed him with my silver blade until he was holier than Palm Sunday, not that he noticed. I had my mandate from the Court not to kill him, but I figured it was going to be either him or me. I have a DNV on file with the Court, but I trust them to honor it about as much as I trust a rattlesnake not to bite."

"A DNV?"

"A *Do Not Vamp*." She gave him another humorless smile. "It's the vampire equivalent of a *Do Not Resuscitate*. In other words, if I croak, don't turn me. All employees of the Court must make their wishes clear."

"But they don't always honor those wishes?"

"Exactly. Legal or not, if it's to the vamps' advantage, sometimes important documents or records go missing." She got up, walked to the wall opposite the couch, and crossed her arms. "So, anyway, I decided I'd had enough of being Strung-Out Harry's chew toy and pulled my stake...and that's when the Hunters showed up."

He read her expression and felt himself go cold. "The Court used you as bait."

"Yup. And I think they wanted him to kill me 'accidentally' so one of them could turn me." She leaned against the wall. "Charles Vaughan and another member of the Court, Amira, said more than once that I would make an ideal Hunter or vampire. I think they meant it as a compliment, but to me it was a huge warning to watch my neck."

"And a good reason to believe they might not honor your DNV, as you called it." He absorbed her words. "I assume the only reason you haven't found and staked Farrell is he has the Court's protection?"

"You assume correctly." She flexed her hands. "Farrell belongs to David Noble's line, and Noble is a longtime member of the Court. I can't stake Farrell for biting me. If he's involved in other criminal activities, however, especially human trafficking not sanctioned by the Court because that's super-duper illegal, he might end up on the sharp end of a stake for that. And the vamps will let that slide."

"Because the truth would reflect poorly on them," Ronan finished. "And this endearment Mora used?"

"That's what Farrell called me all the time he was biting me: *my sweetness.*" She took a deep breath and let it out. "I don't believe in coincidences. I think Henry Farrell is mixed up in this trafficking thing and Mora knew him at least well enough to pick up that phrase."

"As well as a deadly *geas* to prevent him from talking about Farrell." Ronan nodded. "It's a strong lead."

"Yes, it's a lead. So yeah, technically you won our wager." She watched him. "No one outside the Court but you knows about what Farrell did. I expect it to stay that way."

"No hint of this will ever pass my lips." He pulled a knife from a sheath on his belt. "I will swear a blood oath if you wish it."

"Shit, dude, and here I thought *Malcolm* was dramatic." She went to him and raised her right hand. "Put your knife away. I'll take a pinky swear."

He hooked his pinky with hers. "*Dude?*" he asked with raised eyebrows and released her finger.

"Ugh, embarrassing." She winced. "I picked that up from Malcolm."

"He's a good man and an even better ally."

"And friend." She sighed. "He's a pain in the ass but I love that bratty little ghost. Don't you dare tell him I said that."

"Our secret," he promised. "So, where do we find Henry Farrell?"

"He's still manager of Nyx, so I bet he's there. We'll have to be careful. The moment he hears we're looking for him, he'll probably go to ground, if he hasn't already. He might have heard about Mora and decided to make himself scarce in case someone's on his trail."

Ronan considered her words. Surprise was almost always the best route, but there were exceptions to the rule. The way Farrell had come at Arkady the first time indicated the young vamp thought the best defense was a good offense. Ronan tended to think the same way.

"Not necessarily," he said finally. "That rather depends on what he's expecting, does it not?"

"Fair point." Arkady grinned. Rather than upsetting her, talking about Farrell's attack seemed to have rekindled her impatience to get back to work. "So, what's your plan?"

"Another trap." Ronan gave her his own hunter's smile. "If you're up for it, that is."

"I'm *always* up for it, sweet pea." She glanced down at her boots. "But if I'm going to be bait again, I need to change clothes—unless you think our target's kink is blondes in ass-kicker casual."

"No, that's *my* kink," he said, because he wanted to hear her laugh again, and because it was true.

Instead of laughing, however, she straddled his lap so they were at eye level. Then she kissed him so fiercely and for so long that for the first time since Michael cast him out he forgot all about his mortal body and bound wings. Nothing else mattered but how good she felt against him. They had places to go and people to kill, but his body had other priorities. He grew hard again.

Rather than thinking about cold showers, he reveled in the raw desire she kindled in his body and soul. He cupped her ass with both hands and kept her from moving away when she broke their kiss.

She chuckled softly in his ear as he gripped her tightly. "Mmm... that feels good," she murmured. "So, it's not just my mouth you like, huh?"

"Definitely not just your mouth." He kissed her again, savoring her fiery taste and scent. "I look forward to finding *all* the parts of you I like."

"Ditto." She glanced down at the very noticeable evidence of his arousal and put her hand to her chest in mock surprise. "Speaking of which...my goodness, is that all for me?"

He wasn't sure which turned him on the most: her precision with a blade, her combat skills, her hunter's smile, or her ability to make him forget all the bullshit in his head.

"Every inch," he promised. "Just say the word and I'm all yours."

"That's the right attitude. I like a man who's ready to rise to the occasion." She stood and offered him her hand like a fellow warrior would. "So, back to this trap you're proposing. Who am I supposed to seduce this time?"

"Nobody." He gripped her hand and rose. "You *will* need a different outfit, Miss Woodall, but so do I. I believe Nyx has a rather strict dress code."

"We're going straight to Nyx?" She licked her lips in anticipation, which distracted him for a beat. "You mean—?"

"Yes." He couldn't help but grin. This was going to be fun. "We're after Henry Farrell. And this time, *I'm* the bait."

8

ARKADY

FROM THE BACK OF RONAN'S HARLEY, ARKADY SPOTTED THE signature purple neon glow of Nyx six blocks before they reached its famous Gothic entrance. The massive club drew hundreds of would-be customers like moths to a flame every night of the week.

Despite the multiple lengthy waivers all who made it past the velvet rope had to sign, most stayed on the main floor. Vampire and human performers provided various kinds of entertainment with just enough of a dangerous edge for the audience to get the rush they sought.

While regular customers sat at floor level, VIPs entered through a different set of doors and watched the shows from luxurious suites with glass walls that ringed the main floor on the second and third floors. Thanks to her time working for the Court, Arkady had witnessed some real horrors in those suites.

As for what went on in the two basement levels, she knew little firsthand—especially about sub-level two. What she'd heard from those who'd ventured there and survived was bad enough, but it was imagining the fates of those who *didn't* walk out that kept her awake some nights. No matter how this played out, or even if she got to stake Farrell tonight, she'd likely be in for more insomnia.

Her phone buzzed two blocks from Nyx's front door. She checked the message, texted back a terse thanks, and stuck her phone back in her pocket.

"What's the word?" Ronan asked in their helmets.

He sounded impatient for action. She felt the same way, even as her stomach churned. The heady combination of anticipation and nervous energy made her skin almost crackle with electricity.

"My source says he's on sub-level two," she told Ronan. "Likely to be there for a while and looking for 'adventurous companionship.'"

"Adventurous companionship." He chuckled. "In other words, someone willing to roll the dice on whether they'll walk out or leave feet-first. Even most hardcore fang-bangers would balk at that, so we shouldn't have too much competition. With any luck, I'll be just his type."

"With any luck," she agreed. "But when we're done, don't forget who gets to stake him."

He squeezed her hand where it rested on his waist. "I won't forget."

"Don't touch me without my permission," she snapped. "Remember who you serve. Don't make me punish you."

"Yes, Mistress." He let go instantly. "I'm sorry, Mistress."

She smiled but kept her voice stern. "Don't let it happen again."

"Yes, Mistress." He sounded truly contrite and subdued, like the perfect submissive.

She shivered slightly, but not from cold. They might have to revisit this role-play later in private. The thought sent another wave of desire through her. She didn't fight it. A vampire's acute sense of smell would note her level of arousal, or lack thereof. They'd have a better chance of getting to Farrell if she not only acted but smelled the part of horny master—or so she hoped.

As they neared the purple carpet at Nyx's front doors, the Harley's deep rumble attracted the attention of the hundred or so people standing in line, hoping to gain admittance. Their arrival was the exact opposite of stealth. But if Ronan was right about Farrell's apparent preference to meet a challenge head-on, their mission had more potential for success if they made an entrance rather than if they'd tried to sneak in unnoticed.

"You had better be right about this," she warned Ronan in their helmets.

She'd forgotten to use her stern voice, but he didn't forget his role of submissive. "I am right, Mistress," he said, stopping the Harley in front of the purple velvet carpet. "I wouldn't dare fail you."

"Then let's do this." She slapped his thigh hard enough for the sound to be audible over the bike's rumble. "Hurry up."

He shut off the Harley's engine and held Arkady's hand to steady her as she climbed off the back. Then he lowered the kickstand, got off the bike, and knelt in front of her.

She took off her helmet, unzipped her newly cleaned and conditioned leather jacket, and shook out her chin-length black hair. The wig was part of her handy-dandy PI disguise kit. The lace bodysuit, red satin bra, and fishnet stockings she'd chosen from her lingerie drawer, and the black short-shorts and tall boots were club clothes she hadn't had a chance to wear in much too long. She was pleased to note they still fit just fine.

As for Ronan's studded leather vest, pants, and matching collar, he'd produced them from one of his bike's saddlebags, along with a leash. She hadn't seen them during her search for a shirt to wear in the Pelican parking lot, but then again, she hadn't dug all the way to the bottom of both bags.

"Dare I ask why you carry fetish gear with you wherever you go?" she'd asked when he returned from the garage looking like just about any domme's wettest dream.

His grin nearly undid her. "We both know sometimes it's better to have doors opened to us than have to kick them down, Miss Woodall. And what is more irresistible and seemingly nonthreatening than a man wearing a collar and leash?"

In the vest, collar, and pants, he was indeed irresistible...but she'd never mistake him for nonthreatening. Then again, she reflected as he knelt on the hard pavement in front of her, not everyone had her training. And arousal could cloud even the most suspicious person's mind. They were certainly hoping it would tonight, at least long enough to get to Henry Farrell.

The entire crowd in front of the club had gone silent, so Arkady's voice carried when she snapped, "Take off your helmet."

"Yes, Mistress." Ronan's voice was muffled inside the helmet. He took it off and set it on the seat of his bike.

She slapped him across the face with her bare hand. "Did I tell you to put it down?"

He picked up his helmet and hung his head. "No, Mistress."

A few people in the line tittered. Arkady ignored them. "You take care of me first."

"Yes, Mistress." Without meeting her eyes, he took her helmet, set it on the seat, and waited.

"Put yours in the gutter," she ordered him.

"Yes, Mistress." He obeyed, his gaze fixed on her boots. "What may I do for you now, Mistress?"

"Hey, Mistress, how do I get one of those?" a blonde woman called. "Is he available for rent?" Several people in the crowd laughed. Many seemed intrigued by their performance. And Arkady would be lying if she claimed having Ronan kneeling at her feet wasn't as much of a turn-on as the prospect of finding, interrogating, and staking Henry Farrell.

"You may look at me." She raised Ronan's chin with her fingertip and tapped her flogger lightly against her leg. "What should I tell her? Should I rent you out?"

When their gazes met, only she could see that his glacier blue eyes sparkled with suppressed laughter. "If Mistress wishes," he murmured, his voice and expression meek. "I will do anything she commands."

She coiled his leash around her wrist and leaned down until her lips were millimeters from his. "Yes, you will." She kissed him, then sucked on his bottom lip until she was sure she'd left a mark on his skin. As she freed his lip from her mouth, someone in the crowd groaned and cursed under their breath.

"Leave the lipstick on your face," she told him. "Now get up. You'll be wanted downstairs." Her words sent a murmur through the crowd. Going into Nyx was one thing; venturing into its basement levels was quite another.

Ronan followed her obediently up the purple carpeted steps to the club's front doors. One of the club's two enormous doormen met them at the top of the stairs. His name was Ivan, as she recalled. Like most of the humans, dhampirs, and vamps who worked at Nyx, he belonged to Court member David Noble. She saw nothing that indicated Ivan recognized her, which was just as well. It wasn't *his* interest she wanted to pique, but that of his boss.

They'd raised enough of a fuss by now that surely someone had directed Farrell's attention to the goings-on out front. She looked up at the camera and stared at its red light to give her quarry a good, long, unobstructed look at her face.

"Ma'am," Ivan began.

She rested the handle of her flogger on his sternum. "*Mistress*," she corrected. "No one touches that Harley while we're inside." In case he hadn't already noticed the amulet dangling from the bike's right grip, she added, "And by that I mean no one *wants* to touch it."

When Ivan's eyes darted to the left, she knew someone was speaking to him in his earpiece. Whatever they said, it was brief—and not at all what he'd expected to hear, judging by the way his eyebrows raised slightly.

"You are expected, Mistress," he said with a bow. "You and your... companion may enter. Your personal host will accompany you downstairs."

"I'm delighted to hear it." She stared pointedly at the entrance. "Well?"

Ivan opened the door for them. Muffled music drifted out into the lobby from the club's main floor. "Come," she commanded over her shoulder. "We are *expected*."

As they'd rehearsed, Ronan hesitated on the threshold. "Mistress... must I?"

She lashed him with her flogger across the patch of bare chest above his vest. He made a show of flinching and cowering, though she hadn't hit him all that hard. "Was that disobedience?"

"No, Mistress." Eyes downcast and trepidation in his expression and body language, he followed her into the club's main lobby. Ivan closed the oversized front door behind them with a heavy *thunk*.

A beautiful dark-haired female vampire in a velvet bodysuit and matching stiletto heels met them inside. The bodysuit was the same dark purple as blood appeared to be at night. Not subtle, the vamps—not if you knew what to notice.

Arkady expected the female vampire to escort them to the host desk to sign the club's numerous waivers. Instead, their hostess smiled and flashed her fangs. "Welcome to Nyx, Mistress. My name is Daniela. I'm honored to be your host tonight."

"Hello, Daniela." Arkady made a show of looking around the lobby with disdain. "What are your duties as our host?"

"It is my privilege to provide you with new and unimaginable pleasures." Daniela studied Ronan with undisguised avarice, then turned her attention back to Arkady. "May I escort you to a suite where you may discover the many ways a woman with your particular preferences can indulge herself?"

"You may indeed." Arkady wrapped Ronan's leash one more time around her wrist to shorten the length of his tether. "We're both anxious to explore these new pleasures."

At her words, Ronan cowered. Arkady had to hand it to him; he was a very good actor.

"Then please follow me." With enough sway in her hips and surprisingly ample rear end to make Arkady feel a bit seasick, Daniela led them to an ornate elevator on the far side of the lobby opposite the double doors that led to the main stage area. "You're clearly a woman who knows what she likes," Daniela added as they entered the elevator. "I'm certain we can find ways to make your night memorable."

"I'm sure you can." Arkady gave Ronan's leash a yank, causing him to stumble. "Sit. Stay."

He went to his knees again and stared at her boots.

Daniela pressed and held the button labeled B2. The doors of the elevator slid closed. They sounded much heavier than normal. Probably reinforced.

Getting into Nyx had proven easier than she'd anticipated. Getting out, however, might be a very tall order. Good thing both she and Ronan were very tall.

As the car descended, the lights dimmed and then went out except for a single purple flame that flickered in a glass fixture above their heads. "I approve of the ambiance," Arkady said. "Very sensual."

"Our goal is to immerse our most adventurous clients in their most personal fantasies from the moment they cross our threshold." Daniela's smile again revealed a hint of fang. "We find the lighting facilitates a certain level of anticipation and arousal. Few are as comfortable exploring their pleasures as openly as you and your submissive."

"I suppose that's true." Arkady stroked her hand over Ronan's hair several times, as if petting him, then rested her palm on top of his head.

Daniela licked her lips. "What is his name?"

"He doesn't have one. He doesn't deserve one." She caressed Ronan's cheek and then gave him another light slap. "How lucky he is to have found someone like me. Who knows what might have happened to him otherwise. Such a helpless thing, isn't he?"

Ronan rested his head against her leg, his expression contented.

Daniela chuckled low in her throat as the elevator came to a stop and the doors opened. "Indeed," she murmured. "If you tire of him, Mistress, do please let me know. I have a particular affinity for helpless things."

Arkady smiled as if the vampire's tone hadn't made the little hairs on the back of her neck stand up. "I'll certainly keep that in mind."

Daniela turned left out of the elevator and led them down a dimly lit corridor lined with doors and gilt mirrors that glowed with soft purple light. The plush carpet made their steps silent.

The doors had no numbers on them, but Daniela seemed to know which was their group's destination. She stopped in front of the fourth door on the right. "I believe you will find this suite more than suitable. You may contact me via the courtesy phone to request any additional amenities. A menu of our offerings is located near the phone. Page three in particular may interest you." She opened the door and gestured at the rooms beyond. "Indulge yourself, Mistress."

The suite was an erotic dungeon containing more than a dozen "sets" where a master could inflict great pleasure and pain—and a few that seemed potentially lethal. The walls and floor were likely soundproof and designed to be easy to clean. Though she had no special magic or psychic ability, Arkady got the distinct feeling the suite had seen a lot of spilled blood.

She strode into the suite with Ronan following on his leash. "This will do," she said over her shoulder to Daniela. "We'll let you know if we need anything."

"Enjoy." Daniela shut the door.

Out of curiosity, Arkady picked up and perused the menu Daniela had referenced. Pages one and two contained a wide selection of very personal services offered by the club and its employees. Most weren't all that different from a menu at any bordello—albeit with a lot more emphasis on bloodletting.

But page three...*yikes*. She read through the list partly because she was playing a role and a domme wouldn't hesitate to do so, and partly out of curiosity. *Double yikes*. Nothing on page three counted as BDSM in her book. Those items were nothing but torture. The black marks beside some seemed to indicate those selections might result in death. People had likely been murdered in this room, all in the name of someone else's pleasure. Suddenly queasy, she closed the menu and put it back on the table.

Ronan stepped close to Arkady, his gaze fixed on hers. It was the silent signal they'd arranged beforehand. He'd seen, heard, or sensed surveillance in the room. That didn't surprise Arkady in the least. The surveillance probably had very little to do with liability and everything to do with gleaning information about the club's clients—information that could be leveraged later.

"Mistress." The raw desire in Ronan's low voice distracted her from her disgust at the menu and made her shiver. "The things I would like you to do to me in this room..."

She cupped his face and ran her thumb across his bristly chin. "Oh, the things I'd like to do to you in this room, given the opportunity. Unfortunately, I don't think we'll have the chance to really indulge ourselves, do you?"

"No, I don't, Mistress." His eyes twinkled. "Not to *really* indulge ourselves, but perhaps I'll indulge myself."

Despite her trepidation at their surroundings, she was intrigued.

"How so?"

"May I touch you?"

She repeated what she'd said earlier in her garage when he'd asked the same question. "Touch me where? Why?"

"Where? Here." His gaze on hers, he slid his hand up her thigh to the inside seam of her shorts and rubbed her gently but very deliberately through the fabric.

Oh, God. She let out a gasp.

"As for *why*," he continued, "to hear you moan, of course."

She wanted to resist, but she'd been turned on from the moment he'd kissed her in her kitchen. Even a bit of self-indulgent relief in the shower hadn't eased her arousal much—just made her yearn for more. Add that to their role-playing and the contents of this room, and she was as tightly wound as she could remember being in recent memory. She couldn't stifle a moan.

With that green light, his fingertips slipped under the hem of her shorts and explored further. His eyes widened almost imperceptibly. "Crotchless stockings?" he murmured in her ear.

"It's the only pair I had." Her voice sounded ragged. "Don't look so smug. It has nothing to do with you." He could probably tell that was a lie. Her choice of stockings had everything to do with him.

They had to stop. Henry Farrell could be right outside the door. She grabbed Ronan's wrist.

"If you want me to stop, say stop." He nuzzled her jaw, smelling like leather and pure hot-blooded male. "You want me to stop?"

She wanted him so badly she couldn't think. *Fuck it*, she thought. She'd fight better if she wasn't so wound up. And if someone was watching, she didn't care.

"No, I don't want you to stop." She pulled him with her until her back hit the wall. She hooked her leg around his thigh to make it easier for him to slip his hand back into her shorts, grabbed his hair, and drew his face down to hers. "I want you to keep your promise about earning that blowjob," she said, her mouth an inch from his.

He let out a guttural sound and kissed her so hard that her busted lip throbbed and she was sure she'd be bruised. *Totally worth it.*

With one hand under her raised thigh to hold her steady, his warm fingers stroked the slick, delicate skin left bare by the stockings. When he discovered how wet she already was for him, he smiled. Arkady wanted to be mad at him for looking so pleased with himself, but she couldn't manage to feel anything but pure white-hot desire.

When two of his fingers slipped inside her, she arched her back against the wall. "More," she ordered.

"Yes, Mistress." His smile turned wicked as she shuddered and moaned. "I wanted you to come for the first time with me with my mouth on you," he said softly into her ear. "But since we're so pressed for time..."

In her haze of pleasure, she'd barely registered his words when he finally, *finally* rubbed her just right. A few deliberate strokes were all it took to send her over the edge.

Her hand clenched reflexively and pulled his hair as she let out a series of gasping cries into his mouth. He held her up with one hand still under her leg while she writhed. And he continued stroking her until she had no more strength to stand.

It occurred to her that if Ronan was this good with his fingers, actual sex with him might land her in the hospital. The thought of it sent one last shiver through her entire body as he released her leg. Her knees trembled, but she could stay upright with two feet on the floor and her back against the wall.

"I needed that," she said with a sigh.

"I know." He leaned in to kiss her with surprising gentleness. "Some claim an orgasm speeds up reflexes and sharpens the eye," he said, his mouth near her ear. "I have only anecdotal evidence to support that theory, but perhaps my Valkyrie will find it to be true."

He froze. His expression indicated he thought he'd just stepped on a landmine.

Ronan had been so annoyingly self-assured and unflappable all night that Arkady couldn't miss such a great opportunity to needle him. She put her hands on her hips. "*Your* Valkyrie? So you give me one decent orgasm and now you think I'm yours? That's not how it works, sweet pea."

"That wasn't...damn it." He scowled ferociously, which amused her to no end. Though he wasn't a shifter, his glower would give even

Sean's alpha stare a run for its money. She made a mental note to mention that to Sean the next time she saw him. Both she and Alice would get a good laugh out of his reaction.

"I mean, don't get me wrong—I'm not ungrateful." She gave Ronan another dose of her most annoying smirk just to see his scowl deepen. "But we've got quite a ways to go before anyone starts throwing around declarations of ownership."

He muttered something under his breath that she didn't quite catch, but might have been some variation on *oh, fuck it*. "I don't suppose it would make the situation any worse if I told you I thought of you as *my Valkyrie* back at your house," he said.

That was true, she decided after studying his face. *My Valkyrie* might have been a slip of the tongue just now, but it wasn't something he'd thought or said only in the wake of getting her off.

A shockingly honest man, she'd called him at Bella's. A man to whom she had nothing to prove, who'd knelt in front of her in public, told her with zero hesitation that he'd wanted to make her come with his mouth, and given her a much more than *decent* orgasm in a vampire club sex dungeon simply because she needed one.

He stilled, his whole body going taut. "Mistress."

"Oh, shut up." She put her index finger on his lips. "For tonight, for the next week, or for however long we can stand each other, I have no problem being your Valkyrie."

He seemed to be struggling not to laugh. "Glad to hear it, but we have company."

When he stepped aside, Arkady went cold.

A familiar dark-haired vampire in a tailored designer suit leaned casually against a rack of leather restraints. He'd loosened his tie and held a glass of what might have been bourbon in his pale, thin hand. How had he gotten into the room? They'd been a bit distracted, but Ronan had damn good hearing, and if he'd heard a door open, he wouldn't have ignored the sound.

As if he'd heard her thoughts, Ronan caught her gaze and then looked at the wall just to the right of the restraints. She followed his stare and spotted an almost imperceptible dark line on the wall. It must be a hidden door that operated so soundlessly that even Ronan hadn't heard it.

She felt no fear—only calm and focus. Maybe that was because she'd told Ronan the story of what had happened and it no longer seemed like a shameful secret. Maybe facing her attacker was now part of a different, bigger mission, and her personal feelings seemed less important. Or maybe Ronan was right about the effects of a good orgasm. Could be all three.

Meanwhile, Ronan studied the intruder with an even colder gaze than her own. His expression reminded her of Alice's flat stare when facing down an enemy. The observation got Arkady no closer to figuring out what Ronan was, but it cemented her certainty that she was glad to have him at her back.

"Hello, my sweetness," Henry Farrell said to her, smiling to show his fangs. "I am so very pleased to see you again."

9

RONAN

"IT IS SUCH A LUXURY TO HAVE MY DINNER COME TO ME," THE vampire added. The way he leered at Arkady made Ronan's skin crawl.

Every word out of Farrell's mouth put Ronan on edge, practically dared him to reach out and crush the vampire's pale throat—but there was something about that pet name, intimate and patronizing and tinged with a hundred past abuses, that made him want to send a message when he did it.

From the earliest eons of his existence, the creatures Ronan had the least use for in all the universe were those who preyed on those less powerful than themselves. Given her reaction to the demon minions they'd dispatched at the Pelican, he suspected Arkady shared that sentiment.

Over the intoxicating smell of her most personal scents that still lingered on his skin and in the air, Ronan caught a strange odor coming from Farrell. A human nose probably couldn't have detected it, but the vampire's natural wine-and-spice scent had a distinct sour note that made Ronan want to sneeze. The unsettling odor reminded him of rotting fruit and spoiled meat. He recalled Arkady's claim of a drug epidemic among the vamps, but he saw no sign that Farrell was under the influence of anything.

An even more disturbing possibility came to mind: was the vamp diseased? He had no knowledge of any illness that could affect a vampire, but that spoiled-food odor couldn't be ignored. Something was very, very wrong with Henry Farrell.

Beside him, apparently oblivious to Farrell's odor and Ronan's reaction to it, Arkady shifted her weight, ready to defend herself or attack. Ronan hadn't seen her palm one of the small blades she'd hidden on her body, but he caught a glimpse of matte black metal in her hand. The steel blade wouldn't kill the vamp, but a strike to his eye or heart would at least incapacitate Farrell for a few precious seconds.

"You must have enjoyed our last meeting, my sweetness, to come back to me so soon." Farrell sipped his bourbon with what Ronan interpreted as the casualness of a man who believed himself untouchable.

"I'm not your sweetness," Arkady stated. "And I'm not your dinner either."

"I must disagree." Farrell showed her his fangs again. "You were a truly marvelous meal. I can still taste your sweet, hot blood on my tongue."

"It's pathetic that you have to resort to preying on victims for lack of *willing* meals," she said as if Farrell hadn't spoken. She shook her head in disgust. "You must be your maker's greatest shame."

Ronan palmed his own knife.

Among vampires, the accusation of lacking willing donors was an insult of nearly breathtaking proportions. One of the few slurs even more insulting was being accused of bringing shame to a master vampire's line. Farrell's maker was a member of the Vampire Court, making Arkady's comment even more daring. She'd just leveled not one but *two* scorched-earth insults in a single breath.

Whether she'd done it to get Farrell to attack in a blind rage, or just to screw with him to see how he'd react, Ronan wasn't sure. Sometimes her motivations seemed less clear to him than any human he'd ever known. In any case, Ronan fully expected the vamp to attack.

Instead, Farrell threw his head back and laughed.

Ronan's skin prickled warningly. Meanwhile, judging by her

expression, if Arkady had been a cat, she would have arched her back and hissed at the sound of Farrell's laughter.

He pressed his mouth to her ear and warned, "Farrell is not well."

"No shit, Sherlock." She spun her blade reflexively in her hand without having to look at it. "Seems to be a couple fries short of a Happy Meal."

"It's more than that," he insisted. "I can smell—"

Farrell's maniacal laughter cut off abruptly, replaced with a choking sound. His eyes had gone completely black. The sickening odor intensified.

"Phew." Arkady wrinkled her nose. "Somebody's a stinky little vamp."

"I...had...her...first," Farrell gurgled. His eyes bulged slightly as he met Ronan's gaze. "Your Valkyrie...is...*mine*."

Ronan worried Farrell's taunt would hit a nerve. But when he glanced at Arkady, she smirked. "Yours?" she scoffed. "In your dreams."

Farrell's mouth opened impossibly wide, stretching the pale flesh of his cheeks until it tore. His jaw broke apart with an audible sound and hung loose from his face, held in place by torn skin and tendons.

"Ruh-roh," Arkady muttered.

A horde of screeching four-winged insects spewed out of Farrell's mouth. No, not large insects, Ronan realized immediately—tiny demons. Hundreds of them, all wearing armor and wielding razor-edged swords likely dipped in poison. His angelic ability to sense the presence of demons remained, even if most of his other powers had been taken away. Farrell crumpled to the floor, apparently insensible.

Minor demons like these had posed no threat to Ronan as an archangel. He would have swatted them as easily as the flies they resembled.

As a mortal man, however, he could be sickened and even incapacitated by their poison. And Arkady, for all her knives and unrelenting cockiness, could absolutely die from it.

The horde of tiny demons made a beeline for them, their deadly swords leading the way.

Though Ronan doubted she'd ever seen such creatures in her life, the sight didn't seem to faze Arkady in the least. Brandishing knives in each hand, she ran straight toward the horde with a banshee yell.

A frontal assault was a tactic clearly neither he nor the demons had anticipated. Caught off guard, the demons seemed conflicted about whether to attack or get out of the way of the much-larger human woman about to plow into them. While they had numbers on their side, minor demons weren't terribly bright. It was a weakness he and Arkady would have to exploit to survive.

Just before she reached the horde, Arkady dropped to the floor with one leg outstretched and the other bent like she was sliding into home plate. Her momentum carried her past the confused demons. Unfortunately, the less-befuddled ones managed to stab and slash her as she passed. His stomach lurched as they left bloody wounds on her face, neck, and chest. How much of the poison could she withstand?

Once clear of the horde, Arkady jumped to her feet and dashed for the dungeon's bedroom. He had to assume she had a plan and wasn't just running for cover. That meant he needed to buy her time.

His celestial sword would have incinerated the demons without even touching them, but he couldn't wield it. Instead, he drew his hidden and enchanted, but much less powerful, sword from the scabbard on his back.

On impulse, he picked up Arkady's discarded flogger. When she'd produced it back at her house to use as part of their ruse, it had appeared fairly well used. Arkady seemed to have an appetite for adventurous sex. Which was why when they'd first entered this dungeon all he'd been able to think about was how much fun they could have had here if they hadn't been after Farrell.

Sword in one hand and flogger in the other, he charged the demon horde.

The tiny flying demons might have been confused about how to react to Arkady, but they had no such trouble attacking Ronan. Maybe they sensed his angelic origin or celestial sword and attacked him instinctively. Or maybe they recognized him as the greater threat. Either way, they swarmed him like bees.

As the demons reached him, Ronan lashed out with the flogger, dashing a dozen demons at a time to the floor, where they lay dazed.

The dozens of thin leather strips were far more effective than his knife would have been. But for every one he hit, a dozen sank their tiny swords into his flesh. The poison raised welts that burned white-hot like they'd been made with branding irons. He gritted his teeth and swung his weapons harder and faster.

Pale and a little unsteady on her feet, Arkady emerged from the dungeon's bedroom carrying the black sheets from the king-sized bed. He was horrified to see her wounds had turned black and oozed blood. Her breathing sounded labored.

Halfway across the room, she stumbled and almost fell. "Son of a bitch, that hurts," she gasped. She flung one of the sheets at him. "Let's...get 'em."

Her plan was obvious. He caught the sheet, returned his sword to its scabbard on his back, and fought to trap as many of the demons in the sheet as possible. While the demons' swords could inflict painful wounds and armor safeguarded their bodies, their wings had no protection. Once the demons were entangled and immobilized in the sheet, he and Arkady could stomp them until their wings broke off, leaving them to writhe and screech on the floor.

They quickly discovered that de-winged did not mean disarmed or helpless. Arkady flinched and plucked several toothpick-sized blades from her forearm. "Son of a—they're throwing their swords!"

Ronan pulled a half-dozen swords from his own skin and tried to keep the demons focused on him.

Arkady, her teeth gritted, somehow managed to stay on her feet until the last of the tiny demons had been de-winged. "What do we do with them?" she asked, panting. "Can't cut them up. That armor's made of mithril or some shit."

With a growl, Ronan covered the wriggling horde with both bedsheets, then toppled a heavy rack of whips, chains, and restraints on top of the sheets. The demons' shrieks at least were muffled now. "That ought to hold them," he said. "We'll let disposing of them be the vamps' problem."

Arkady swayed on her feet. He caught her before she fell. "Little assholes," she wheezed into his chest. "I think they poisoned me."

"They did." He kissed her forehead. Her skin felt clammy. "We must find a healer with antidotes to demon poisons."

"I know someone, but I think we're going to have a tough time getting out of here." She doubled over with a groan. "Demon poison," she rasped. "That's a new one. Wait—what the ever-loving, blood-sucking hell?"

Somehow, despite having disgorged five hundred or so tiny flying demons armed with poisonous swords from his gullet, Henry Farrell staggered to his feet. His jaw hadn't yet healed completely, but his cheeks were no longer torn. He looked emaciated and weakened, so much so that Ronan wondered how he managed to stand at all.

Trembling with what must have been excruciating pain, Arkady freed herself from Ronan's arms and faced Farrell. "We found you through Oliver Mora," she told the skeletal vampire. "He told us how he delivers people to a broker. He works for you. You're a trafficker."

"What is it to you, my sweetness?" Farrell gave her a grotesque, lopsided smile. His broken jaw still hung loose. "Our concerns are much more personal, I should think."

"To you, maybe. To me, this is just business." Before she finished the sentence, she threw her knife. It was an exceptional throw, especially given her physical condition. In Ronan's expert opinion, the blade would have buried itself in Farrell's eye if he hadn't still been able to move vamp-fast and dodge it.

Ronan's own blade, thrown a millisecond after Arkady's in anticipation of exactly that movement, caught Farrell in his left eye. The vampire went down with a scream.

"Yay team," Arkady said dryly. "You're on a roll. You're two for two against bad guys' eyeballs tonight."

He helped her over to Farrell, who lay whimpering on his back with the knife protruding from his eye socket. She retrieved her knife from where it had ended up embedded in a wooden whipping post and crouched next to Farrell. "Tell us where to go from here," she told the vamp. "And I'll pull out the knife."

"Take it out." Farrell tried to make it a command, but his words slurred and his hands twitched. The blade had apparently done enough damage to his brain to affect both his speech and movements. "I will tell you all I know."

"Talk first." She flicked the hilt of Ronan's knife, eliciting a pained groan from Farrell as the blade wobbled. "Better hurry. If your eye heals around that blade, it's going to hurt a hell of a lot worse getting the knife out." She paused. "No, wait...on second thought, take your time."

Farrell let out a garbled sound Ronan realized was a laugh. "No wonder you taste so sweet," the vampire mumbled. "You have a vampire's black heart. They are right to want to turn you. You will be greatly feared when you become one of us."

"I'm feared *now*, sweet pea." Arkady leaned forward so the vamp could see her face. "Or hadn't you wondered why they haven't tried again?"

Farrell went for her throat.

Maybe she'd hoped he would. Ronan had noted the way she'd presented her bare neck to Farrell, knowing full well he was desperate for blood to heal as well as payback. Farrell probably thought she was in bad shape after getting stabbed and poisoned by the demons.

And so had Ronan, until Arkady whipped a small tactical stake from her boot almost as fast as he could have pulled one and jammed it into Farrell's ribcage just deep enough to graze his heart. It was a perfect stab, and she'd done it reflexively.

She was far less affected by the poison than she'd led them both to believe. He'd even used that ruse himself a dozen times, and he still hadn't realized her behavior was a ploy. He would have been furious at being tricked if he hadn't been so relieved.

The vampire went preternaturally still in the way only the undead could. Any movement would drive the tip of Arkady's stake into his heart and turn him to ash.

"Now," she said conversationally. "Tell me everything you know about this trafficking ring. Start with who cursed you to puke tiny demons."

"The demon horde was a gift, not a curse." Farrell smiled despite the dark blood dripping from the corner of his mouth. "Protection against those who mean me harm."

"Shame your so-called protectors could be foiled by satin bedsheets and a rack of sex toys, then." Arkady flicked the knife hilt again. "Your fairy godmother didn't give you much of a defense, if you ask me. Give us a name and tell us where they're holed up."

Farrell flashed his fangs. "My sweetness, if you asked the same question of Mora, you know I cannot speak of my benefactor and live."

So the *geas* that had killed Mora wasn't Farrell's handiwork, but a demon's. Given the odor of sulfur on the minions at the Pelican, it didn't surprise Ronan that a demon was behind the trafficking ring.

"I have failed my benefactor," the wounded vampire continued. "You might as well stake me."

"Not if that's the kinder way for you to go," Arkady retorted. "I'm not into merciful quick ends for worthless slime like you."

"Perhaps not." Farrell glanced at Ronan. His smile grew. "You think *I* am worthless, but you freely debase yourself with a disgraced, fallen—"

With one lightning-quick move, Ronan slammed his palm on the hilt of Arkady's stake and drove it through Farrell's heart. Farrell crumbled to ash before he could even cry out.

Arkady sucked in a breath. "You *bastard*." She staggered to her feet and confronted Ronan, her fists clenched. "We had an agreement!"

Even as Ronan had staked him, he'd known Farrell had baited him on purpose. Farrell might have been a few fries short of a pleasant meal, as Arkady had noted, and not the smartest of vampires, but he'd clearly guessed Ronan would kill to keep his angelic origin a secret and used that to deny Arkady her revenge, safeguard the identity of the demon behind the trafficking ring, and ensure Ronan and Arkady would have a hell of a time getting out of Nyx alive.

In a fit of pique, Arkady kicked the ash and crumpled suit that was all that remained of Henry Farrell. Her movement caused her to cough thickly and stumble. Ronan reached out, but she smacked his hands aside and grabbed a handful of his vest so she could snarl in his face. "Did we or *did we not* have a fucking agreement?" Her rage appeared to give her additional strength despite the effects of the demon poison. "You selfish asshole. Whatever he was about to call you, you had no right to do that."

She was the second woman to rightly call him an asshole tonight, and by his estimate about the hundredth in the past year alone. While he'd felt guilty for brushing aside Mireille's offer of help, he hadn't cared one iota about her opinion of him, or anyone else's, except perhaps Alice. Truth be told, he'd not-so-secretly reveled in his asshole status more than once.

Which was why he was totally unprepared for the uneasy feeling Arkady's words caused.

He might not have cared if anyone else in the cosmos thought he was a selfish asshole—and might have actively cultivated that opinion, in fact—but he *did* care that Arkady Woodall thought so, especially when he'd put some very uncharacteristic effort into convincing her otherwise.

With visible disgust, Arkady let go of his vest and took a step back. "How are we going to get out of here?" She picked up her stake and dusted it off before sliding it back into its hiding place in her right boot. "They're going to know he's dead soon if they don't already. If he's got any offspring, they felt him die, and if anyone was watching the surveillance cameras, they saw what we did."

Ronan put more personal concerns aside and focused on their immediate problem. "If someone had been watching, they would likely have come in here when he spewed flying demons," he pointed out. "Certainly when I put a knife in his eye. He must have turned the cameras off to make sure no one watched him confront us."

"That makes sense."

"But you're right—they will know soon." He crouched, lifted the edge of the satin sheets, and picked up one of the wriggling demons between his thumb and forefinger. "How good of an actress are you?"

"You ask me that after you saw me convince Mora I wanted to sleep with him?" She snorted. "I deserved an Oscar for not vomiting every time that slimeball touched me."

"A fair point." He stashed the disarmed and de-winged demon in one of the zippered pockets of his leather pants. "I suggest we use these vermin as our means of escape."

"What, find two that still have their wings, shrink ourselves, and ride them out of here? 'Cuz I'm all out of shrinking spells and I don't see any saddles laying around." She glanced at their surroundings and raised her eyebrows. "Well, not tiny ones, anyway."

"A wonderfully creative but impractical solution." Ronan grabbed the toppled rack to test its weight. "I'm going to suggest a slightly more feasible scenario."

"Fine." She studied him, her expression cold. "When we make it out of here, you and I are going to discuss at length the extent to which you just fucked up."

"I have no doubt we will." Grimly, he adjusted his grip on the heavy rack and braced himself to lift it. "But first, I need you to scream."

ARKADY

ARKADY POUNDED ON THE DUNGEON'S THICK DOOR AND SCREAMED bloody murder. "Help! *Help!* Somebody, *HELP!*"

She hurt so badly from the demon poison that even tiny movements sent waves of agony through her entire body. Banging her fists on the door almost made her black out. She held onto consciousness with all her might and stayed on her feet because she'd be damned if either the vamps or Ronan would get the satisfaction of seeing her sprawl on the floor.

Ronan. She wanted to put her boot so far up his fine ass that he'd be spitting out her shoelaces. And to think she'd put on crotchless stockings for him.

The door flew open so fast that it would have sent Arkady flying if she hadn't been standing to the side. Daniela stood frozen in the doorway, staring in horror at the sight of the hundreds of tiny, wriggling, screeching demons crawling over the pile of ash that had once been Henry Farrell. Whether or not Daniela recognized the clothing, Arkady wasn't sure, but it wouldn't be long before the vamps figured out the dead man was Farrell. She wanted to be gone before that happened.

"Let us out of here!" Arkady wailed. She yanked on Ronan's leash and elbowed past the dumbstruck female vampire. In the hallway, she shouted, "This place is infested with *demons*! They just killed someone!"

An alarm went off. Who or what had triggered it, she had no idea, but it accomplished what she'd hoped it would. All hell broke loose. Club employees—vampires, dhampirs, and a few humans—converged on the dungeon suite. Even the vampires seemed shaken and confused by the swarm of screeching demons and the remains of one of their own.

To get through the crowd, Arkady acted increasingly hysterical. The vampires, with their sensitive hearing, seemed more than happy to let them pass. Some even averted their eyes as if the sight of a panicked human offended them.

Unfortunately, they didn't make it more than halfway down the hall before the effects of the damned demon poison caught up with her in earnest. Her vision swam. She stumbled into the wall and had to hold onto a sconce to keep from falling.

Without missing a beat, Ronan scooped her up like she weighed nothing and ran for the elevator. "My mistress needs help!" he pleaded to everyone they passed. "The demons hurt her, and they killed a vampire."

None of the club employees bothered to reply. They rushed in the opposite direction, clearing a path to the elevator.

"I'm going to hurt you for this," Arkady said very distinctly as Ronan jabbed the elevator button. "Nobody carries me like some damsel in distress."

"I know, Mistress." His eyes appeared feverish. "Add it to the list of ways I've fucked up tonight."

She wondered if the demon poison had affected him after all. She'd assumed he was immune to whatever they'd had on their blades. Maybe not. He didn't look well. He looked ill...and worried.

Worried about her? Surely not. Unless he knew something about that poison she didn't—like it was deadly to humans. She would have expected him to tell her if that was the case, but who the hell knew what went through his idiot mind. He'd staked their best lead after promising not to. Maybe she'd given him more credit for brains than he deserved.

She was still processing that a vampire had puked a swarm of tiny flying demons with poisoned swords at them. She'd thought *Alice* was the one in their partnership who got herself into this kind of jam. Starting a bar fight—or any kind of fight—was more Arkady's style, and here she was doing everything she could to avoid fighting their way out of Nyx. She would have laughed if she hadn't thought it would attract attention, and if she didn't hurt like she'd been run over by a steamroller.

The elevator doors finally opened. Ronan got on and hit the button for the main level. The doors closed, but nothing happened.

"Put me down," she ordered him, because if they were about to be ambushed she wasn't going out being held like a child. He set her on her feet and she leaned against the elevator wall. "I didn't see her put in a code."

"The buttons might be biometric." Ronan pressed his index finger to the button and held it. Again, nothing happened. "Yes, biometric," he confirmed, though she hadn't seen or heard anything. He must have felt something. "We need Daniela's hand."

It didn't escape Arkady's notice that he didn't say they needed their hostess to be alive or even in one piece—just that they needed her hand. Truth be told, she'd had the same thought.

"I don't think we've got any such favors coming our way, so we better get on to Plan B." She glanced up. "Give me a boost."

Ronan followed her gaze to the emergency hatch on the ceiling. "You are in no shape to climb." His tone was matter-of-fact, not critical or mocking, but it pissed her off nonetheless.

"I bet I'll beat you up the ladder." She steadied herself against the side of the elevator and shook her head to clear her vision. "Unless you're scared to lose?" She'd easily manipulated him that way several times already tonight so she figured it was worth a shot. They might not have anything to prove to each other, but they both had competitive streaks a mile wide.

"You are impaired and will require help to climb a ladder," he argued implacably. "I need my hands free in case we encounter resistance. We need another escape route. There must be stairs."

"Impaired my ass," she fumed. "I've climbed ropes wearing a fifty-pound backpack while I had the flu and had to stop along the way to puke and still beat half my squad's best times. Hurry the hell up before someone tries to use the elevator."

"If I end up carrying you over my shoulder, I will be obliged to never let you forget it." He opened the hatch and laced his fingers to create a foothold. "Whenever you're ready, Miss Woodall."

"If you ever try to carry me over your shoulder, I'd better be dying, or you *will* be." She rested her hand on his shoulder for balance, placed her boot in his hands, and looked up at the hatch to make sure she was centered under it. "Alley-oop."

With one smooth movement, he sent her flying up and through the open hatch. It wasn't so much a boost as being shot out of a cannon. She managed to control her flight enough to land semi-gracefully on the elevator roof and only stumble a little.

Ronan jumped, grabbed the edges of the hatch, and pulled himself up and out of the elevator car without noticeable effort, despite his own wounds. His movements emphasized the size and strength of the muscles in his upper back, arms, and chest. She licked her lips without meaning to. Which of course he noticed.

She scowled and started up the emergency ladder as he shut the hatch behind them. "By all means take your time, O Great and Mighty One," she said over her shoulder. "We've got all night."

His quiet snort echoed in the elevator shaft.

For all her bravado, she made it up only about six or seven rungs of the ladder before the weakness and pain in her arms, legs, and joints reached excruciating levels. She hauled herself up one rung at a time, well aware Ronan couldn't miss either how slowly she was moving or her ragged breathing. She cursed under her breath.

"Talk to me," Ronan said from below her. "How are you doing?"

If it had been anyone else asking, even Alice or Malcolm, she would have said something sarcastic or just ignored them. But since she had nothing to prove to Ronan, she gritted her teeth and said, "It hurts. A lot."

"I know." Gently, he stroked the back of her calf with his fingertips. Some kind of magic passed between them, warm and prickly. The feeling reminded her of the magic he'd used to heal her cut hand. It took the edge off the pain.

"Thanks." She resumed climbing, no faster than before but without having to stifle a groan or curse with every movement.

"Excellent screams back there, by the way," Ronan said as they climbed. "Surprisingly convincing."

"I watch a lot of slasher movies. And it wasn't the first time I've used that ruse. Lots of people think women are helpless, hysterical, and in perpetual need of rescuing. Might as well use that to my advantage."

He chuckled. "A wise warrior knows their own strengths *and* the weaknesses of their enemies and uses both to their advantage."

"Exactly." She heaved herself up another rung. Either Ronan's pain-relief magic was already starting to wear off or the poison's effects were worsening. "Is this demon shit going to kill me?"

"I don't know." His voice sounded grave. "But it hasn't yet, which gives me hope. Demon poison is usually immediately fatal if it is designed to kill."

She grunted. "Good to know."

He spoke like he dealt with demons on a regular basis. She'd guessed as much after seeing his reaction—or lack thereof—to the swarm's appearance. It was another clue to what he was, but like all the other hints she'd caught, it wasn't enough to arrive at any particular conclusion.

When they reached the main level, he surprised her by saying, "I suggest we continue to the next floor and make our way out without venturing through the lobby. The less attention we attract, the better."

"They've got cameras and security everywhere, especially on the upper floors where the VIP suites are," she reminded him. "We can't just stroll down the hallways. Odds are, whoever's watching the live feeds saw us climb out of the elevator and they've got a squad of vamps waiting for us to appear. I've got one more of those *Exit* spells, but I don't think its range covers all of this place."

"What do you suggest?"

"I'm assuming you don't have a big flex that'll get us out of here?"

"I do not." He climbed up the ladder to reach her eye level. She hung onto the side to make room for him to join her. The ladder was wide to accommodate first responders carrying emergency equipment, but he was a mountain of a man and she wasn't exactly petite. "Will your affiliation with Alice's pack benefit us?"

"I'd rather not drag Alice and Sean into this if I can help it. They've got enough on their plate and Alice *really* does not want to get tangled up with any vamps again." She hummed under her breath. "You know, vampires love making deals. We might be able to buy our way out."

"With what?" He raised his eyebrows. "I know you are a woman of many talents, and I have some of my own, but what can we offer the vamps that might entice them to grant us passage after we witnessed the death of the club's owner by a demon horde? Money doesn't interest them unless it's in *very* large sums, which neither of us have, unless you have vast resources at your disposal."

"I don't have vast resources, but I do have something of great value." She gave him a smile that probably looked more like a grimace. "We're in a vamp club full of customers thirsting for danger and blood. How about an act they've never seen before? Live on their center stage, tonight only. Something so twisted it'll be legendary."

"Miss Woodall, I'm fairly certain whatever you're about to propose, I'm not going to like it."

"And I'm fairly certain we don't have a lot of choices." She took an uncharacteristically shaky breath as a wave of pain rolled through her entire body. "I have a spelled blade magicked by the same witch who made the *Exit* spells. I got the idea for what it does from Alice."

His eyes narrowed. "I know Alice well enough to not find that reassuring in the least."

"Well, you should. If anyone knows how to survive, it's Alice. Last year, she had to save Sean from an ancient shifter artifact. It was a cuff that latched itself onto him and would have killed him if she hadn't intervened and broken the spell."

"Intervened how?"

"She put on the matching cuff and died, and then was resurrected by magic."

"Given Alice's headstrong and self-sacrificing nature, I have no trouble believing you." Ronan shook his head. "Are you suggesting what I think you're suggesting?"

"Absolutely yes. You'll kill me in front of a whole crowd of people, and then I'll come back to life backstage and we'll get out of here." She leaned close and inhaled, enjoying the smell of leather and man. She slipped a knife from her waistband and put its hilt into his hand. "You got us into this mess," she murmured, her lips against his. "Now get us out."

He kissed her hard and for long enough that she almost forgot how pissed off she was at him for staking Farrell. Almost forgot, but not quite.

To her surprise, he gave her the knife back and cupped her cheek. "I got us into this mess," he agreed, his teeth grazing her lower lip in a way that made her think of other places she'd like him to do that. "So I *will* get us out, and *without* killing you."

Aggravated, she returned the blade to its hidden sheath. "And just how do you plan to do that, sweet pea?"

"A big flex. You gave me an idea and now I plan to run with it. I simply ask that you play along."

"I thought you didn't have a big flex!" she protested.

"Technically, I don't." The more annoyed she became, the bigger he smiled. "But no one but us knows that, do they?"

"Fine." She hung onto the ladder with a white-knuckled grip as another wave of pain ran through her. "Whatever you're going to do, do it fast. I feel like refried shit over here."

"Your wish is my command." He removed his leather collar and handed it to her. "Hold this for me, Mistress, please, while I terrify some vampires."

Vamps didn't terrify easily, but he said it like he fully expected to scare them shitless. And damned if that didn't turn her on. She owed him an ass-kicking and he owed her an explanation—not necessarily in that order—but for now she'd settle for seeing him fake a big flex.

"Get behind me," he said. When she started to protest, he kissed her forehead. "Play along," he reminded her. "I promise to make it worth your while."

"You better." Grudgingly, she moved a few rungs down the ladder and glared at his boots.

Above her, Ronan climbed up to the closed elevator doors and braced himself by hooking one leg through the rungs. He took two very deep breaths, rolled his shoulders, and muttered something under his breath.

Her skin prickled as sea-scented magic and power rose. She held on tighter.

Moving so fast that he almost blurred, Ronan punched the elevator doors with both fists. Silver light flared so brightly that she instinctively turned her head. With a *boom* and a crash that must have shook the building, the elevator doors blew out into the lobby.

When she looked up, Ronan was silhouetted in the now open doorway. He appeared suddenly much larger, though that might have been a trick of the light, and shrouded in unnatural shadows. Something rippled in the air behind him and around his shoulders with a sound like giant birds taking flight. What the hell?

No big flex, she thought. *Riiiiiight.*

She climbed up the ladder to the opening. This close to him, she could feel his aura as well as see it. The searing sensation reminded her of how Alice's magic felt when she was furious. The smell was different, though. Alice's big magic smelled like ozone. Ronan's reminded her of the time she'd been stationed on the Gulf Coast and she'd gone outside during a hurricane when the eye of the storm passed over. If ever raw power and danger had a scent, Ronan's aura did.

As she stepped carefully into the lobby, she saw a group of black-clad Nyx security guards and vampires between them and the club's main doors. The dhampirs had frozen in place, while the vamps seemed more wary and apprehensive—and very interested in figuring out what Ronan was. Arkady could empathize with the latter. She eyed the vamps and tried not to let on that she was having trouble standing without swaying.

"My human lover and I came here tonight for entertainment," Ronan rumbled. "Instead, we were attacked by demons who circumvented your security with ease and inflicted injuries. I demand redress for this outrage."

His voice had that same haughty, formal edge she'd heard back at the Pelican, like a king addressing peasants. He also sounded strange, as if several people were speaking at once rather than a single voice, and his icy tone made her want to rub her arms to banish the chill. His emphasis on *human lover* very strongly implied he wasn't human, as if his power and aura hadn't already made that clear. And he'd taken on this imperious persona with very suspicious ease.

"My...lord," one of the vampires said, clearly unsure who he was addressing or what Ronan's proper title might be. "Our sincerest apologies. Nyx has never experienced such a breach in security. We have no explanation—"

Ronan somehow seemed to grow another half a foot. His glower made the vampire take a half step back. "I have no interest in hearing your excuses. You will beg our forgiveness and remove yourselves from our path."

The vamps exchanged glances. "My lord, if you will but wait a few moments—" the same vampire began.

Ronan took two steps forward. Arkady stayed at his side, her knees locked to keep from stumbling. The vamps and guards took a collective step back.

"Was I not clear that we are leaving the premises?" Ronan asked, his voice now quiet and exceedingly dangerous. "You are fortunate I am more concerned with my lover's well-being than in destroying this vermin-infested pit."

The shadows he'd summoned hid it from the others, but Arkady saw lines of strain in Ronan's face. Whatever he was doing, it took a lot of power. Maybe too much. And the longer they stood here, the more dangerous it became. If the illusion broke, they'd be neck-deep in a shit stew in a hurry.

She gritted her teeth. "My lord," she said, letting her voice quaver. "I feel faint." She let her aching legs give way and collapsed.

She wasn't surprised in the least that he caught her well before she hit the floor—or that he put her over his shoulder so he'd have his hands free to fight if need be. At least her shorts covered her ass just enough that she didn't flash her lady bits at the vamps, which she supposed was worth something. She'd opted to go this route to expedite their departure, but even so she was so pissed at being hauled around like a sack of potatoes that her eyeballs felt hot.

Ronan's whole body trembled with the strain of maintaining his aura of power. How long before the aura faded, or he stumbled? He had to be down to sheer force of will at this point.

As if he'd heard her thoughts, Ronan strode toward the front doors. "We are leaving," he said coldly. The vamps and enforcers moved aside.

They were only a few feet from freedom when Daniela appeared from a hallway to their left, flanked by two other vampires Arkady recognized as Farrell's assistant managers. "Stop!" Daniela shouted.

With a bellow that made Arkady's hair stand on end, Ronan charged through the club's front doors like a bull. She couldn't reach her own knives, so she pulled one of Ronan's hidden blades and threw it. She worried her aim would be off because Ronan was running, but the blade still caught Daniela square in the throat. She went down gurgling.

Once they got outside the club, where a hundred witnesses waited behind the velvet rope, she figured the vamps wouldn't make a scene by chasing them or firing their weapons.

She'd figured wrong.

Ronan sent Ivan the doorman flying with a kick and he stayed down, but two vampires emerged from the club, guns drawn. They fired a half dozen shots. The bullets missed by inches. Bystanders screamed and ran for cover.

Hanging over Ronan's shoulder as he ran down the club's front steps was killing her ribs, but if he slowed to put her down, that might be the end of them both. On the other hand, she had no intention of getting shot tonight, especially while being carried over someone's shoulder with her ass in the air.

They made it to Ronan's Harley just as another gunshot rang out. Ronan grunted, swung Arkady around, and dropped her roughly onto the seat behind him. She wrapped her arms around his middle as he started the bike and took off so quickly that she almost lost her grip. Their helmets remained behind on the street.

His vest was slippery. Under a streetlight, she looked at her hand. It was covered with blood.

"You're hit!" she shouted over the bike's engine.

"No shit," he said through what sounded like gritted teeth. "I think it's lodged in my ribs." He let out a groan that she felt rather than heard because of the motorcycle. "It's spelled. Feels like black magic. Probably for tracking."

Grimly, she recalled the single shot just before they'd gotten on the bike. Now it made sense. That shot wasn't designed to kill, but to provide a way for the vamps to find them.

"Can't you heal the wound like you did your hand earlier?" she asked, her mouth close to his ear.

"Apparently not," he replied. "The spellwork on the bullet interferes with my ability to heal."

She had a healing spell that might stop the bleeding, but it wouldn't get the bullet out. Not that she could use it while they were moving anyway. No matter what he was, he wouldn't be able to keep them upright during the magic and pain of the spell.

"We need help," she told him.

"I'm not bringing the vamps to Alice's door."

"I wasn't thinking of Alice," she retorted. "We need black magic to fight black magic. We're going to see a witch."

"Assuming we can get there." His chest rumbled. "They're behind us."

She hadn't heard anything or seen headlights, but when she glanced over her shoulder she saw two small black SUVs, their headlights off, two blocks back and gaining fast. "Are they tracking the bullet?" she asked.

"Probably not. Visual tracking most likely. It's hard to do that kind of magic in a speeding vehicle."

That was moderately good news, at least. She took off her jacket, found the bullet wound in Ronan's side, and made sure the jacket was wedged tightly between them so its lining would soak up his blood.

"I suggest you lose them," she said, wrapping her arms around his waist again. "And do it fast, before you faint from blood loss and wreck us. We don't have our helmets, and you promised you'd get us out of this without killing me."

He shook slightly with what she thought might have been silent laughter, though with a bullet in him it must have hurt like a son of a bitch. "Hold on to me, my Valkyrie," he said and twisted the throttle.

With a roar of horsepower, the Harley shot ahead. She squeezed him as tightly as she dared and watched over her shoulder as the SUVs fell back initially, then began closing the distance again. When it came to vehicles, as a rule the vamps loved luxury and engine power, and their pursuers were no exception.

Ronan slowed and took a right at a cross-street, an immediate left, and another much sharper right. She made the turns with him, leaning forward slightly, her elbows low and grip tight on his waist. A few blocks later, the SUVs reappeared behind them, now only about a hundred yards away. They must have found a shortcut. The back of her neck prickled.

"We didn't lose them," she said into Ronan's ear. "They probably want us alive, but that might not be a mandate."

He knew these streets well for a relative newcomer to town, she thought. She'd been here for several years, but this part of town wasn't the area she knew best. Then again, the Harley had a GPS on its dash that showed their location and the immediate surroundings, so maybe he was relying on that too.

"We want to head north and east toward the witch's house," she told him as they took another corner and sped down an alley.

He made a left, heading east. She no longer saw the vamps, but she had no reason to think they were in the clear. Her suspicions were confirmed when one of the SUVs appeared once again behind them.

She wanted to text their would-be helper and warn of their arrival, but she had to keep her attention on what Ronan was doing—not to mention she needed both hands to hold on as he tried to lose their pursuers. Her jacket squelched with his blood when she moved. He was breathing hard, and she could feel his heart pounding as the chase went on. That meant he was losing blood even faster.

"How are you doing?" she asked as they turned another corner, echoing his words to her in the elevator shaft.

"I'm lightheaded," he said grimly. "I can't keep going much longer, and they'll be able to start tracking this bullet before long. All they'll need is someone who can scry."

She spotted a familiar building ahead. "Turn into that parking garage."

"A parking garage is a death trap, not an escape route. Using one to lose a tail only works in movies."

Her temper flared. "Just do it, damn it!"

He slowed and made the turn into the entrance. The gate was down for the night, but the Harley made it around the barricade through a very narrow gap between the gate and the curb. The SUV would probably drive right through the gate.

When he headed for the ramp that went up, she poked his shoulder. "Go down."

"Down?" he echoed disbelievingly. "You've got to be joking." But he obeyed, steering the Harley down the ramp to the garage's below-ground parking levels.

"First, they'll never believe we'd go down instead of up. That'll buy us a little time," she said as the Harley made it to sub-level one. She pointed to the narrow pedestrian ramp to their right. "And second, they can't fit up that ramp. If I remember right, it comes out on the terrace of a conference center."

"Good thinking." He revved the Harley's engine and headed for the ramp. She braced herself and held on tightly.

They went up the ramp far more quickly than even she would have attempted as a single rider. At the top, Ronan scanned the terrace, located a ramp down to street level, and followed that path to a street Arkady knew much better than the area of town around Nyx.

Best of all, she saw no sign of the SUVs. They might still be lurking, but judging by Ronan's labored breathing, they'd run out of time to screw around. If the vamps caught up with them, they'd just have to deal with it. They needed a witch, and they needed her *now*.

She gave Ronan the address of their destination and pulled out her phone to send a quick text. *Coming in hot with a man wounded by a bullet spelled with black magic. I've been poisoned by demons. Need first aid and an umbrella.* *Umbrella* was code between them for protection and hiding.

The full minute that passed between her message and the response had Arkady's already frayed nerves even more on edge. Finally, an answer came: *Go straight to Carly's*, the text read on her phone's screen. *I'll meet you there.*

Arkady let out a breath and tapped on Ronan's shoulder to give him the new address. A painful cramp in her stomach made her groan. Ronan put his hand on hers and squeezed.

In her worry about his bullet wound and their pursuers, she'd gotten enough adrenaline to hold off her own pain. Now the agony came back with a vengeance. She swallowed hard and rested her head against Ronan's warm back. All she could smell was leather and blood.

We have to get to Carly's, she thought, a little hazily. *Just get to Carly's. Then we'll be okay.*

The Harley continued its journey block after block, mile after mile, until she lost track of where they were or even where they were going. All she knew was she needed to hold on to Ronan and not let go.

11

RONAN

IS THIS WHAT DYING FEELS LIKE?

During the last few miles of their journey, Ronan didn't so much steer the Harley as aim it in the general direction they needed to go. By the time they arrived at the witch's house, his sight and hearing had diminished noticeably and his ears rang.

All of which suddenly seemed unimportant when Arkady let go of his waist, slid sideways off the motorcycle, and crumpled in the grass between the sidewalk and the curb.

He managed to put the kickstand down, staggered off the bike, and dropped next to her. His chest had long since gone numb, and he could no longer feel either the pain of the gunshot wound or the sharp agony of the bullet that had lodged in his ribs. He had enough experience with serious injuries to know lack of feeling was not a good thing.

Though his mortal senses were beginning to fail him, his other senses felt the steady thrumming of very powerful witch wards on the otherwise charming and nondescript blue bungalow in front of them.

His fumbling fingers found a thready pulse in Arkady's wrist. When he kissed her, her skin felt cold and damp—far worse than before. The demon poison might yet prove fatal.

"Not dead," she murmured when he pressed his lips to her

forehead. The irritation in her voice lightened his heart because it meant she remained as fiery and defiant as ever. "You're not getting out of this that easily," she added.

He was about to ask her what she meant by *this* when a second, larger set of witch wards flared. The streetlights on the block buzzed and went out, plunging the street into darkness. The wards formed a protective, magic-dampening bubble around the house and yard. That muted the magic on the bullet in his chest so he couldn't be tracked. Unfortunately, it also dampened his own power almost completely.

A brisk female voice came from behind him. "You'll have to get yourself inside. We might be able to carry Arkady, but we *definitely* can't carry you."

The speaker was a petite young woman with vibrant pink hair in long braids, wearing a threadbare punk band T-shirt and yoga pants. If the smell of parchment hadn't already tipped him off that she was a witch, the intricate Triple Goddess tattoo on the inside of her right forearm would have.

Arkady snorted softly and disguised a wince as an exaggerated eye roll that Ronan found strangely charming. "Can't you see we're wounded?" she asked. "Where'd you learn your bedside manner?"

"She came by it honestly, same as you." A second woman appeared out of the darkness. The newcomer was a petite brunette with dark hair and bare feet, wearing jeans and a T-shirt that read HEX APPEAL. "Get inside, both of you, before you either pass out or bleed out."

Ronan recognized her voice as well as her magic. This was Alice's close friend, the powerful witch who'd visited him while he lay in a coma and helped heal him with amulets and prayers.

Together, he and Arkady staggered to their feet and made their way to the gate that led to the house's front yard. Both women watched their every move as only witches did, at least in Ronan's experience.

Vampires had an aloof predatory manner, since they considered all others prey, even their own kind. Shifters watched for signs of aggression and readied themselves to attack or defend. Mages like Alice and Malcolm stayed constantly hyper-aware of their environment and attuned themselves to the natural sources of power around them, their nimble fingers always twitching, ready to create a spell or use their magic.

Witches noted and mentally catalogued everything in an almost clinical way, because everything and everyone was either a source of power or knowledge, or both. In all his long eons of existence, he had yet to encounter anyone as observant as a witch. That skill above all others was what made them so disconcertingly canny and dangerous.

At the moment, the brunette witch studied him in a way that implied she knew everything about him there was to know and then some. Possibly Alice had confided in her about his origins so she could provide the type of healing he'd needed.

Demonstrating the very skills Ronan respected most among witches—observation and keen insight—she touched his arm as he passed. "I don't speak anyone's secrets," she said quietly once Arkady was out of earshot. "But such things have a way of finding the light, whether you want them to or not. Better she hears it from you."

A witch's *other* trademark: unsolicited wisdom.

Arkady had already made it to the top of the steps. Since they had an audience, she hadn't used the handrail, so neither did he.

"Arkady already knows me, of course," the brunette witch said when they reached her front door. "Ronan, I am Carly Reese, High Priestess of the Emerald Star Coven. We've met before, at Alice's house, though I'm sure you have no memory of it." She touched his arm again and then Arkady's as well. Even with his magic dampened, he sensed a little frisson of power. "You are both welcome in my home."

She'd spoken formally, so Ronan responded in kind. "I'm most grateful for your hospitality, High Priestess. I am honored to visit your home."

"Call me Carly," she said. "Hurry inside. You're both in immediate danger of expiring on my front porch, and I try to avoid that kind of negative energy as a general rule."

"I'm Katy Clark," the pink-haired witch added. "Your friendly neighborhood black witch gone good-ish."

Ah—probably the source of Arkady's Exit spells, then. "A pleasure to meet you," he said.

As they crossed Carly's threshold, Ronan smelled a hundred scents: drying herbs, incense, smoke, even what might have been the lingering smells of elixirs and spells that hung in the air long after their creation thanks to the magic used to mix them. He also detected the aroma of something baking, which reminded him that he'd consumed only tequila since lunch.

"A kitchen witch, I take it?" he asked as Carly led the way to her living room.

"A very eclectic witch." She smiled kindly. "But you can think of me as a kitchen witch if you like. That reminds me—Katy, take the scones out of the oven. Our guests will be hungry when we're done. And finish brewing Arkady's healing tea."

Obediently, Katy disappeared into the kitchen. Meanwhile, Ronan surveyed Carly's living room. She'd set up an altar and a nest of cushions in the middle of the floor, draped with a tarp to keep blood off the carpet and furnishings.

"Lie down now," she told him. Her tone was still kind, but firm. "Before you fall."

"Help Arkady first," he countered. "I'll wait."

In his defense, his pain and the itchy sensation of the dampening spells had made his temper short, but he should have known better than to issue an order in a witch's own house. Carly's stare and the odor of burned paper made it clear he'd just added yet another item to the list of ways he'd fucked up tonight. Katy appeared in the kitchen doorway, a kettle in her hand, and gave him a matching glare.

"I apologize," he said. "But I won't accept treatment while Arkady suffers."

"Katy will tend to Arkady while I take care of you," Carly informed him. "Either trust us to care for you both or go. I need my energy for protecting my coven and healing people who get themselves shot and poisoned, and I won't waste it arguing with you."

"Lie down, you horse's ass," Arkady snapped. She leaned against the wall with her arms folded over her abdomen. "Katy's got me. She's not going to let me suffer."

"Not much, anyway," Katy interjected. At Ronan's glower, she shrugged. "Hey, I'm a black witch. You want black magic to undo black magic, you gotta be prepared for some pain."

That was true, he reflected grimly. Blood and pain were the primary ingredients in black magic, along with thirst for power.

He gave in and lay down in the bed Carly had prepared, with his head in front of the altar and his feet toward the south wall of the house. Apparently satisfied that the conflict was over, Katy went back to the kitchen to finish preparing some kind of healing elixir for Arkady.

As Carly busied herself at the altar, Arkady tossed a throw pillow on the floor and sat down next to him with an almost inaudible groan. He patted her knee. "No need to fret over me so much, Miss Woodall. I have no plans to die tonight."

She glared at him. "I'm just here in case you start crying and need these." She pushed a box of tissues closer to him. "We all know what a big baby you are."

He snorted without thinking and couldn't hide his flinch. She covered his hand with her own. "Okay, okay, cut the dramatics," she said. "Just hold on to me, you big baby."

Despite her mocking words and tone, the worry in her eyes nearly undid him. She stroked her thumb over the callouses created by his long years of fighting and practicing with his sword. Her gentle touch soothed him.

Carly rested her hand on top of Arkady's head and murmured something even Ronan couldn't quite hear, but that seemed like a prayer or blessing. Whether actual magic passed between them he couldn't tell, but some of the tension went out of Arkady's shoulders. Carly stroked Arkady's head like a child's, then busied herself at her altar.

Ronan was hardly new to working with witches, and much of what Carly had on her altar was familiar to him. The pentagonal altar had a statue of a goddess at the top—probably the Morrigan, given both he had Arkady had fallen victim to black magic and demon poison. The top right point had a bowl of river water, since the movement of water would help carry the poison from their bodies. A twelve-inch red taper candle in the lower right corner added strength to Carly and her magic and would help burn away negative energy released when she took out the bullet.

The bowl of what he thought might be graveyard dirt in the lower left corner was the most unsettling item on the altar. If he'd guessed right, its presence indicated Carly thought he and Arkady might be in danger of dying. On a less-dire note, it would also help absorb any death energy in the demon poison or black magic spellwork on the bullet. In the upper left corner, she'd arranged a pile of loose white sage mixed with what smelled like palo santo and sweetgrass to keep the energy in the circle cleansed and positive.

In the center of the altar was a basket full of implements and one of the most beautiful athames he had ever seen. Its power was so great, and so pure, that it reminded him of a full moon shining brightly on a clear night. Everything on the altar was designed to protect, purify, strengthen, and care for bodies and souls.

Carly and her altar reminded him it had been entirely too long since he had interacted with a true white witch—so long that he'd forgotten how simply being in their presence felt like a healing.

Athame in hand, its blade pointed at the floor, Carly walked around the bed and altar clockwise. "I close this circle with love," she said on the first turn. "I close this circle with healing," she added on her second turn. Finally, on her third pass around the circle, she said, "I close this circle with comfort." She knelt, pricked her finger carefully on the tip of her athame, touched the edge of her circle, and said, "With my blood I give this circle my strength and protection."

The scent of warm parchment and the contents of her altar swirled in the circle. Ronan took as deep of a breath as he could and let her magic settle over him.

Carly rose, placed the athame back on the altar, and stood in front of it with her hands outstretched, palms up. "I call upon the goddess Morrigan to enter this circle to help me rid Ronan and Arkady of the demon energy that flows through their veins. Lend your strength and knowledge to my mind and guide my hands to do whatever needs to be done."

She knelt at Ronan's side, across from Arkady, and picked up a cup from the altar. "Help me raise his head so he can drink," she told Arkady.

Together, they lifted Ronan's head. Carly pressed the cup to his lips. The warm liquid smelled and tasted like Carly's house: a hundred distinct flavors and odors blended together. And not one drop of black magic, he decided after a few sips—pure white magic, designed to calm and heal. It eased the pain caused by the demon poison in his bloodstream, and it soothed his body and soul.

At Carly's urging, he drank the remainder of the tea in a few gulps, rested his head back against the cushion, and focused on the steady, even strokes of Arkady's thumb on his hand. Under the influence of the tea, her gentle touch became hypnotic. Everything taking place around him grew blurry, but not in the same way he'd become hazy from blood loss. He felt...peaceful, for the first time in a very, very long time.

His serenity was short-lived. Carly took a pair of scissors from a basket at her side. "I need to remove your vest," she told him.

He grabbed her arm before he realized he'd moved. His sudden movement startled her. "I have magic, but not the kind that can remove the bullet or treat the wound through your clothing," she said. "Don't worry about what's under the vest. Your secrets are safe with us."

He gritted his teeth. "You've seen, then?"

"Yes," she said simply. "I did what I could at Alice's house to heal your body and spirit, but some things are beyond my power." She did sound regretful about the last, but it was the unvarnished truth— another specialty of white and gray witches.

He should have been angrier that she'd seen his scars, but the tea she'd given him muted everything, even his fury. He blinked slowly, and time seemed to jump ahead a bit before he opened his eyes again.

He managed to focus on Arkady's face. "Go to another room," he rasped.

She brushed hair back from his face. "Don't worry about me. Like Carly said, your secrets are safe with us."

"I don't want you to see." The tea had made him even more honest, or perhaps he'd run out of gentler ways to say it. "Turn your back." He coughed thickly and tasted blood.

"Arkady, we are running out of time." Carly's firm voice cut into their argument. "Tell him and let's move on."

Ronan sensed sudden tension in Arkady's grip on his hand. For the first time all night, she avoided his gaze. "Tell me what?" he demanded.

"Damn it, fine." She cursed under her breath. "I've already seen your scars, Ronan. I saw them the day you showed up at Alice's house."

Despite the effects of the sedative tea, he went cold with anger. She'd had every chance to tell him she'd seen his scars, but she hadn't, even after he'd made it clear how heavily they weighed on his mind. That she'd chosen to pretend she hadn't seen them felt like a far worse betrayal than the fact she'd seen them at all.

When he'd asked Michael to return him to Alice's house, he'd resigned himself to the fact Alice and Sean would see his wounds. He'd had every intention of keeping them hidden from every other living thing. Carly had seen them, but in her capacity as a healer, so he couldn't hold it against her.

He pulled his hand out of Arkady's and turned his attention to Carly. "Do what you need to do," he said curtly. "I'm grateful for your help, as well as your respect for my person."

Without a word, Carly cut through Ronan's bloody vest. He kept his gaze on Carly's face and didn't look at Arkady. Arkady, for her part, went silent except for quiet, raspy breathing.

She didn't angrily defend herself or even offer excuses or explanations—not that he would have been particularly interested in hearing them. That was, he reflected, possibly why she didn't offer any.

Carly finished cutting through his vest and peeled it back, baring his bloody chest. He wanted to cover the scars with his hand, but her touch on his arm dissuaded him from moving.

With her fingertips, her brow furrowed in concentration, she pressed lightly on his chest in a spiral pattern until she found where the bullet had lodged. "It's not too deep, for which we should all be grateful," she said. "I'll have to cut it out."

"Not the first time someone has cut a bullet out of me." He managed a bitter smile. "Do you have tequila?"

"No, but we have this." She picked up a small bowl filled with a foul-smelling paste. "Katy's special anesthetic. It won't knock you out, but it'll make this process easier to bear."

"What's in it?"

"Never ask a black witch what's in her potions." Katy appeared in the living room with a teapot and a ceramic cup covered with runes. "It does the job, and that's all you need to know."

He blinked slowly and lost track of time again, this time for much longer. When he woke, Carly was bent over him, focused on her work. He felt strange pulls and tugs in his chest. She must still be trying to extract the bullet.

Rather than look at what she was doing, he glanced to his left and was surprised to find Arkady had vanished. His stomach lurched. "Where—" he mumbled.

"Don't talk while I'm working on you," Carly said sharply. "She's ridding herself of the demon poison."

He stared at the ceiling. From another room, he heard someone chanting—presumably Katy—and someone else vomiting violently. Despite his anger, he flinched at the sound.

"It's worse than you're imagining." Carly went back to digging out the bullet. "You're lucky you'll only need a small dose. And you're *very* lucky you got here when you did. Neither of you would have made it another hour."

Finally, she squinted, leaned closer, and did something that caused a dull pain despite Katy's anesthetic. "Got you, you little bugger." She held up the bullet in a large pair of tweezers. Though the slug was deformed by its travel through his back and getting lodged in his rib, he saw the black magic spellwork cut into its nose, where its trip through the gun barrel wouldn't mar it.

Carly placed the bullet in a saucer with her own spellwork carved into it and draped a cloth over it. "Done. No one will be tracking you now." She wiped her gloved hands with a rag, which she put in a bucket. "I'll burn everything with your blood on it," she said in response to his unspoken question. "Now, a healing spell will get you closed up, but you've lost a lot of blood, so I don't want you to move or talk right now. Blink once for yes. Do you have access to a blood transfusion?"

He blinked.

"Good." She held up a purple crystal. "Alice gave me a couple of these strong healing spells for emergencies. I figured you'd be more comfortable with her magic than anyone else's. I'm assuming you've used one before and you know it hurts."

Again, he blinked. From a back room, he could still hear Arkady being sick. She must have gotten a much larger dose of the demon poison than he'd realized. The fact she'd survived long enough to get to Carly's house seemed something close to a miracle now. Her dishonesty still angered him, but he'd take her place in a heartbeat to save her from this much suffering, not to mention the indignity.

When Carly's voice drew his attention back to his own condition, he focused on her face. "You want something to bite on?" she asked.

He blinked a third time. She pulled his belt from its loops, folded it in half, and put it carefully between his teeth as if she'd done this before. She probably had, he reflected. A coven High Priestess would not be a stranger to painful healings.

Carefully, she placed the healing spell on his chest near where she'd been cutting and pressed his hand on top of it. "The invocation is *Helios*."

The magic rose as if it anticipated his need. He recognized it as Alice's, and a powerful spell at that. At least he was no stranger to pain. "*Helios*," he rasped around his belt.

The healing spell pulsed through his body in waves of white-hot agony. He grunted, breathed in and out between waves of magic, and bit down on his belt so hard he imagined he might bite right through it.

Slowly his injuries healed. The intensity of the magic pulses increased and then began to wane. By the time the last of the magic passed through his body, he felt unexpectedly nauseated in addition to shaky from the spell's effects. *Mortal frailty*, he thought savagely as he dropped the crystal and took the belt from his mouth.

Ever observant and insightful, Carly must have noticed his anger and guessed its cause. As she picked up the crystal and set it aside, she said, "Something to consider. A mortal body may seem weak or fragile compared to what you're used to, but it can withstand far more than you give it credit for. And a mortal heart offers more joy than any immortal life could ever experience." She glanced in the direction of the back room, which had gone quiet finally. "Especially when you choose to share it with another."

More unsolicited wisdom. "She lied to me," he said, his tone flat.

"Did she?" Carly raised her eyebrows and pulled off her bloody gloves. "Maybe. But you have to ask yourself why."

He pushed himself up to a sitting position. The room went a bit hazy, then his vision cleared. He wanted to argue the why didn't matter, but of course it did. Hadn't he had that argument with Michael? But what good reason could Arkady have had to lie about this?

Carly rose, picked up her athame again, and opened the circle with a quiet prayer of thanks. He got to his feet, still nauseated and unsteady, and eyed the blood on the tarp. It looked worse than it was, he decided.

"Arkady's in the shower in my room," Carly informed him. "You can use the guest bathroom. Towels are in the cabinet."

"We need clothes to change into. They're in my saddlebag outside."

"I'll bring them in."

Before he went to clean up, he unzipped one of the pockets in his pants and withdrew the tiny wingless demon he'd brought from Nyx. It wriggled between his fingers and let out a weak screech. "This is our only lead on where to go next," he said. "If I may ask yet another favor, do you have any means of tracking its master?"

"I assumed you had a good reason to bring such a foul thing into my home." Carly studied the creature with obvious distaste. "Why do you need to find its master?"

He explained why he and Arkady were tracking down the demon they believed ran the trafficking ring. Carly's expression went from distaste to disgust and then anger as he described what they'd uncovered so far.

When he finished, she had him drop the little demon into a wooden box covered with intricate spellwork. "Katy has a strong gift for scrying," she said, shutting the box. "I'll ask her about this when she's done helping Arkady. If she hasn't used too much power tonight and she's willing, she'll try to get you an answer."

"That's all we can ask. Thank you."

"Shower." She made a shooing motion. "Try not to track blood all over my house."

He hurried to the guest bathroom. He passed Katy coming out of the master bedroom with Arkady's clothes in a bucket.

She handed it to him. "Put yours in here too. We'll burn it all at once and I'll disperse the ash and traces. No one will know you were ever here."

"Thank you." He set the bucket in the bathroom. "How is she?"

"Pissed at you." Katy crossed her arms and leaned against the wall. "And sick enough to call me names I've never heard, and I thought I'd heard them all. We got the poison out, though, eventually. I'll bring your cup of elixir and leave it on the counter in the bathroom. Don't worry—it's a small dose compared to what she needed. You'll be a little sick but fine."

He thanked her again, went into the bathroom, and shut the door. As he stripped off what remained of his clothes, he looked himself over in the mirror. The healing spell had done its job. He was covered in blood, but no wounds remained except his scars.

They'd healed enough to no longer hurt, burn, ooze blood, or glow faintly with angelic power, but he remained aware of them all the same. They were a constant nagging sensation that never let him have a moment's true peace. Even whole bottles of tequila couldn't banish the feeling—and he'd tried. The only times he'd managed to ignore them were during fights...and when Arkady smiled at him.

No, that wasn't the whole truth. When he'd watched her come in the dungeon at Nyx, he'd forgotten about them completely.

In the shower, he stood under hot water and soaped himself from head to toe twice until he felt clean and the bathroom filled with steam. And all the while, his thoughts circled back to the same words again and again:

She lied to me.

You have to ask yourself why.

The bathroom door opened and closed quietly as he scrubbed his face one last time under the hot spray. Probably Carly dropping off his clothes and his dose of Katy's demon poison antidote. He doubted he'd need to drink it now. The poison's effects seemed almost gone. Maybe Alice's healing spell had helped in that regard too.

He shut off the water, pulled back the curtain, reached for a towel...and stilled.

Arkady sat on the bathroom counter next to his clean clothes, eating what looked like a blueberry scone and wearing the change of clothes she'd put in his saddlebag: jeans, boots, and a tight dark gray T-shirt.

"Hey," she said and tossed him a towel. "We need to talk."

12

ARKADY

IF SHE'D THOUGHT RONAN LOOKED DAMN GOOD IN LEATHER AND motorcycle boots, that was nothing compared to how fine he looked in water and nothing else.

He caught the towel she'd thrown, but he didn't wrap it around his waist or even make a move to dry himself off. He did, however, step out of the shower onto the mat so they were only about a foot apart. He smelled of Carly's homemade herbal soap and hot skin. Judging by the thick steam in the air, he'd showered in scalding water. She'd done the same. It had been the kind of night that demanded a good hot scrub-down, and it wasn't over yet.

"So talk," he rumbled.

That was unmistakably a challenge: have a conversation while he stood naked and dripping wet only inches away, with all that muscle and other glorious things on full display.

His scars looked much better now than when she'd seen them at Alice's house. Back then, they were bloody cuts that indicated just how cruel his tormentors had been, especially their desire to inflict suffering and shame.

In the interim, they'd healed enough to become slightly raised lines forming neat rows of runes. Looking at his scars now, she suddenly understood Ronan's impulse to kiss her throat where Farrell had bitten her. She wanted to run her tongue over them and make them into something different. At the moment, however, she had some business to settle.

She ate another bite of her scone and met his stony gaze. "I'm only going to say this once. You can accept it or not. I saw your scars because I happened to be standing next to Alice when she looked at them, not because I pulled back your covers while you slept. And I didn't look at them again, even when Alice and Sean left me alone with you. It didn't occur to me to do so. At least give me *some* credit. I wouldn't have wanted someone to look at my wounds if I'd been in your condition."

His expression didn't change. "And the reason you didn't tell me this earlier?"

"I wanted you to show them to me on your own terms when you were ready. I figured it would hurt you to find out I'd seen them without you knowing. I made the choice I thought would hurt you less. Maybe I chose wrong. I suppose I should have known it would come out anyway." She offered him the other half of her scone. "Want a bite? You've got to be starving."

"You finish it. You need the nourishment. I'll get my own." He moved closer until he was between her thighs, as he'd been hours earlier in the parking lot at the Pelican when she was sitting on the hood of Ren and Stimpy's car. He was naked now, however, and unlike that earlier confrontation their mutual desire stirred the air between them.

She took a chance and leaned close enough to gently lick his wet, scarred skin. He tensed but held his ground as her tongue explored the lines. He tasted of soap and sea water, though the shower had certainly used fresh water. Another clue to his true nature, she supposed.

When he didn't move away or stop her, she continued her careful explorations, moving across his scars and then to his chest, where her tongue curled around his nipple. She grazed him with her teeth there too, and smiled when he twitched in response.

"Carly told me a mortal heart offers great joy." He raised her chin with his fingertips. "So far, mine has only felt pain and loneliness."

"That doesn't mean it has to stay that way." She entwined their fingers, causing him to drop the unused towel at his feet. "You remember what I told you about scars?"

The corners of his mouth turned up. "They only have power if you let them?"

"Yes." She ran her tongue along his breastbone, licking up the water that clung to his skin. "I don't need to know what the scars are about. They're battle scars and that's enough for me. You can see all of mine too, if you want."

"I will," he promised, his lips close to her ear. "Every single one."

Despite the near-tropical heat in the bathroom, she shivered. "Whatever your scars meant to begin with, now they're proof that you got back up when you weren't supposed to. They were meant to crush you, body and soul. Instead, here you stand, a man fighting for the life he wants *and* the lives of those who can't fight for themselves." She looked up into his startled eyes. "They're your medals of valor."

His face lost all expression, and he said nothing for a long time—so long that she thought he was going to reject what she'd said. But when he finally spoke, his voice was suddenly thick with emotion. "My medals of valor. Because you said so?"

Exasperated, she let go of his hand. "No, you asshole—because *you* said so."

With a low growl, he pulled her against his body, cupped her head, and kissed her.

She'd thought he'd been a fantastic kisser before, but those earlier kisses paled in comparison to this one. This kiss contained what felt like his entire being and one hundred percent of his attention. Even in their most intimate moments in her kitchen and the dungeon, she'd sensed he remained reserved, as if he had to keep some part of himself secret or even protected from her. Now he seemed to come alive in her embrace. His power, whatever it was, grew until it thrummed in the air.

Maybe it was that hum of power that filled her with longing, or maybe it was the raw hunger in his eyes, but she couldn't resist the urge to see him lose himself in pleasure. She pushed him back, slid off the counter, and went to her knees in front of him. Before she could lean forward, he stopped her with a gentle touch on her shoulder. "You don't need to," he told her, though she could see the desire in his eyes, and his body quite obviously voted in favor of the idea.

Equally irritated and aroused, as she'd been for almost the whole time she'd known him, she brushed his hand off her shoulder. "I know exactly what I need, and what *you* need," she retorted. "So shut up and enjoy what you've earned."

He chuckled softly. "Your wish is my command."

She began by stroking him lightly and teasing him with her tongue, enjoying the way he reacted and the sounds he made. He was every bit as magnificent as she'd guessed and then some. And delicious as well —even more so the more of him she took into her mouth. And try as she might, no matter how much she managed to fit into her mouth and throat, she couldn't take all of him. She watched him as he watched her, their gazes locked as she moved, and his breathing grew heavy.

Despite his need, he let her control the rhythm and intensity for a while, but she wasn't at all surprised when he took over. With one hand on the back of her head to hold her still, he used his other thumb on her lower lip and jaw to keep her mouth and throat at just the right angle. He stroked in and out of her mouth, his head thrown back, as she kept her lips tight around him. She loved watching the way the muscles of his chest, abdomen, and legs contracted with his movement and the intensity of his pleasure, much as he'd probably enjoyed watching her writhe for him at Nyx.

She hadn't planned to get herself off too, but thinking about how he'd touched her earlier and watching him now made it impossible not to unbuckle her belt, unfasten her pants, and slip one hand into her jeans. They'd both stayed quiet, mindful of Carly and Katy in the house, but as Ronan's breathing turned to gasps and the muscles in his abdomen tightened, she couldn't hold back a moan.

When their eyes met, his held an unspoken question. In answer, she gripped his ass with her free hand and held him in place, refusing to let him pull away.

They came together a few moments later, with Ronan's hand wrapped in her hair and her mouth on him. He groaned and shuddered as she drifted in a haze of her own pleasure. When he withdrew from her mouth, she sat back on her heels and gasped for air.

He knelt in front of her, his chest still heaving, and took her hand —the one that had been in her jeans. "Allow me," he said, and brought her fingers to his lips. He licked them clean, one at a time, sucking on each before letting go. Then he brushed loose hair back from her face and cupped her cheek. "I needed that."

"I know." She had to chuckle as they repeated their exchange, with reversed roles, from their intimate moment at Nyx. "I figured we both deserved the opportunity to find out if orgasms improved our eyesight and reflexes."

"Oh, was that your motivation?" He smiled. "What are your initial findings?"

"I'm no scientist, but I think the hypothesis requires additional study."

"I concur." He grew serious. "I am sorry for staking Farrell and denying you your revenge."

She'd been giving that incident some thought herself—specifically, what Farrell had said immediately prior to getting ashed. Other than cursing and fantasizing about what she'd do to this demon trafficker when they found him, she'd had little else to distract herself while puking up her guts. "You killed him because he was about to tell me what you are. And he did it on purpose, to provoke you."

"Yes." He looked grave. "That doesn't mean I don't regret it, for your sake."

She'd started the night wanting nothing more than to uncover what he was. In the hours since, she'd come to understand a lot about this mysterious man—enough to know she cared less about what he'd been than the man he was now.

"I do want to know, but I don't have to know now." She touched his face. "You'll tell me one day."

"Alice, Sean, and Malcolm know." He tilted his head and considered. "Carly as well, since Alice asked for her help to heal me. So why should I want to keep it from you?"

"My guess is, you don't fear they'll reject you, but you think I might if I knew the truth." Arkady shrugged as if that realization didn't hurt. "I suppose that's fair, given you've known me for basically one night."

"I said earlier having nothing to prove to someone is a new thing for me. That's not all about this that's new." He squeezed her hand. "I've never feared anything, not really. But now I fear the truth about me will cause you to walk away." His eyes flashed. "I don't like fear."

She had to laugh at that. "Do you think any of us do? It just comes with the territory. Personally, I like to conquer my fears."

"Of course you do, my Valkyrie. I'm again humbled by you."

He wasn't ready to spill the beans—that much was obvious. She might have been able to force his hand, but she didn't particularly want to.

Someone walked loudly to the bathroom door and knocked. "Get yourselves presentable," Carly called from the hallway. "Katy's ready to scry."

"Thank you," Ronan called back. "We'll be out in a moment."

"Oh, lord...she knows what we just did." Arkady sighed when Carly's footsteps had retreated back down the hall. "Not that I care, I suppose. She probably already knew everything about us in the first ten seconds after we got here. You can't keep secrets from witches."

"Indeed you can't," Ronan agreed. He kissed Arkady on the forehead, rose smoothly, and offered his hand to help her up.

She straightened her shirt and jeans as he dressed quickly in his own spare set of clothing. "What is Katy scrying for?" she asked.

"I gave them the minor demon I brought from Nyx," he explained. "I hoped one of them could see where it came from. It's our best lead now."

"I figured as much." She made a face. "Bummer you already gave it to them, though."

He frowned as he tucked in his T-shirt and fastened his belt. "Why?"

"I wanted to ask if that was a demon in your pocket or if you were just happy to see me. I mean, how often—?"

He laughed and kissed her. "I'll keep that in mind for next time."

"I hope there's a next time," she said, very seriously. "Stomping those little assholes was the most fun I've had in a while." Getting their poison out of her body, not so much. *That* she could do without.

They found Katy and Carly not in the living room, but out back in Carly's garden. Katy sat cross-legged in a circle, her unfocused stare fixed on the surface of a gorgeous round obsidian scrying mirror. The tiny wingless demon lay still in her upturned palm, possibly drugged, possibly dead. Arkady couldn't tell which. Carly sat nearby at a wrought iron table, keeping watch.

As quietly as possible, Arkady and Ronan joined Carly at the table. Their hostess had set out a plate of scones, a pot of tea, and full glasses of juice—two for Ronan and one for Arkady. Her expression made it clear she expected them to finish all of it.

Arkady dove in without hesitation, chugging her juice and then nearly inhaling two whole scones in between gulps of tea. Ronan followed suit. When they'd finished, Carly went back into the house and returned about ten minutes later with a tray bearing three plates full of eggs, sausage, bacon, and toast. Ronan ate every bite on two plates. When Arkady put down her fork, he eyed the remainder of her meal too.

She chuckled and slid the plate over to him. "Go ahead."

Meanwhile, Carly's satisfied expression reminded her of how Sean looked when Alice ate a proper meal instead of her usual ten cups of coffee and half a bag of chips. An alpha wanted all those in his care to be safe, happy, and well-fed, and that went triple for their mates.

Carly was kind of an alpha too, Arkady mused as she sipped her tea and surreptitiously rubbed her full belly. As High Priestess of her coven, she was bossy as shit, with the same desire to ensure those in her care were protected, guided, and healthy in body, mind, and soul.

Katy, with her dedication to black magic and morally gray choices, had proven a challenge for Carly, but they seemed to have worked out an arrangement that suited them both. That came as a big relief for both Arkady and Alice, since they liked Katy and wanted her to find her way within Carly's coven.

As much as she'd enjoyed the food and drink and Carly's peaceful garden, Arkady fidgeted as the minutes ticked by. She found herself playing with the handle of the enchanted knife she'd offered to Ronan as a way of getting out of Nyx. At the time, she'd thought that particularly extreme measure might be their only bargaining chip with the vamps. She was more glad than she'd ever let on that they hadn't needed to use it after all. She wasn't nearly as cavalier about dying and being resurrected as she'd led Ronan to believe.

Before handing over the blade, Katy had reminded her that while the spell would do its job, that kind of magic always had unexpected consequences. Alice's own experience with death and resurrection demonstrated that very clearly. The aftereffects of the incident with the shifter relic had been many and varied—and nearly ended Alice and Sean's relationship to boot.

Unlike Arkady, Ronan seemed uncharacteristically relaxed as they waited, even slouching in his chair, his long legs stretched out under the table. She was just vain enough to think it had something to do with her attentions. She tried not to look smug but probably failed, judging by Carly's knowing smile.

Finally, after what seemed like eons but was probably more like twenty minutes, Katy's voice startled them. "I see a shadow." Her unfocused eyes remained fixed on the scrying mirror, which Arkady found mildly unsettling. "The shadow has two forms and many faces."

"Most demons do," Ronan murmured, his voice pitched so he didn't break Katy's concentration. "We need more."

"The shadow likes to be worshiped always," Katy continued, her tone dreamy. "The shadow sits on her throne."

"*Her* throne?" Arkady echoed in an undertone. "There's a *female* demon in the middle of all this?" She knew relatively little about demons, but she *did* know their male-dominated culture rarely permitted females to operate independent of their male counterparts or lords.

"Katy, where is the shadow now?" Carly asked in a gentle voice.

"Traveling in a car."

"Katy, where's the car?" Ronan prompted, earning an irritated look from Carly. "What's her destination?"

This time, Katy didn't reply and went quiet for a long time as she sat motionless and stared into her mirror. Arkady sipped her tea, trying not to jiggle her foot with impatience.

Finally, Katy raised her head, pale and trembling from the effort. Carly crouched outside the circle. "Katy, tell me what you saw." Her tone was kind but insistent. Arkady knew from previous experience that visions gleaned through scrying could fade quickly.

Instead of speaking, Katy picked up a notepad from beside her altar and drew with a pencil. She filled three pages, then dropped the notepad and pencil, broke her circle simply by cutting its perimeter with the tip of her athame and murmuring a quick prayer, and slumped over onto her side.

With a sigh, Carly checked Katy's condition, then took several deep breaths with what looked like an effort not to lose her temper. When she looked up, she appeared more tired than angry. "She's passed out, but she'll be all right once she sleeps it off," she said, to Arkady's relief. "When she comes to you asking a favor, I expect you to grant it."

It didn't escape Arkady's notice that Carly had said not *if*, but *when*.

"We will," Ronan said without hesitation. "You have my word."

"And mine," Arkady added.

"Take this." Carly handed the notepad to Arkady and rose. "Take her to my room, please. She can sleep in my bed. And then you two need to be on your way." That last part wasn't unkind, but it brooked no argument.

Carefully, Ronan scooped Katy up and carried her inside. Arkady stacked their dirty dishes on the tray and took it to the kitchen. She loaded the dishwasher while Carly cleaned up the scrying circle.

When Carly came inside, she met Ronan and Arkady near the front door and handed them a small wooden box. "The creature's dead. Its master may be able to track it even now, so I've put its remains in here. I'll take the box back when you're done with it."

Arkady gave Ronan the three sheets of paper from Katy's notepad. As he frowned and studied them, she said, "Thank you, Carly. And please thank Katy for us too when she wakes up."

"Of course." Carly leaned against the wall and rubbed her eyes. "Speak to Alice, Ronan. She understands why you left. She's not angry, but she does worry about you a great deal. Ease her fears."

"I will." Ronan gave Carly a solemn nod. "Thank you for your healing and wisdom."

"You're welcome." She opened her front door. "Now scat and let a tired witch get her sleep, before I turn you both into a newt."

"Don't you mean newts, plural?" Arkady asked.

Carly pointed to her porch. "No, I do not."

"We should go." Ronan put his hand on Arkady's lower back and ushered her outside. With a chuckle, Carly shut the door and locked it behind them.

13

RONAN

Katy had managed four very strange drawings before passing out.

"Gimme those." Arkady shoved the wooden box containing the dead demon into Ronan's hand and took the sketches before he had a chance to reply. She studied them under Carly's porch light from various directions and angles, presumably searching, as he had, for something they could use.

The first sketch showed the silhouette of a figure with long hair and unmistakably feminine curves. That by itself seemed straightforward enough, but Katy had drawn four slashes across the figure that reminded him of fingernail or claw marks. The next sketch was a jagged line in the lower portion of a dark shape shaded in with pencil. The third drawing was a simplistic sketch of a bed with a stick figure on it. A shadow hovered above the stick figure.

The fourth seemed their best bet for the demon's location, if only they could figure out what it was supposed to mean. On that page, Katy had drawn a wavy line between two opposing diagonal lines. Above the strange lines was a tall rectangle, unmistakably a building, with an arrow pointing at the top floor.

"Well, she's no great artist," Arkady said with a sigh. "But she tried her best to sketch the things she saw while in a trance before passing out from sheer exhaustion. That can't have been easy. This all means something important."

"It's up to us to figure out what." He stuck the small box into his inside jacket pocket and zipped it closed.

She didn't reply, her attention on Katy's sketches. She seemed back to her all-business self—chomping at the bit, as it were, to get back to the chase. He saw no signs of tiredness or even lingering side effects of the demon poison or purging it from her body. She seemed to run just as well on adrenaline and determination as food and sleep. At some point, however, she'd have to stop and rest, and so would he. He surprised himself by picturing them in bed together, not having sex but sleeping comfortably side by side. It was the first time in all his long existence that he'd imagined such a thing.

As she flipped through the pages yet again, he took advantage of her inattention and leaned close enough to brush his nose against her hair and inhale. She smelled of the same soap he'd used and a dozen other scents he liked—including his leather saddlebags, where her clothes had been stored. If she noticed his shifter-like behavior, she didn't let on.

When she suddenly twitched, he had to jerk back to keep her head from hitting his nose. That was the second time tonight he'd almost gotten a bloody nose from her, he reflected wryly. Unlike her attempted head-butt in the parking lot of the Pelican, however, this time it hadn't been intentional.

"You have a thought?" he prompted.

"Not sure." She hummed under her breath. "I don't want to bias your interpretation. Take a minute to look at this and tell me what you see." She handed him the fourth drawing, crossed her arms, and waited.

Even on his third and most lengthy study of the wavy and diagonal lines, their meaning continued to escape him. "Not any kind of runes, emblem, or crest I'm familiar with," he mused. "The wavy line could be a river—that's a common symbol. But the lines on each side of it don't seem consistent with it being a waterway, unless it's a poorly drawn canal."

Ever impatient, she took the drawing and held it up in front of him. "Forget symbolism. You asked where the car was going, remember? I think this one's more literal."

To look at the sketch now, he had to face away from the house and toward Carly's yard. Arkady moved the sketch up so the bottom of the rectangle lined up with ground level. "Now?" she prodded.

"It's a building."

"No shit. Keep staring until it comes to you."

"A tall, narrow structure." He traced the wavy line that led to the building's front. "At the end of a curving road. And the diagonal lines..." He took the drawing again and held it up for himself. "Those could indicate a steep hill."

"Skyscraper at the top of a steep hill, at the end of a curvy road. Call me crazy, but I think Katy's telling us this demon bitch lives in a penthouse in the infamous Carmody Tower."

"I'm not familiar with it."

"That's surprising." She led him down the steps, along the stone path through Carly's yard, and out through the gate to the Harley. "The most exclusive and expensive condo tower in the Castle Hill neighborhood. In fact, it's *on top* of Castle Hill." She took out her phone and pulled up a photo of an enormous glass condo that he recognized by sight rather than its name. "Opened a couple of years ago. Caused a big ruckus because that whole area used to be Castle Hill Park. Some money changed hands, the city sold it to developers, and up went the tower right where folks used to go on picnics and walk their doggies. Everyone was shocked when it happened. I think they all figured the rich people in the condos around the park would be able to stop it. Guess not."

"If this demon was involved, that might explain how the tower got built against the wishes of what sounds like the whole city." Ronan swung his leg over the seat and settled in with his boots on the pavement. He'd parked badly, too close to the curb and at an angle. He supposed he should be glad he'd managed to park the Harley at all given his condition when they'd arrived. He barely recalled their journey from Nyx, though it had taken place less than two hours earlier. It was possible Carly had not exaggerated all that much when she'd said he and Arkady had been in imminent danger of dying on her porch.

To his surprise, Arkady climbed onto the Harley in front of him and scooted back until her ass nestled comfortably against his groin. How long they'd remain comfortable seemed a very pressing question, given his body was already responding in predictable ways to her closeness.

He rested one hand on her thigh. "What's this?"

"Couldn't resist." He could hear the smile in her voice, though her attention remained focused on her phone screen as she searched for more information on Carmody Tower. "You looked like you needed me to come sit on your lap."

"I wasn't aware my facial expression could lead you to that conclusion." He kissed the back of her neck and enjoyed her little shiver, though it did nothing to help limit his arousal. "I think it's *you* who needed to sit on my lap."

"Delusional as always," she scoffed. "You're not all that, O Great and Mighty One."

"On the contrary, I'm all that and more." He stroked her thigh. "I look forward to proving it."

"I look forward to letting you try." She let him rest his hand on her leg but continued with her online search in a way that made it clear she had other priorities at the moment. His body, however, chose to ignore both her tone and distracted attention. She had to be well aware of his arousal. He got the impression she got some kind of twisted pleasure out of the situation. Despite his discomfort, he had to admit he liked her twisted streak.

He peered over her shoulder as she browsed photos of the tower. "Any luck identifying the residents of the top floor?"

"Not yet. I may have to get home to my laptop and run a search in one of the databases Alice and I spend a fortune each month to access."

"Speaking of which," he asked, "What made you become business partners with Alice?"

"I used to work for the Vampire Court, as I mentioned. When I quit my job, I needed another one. I like being a PI, and the last thing

I wanted was to compete with Alice. She didn't exactly jump at the suggestion, but luckily after she gave it some thought she decided partnership sounded like a good idea. Lord knows that woman needs more people in her corner. I don't know anyone who's as much of a magnet for trouble as her, except me."

"I can't disagree with that assessment." He moved his hand to her hip. "I've always preferred working solo, but the team approach to crime-solving clearly has its benefits. Alice has a ghost sidekick. I have—"

"I have four blades within easy reach," she warned. "So the word *sidekick* had better not come out of your mouth in reference to me."

"Perish the thought, Miss Woodall."

She stuck her phone into her back pocket. "Well, I can't find anything on who lives at the top of Carmody Tower, so we need to go back to my place and get some answers. After that, we'll have to figure out a way to get into the penthouse of the single most exclusive building in town."

"We're going to need a good plan," he agreed. "And possibly different clothes."

"You think?" She snorted. "They're not likely to let us in looking like this. And as much as I hate to say it, your bike's cover has been blown. More to the point, it's not the kind of vehicle that'll be welcome at the tower. We need different wheels too."

He didn't like the idea, but she was right. The Harley attracted too much attention. It had been perfect for their visit to Nyx, but now they needed something else.

"If we need something respectable, nondescript, and dull, we could use your car," he said.

She elbowed him hard enough in the ribs that he coughed. "Watch how you talk about Joanie," she snapped. "She may look cute, sweet, and innocent, but she's feisty when it counts. Kind of like me."

He coughed again, this time for an entirely different reason. "That in no way describes you, Miss Woodall."

"*Four* blades, Ronan. Not that I'd need one to end you if it came to that." She hopped off the bike and climbed back on behind him. "Back to where it all began," she murmured in his ear. "To the Pelican, to get my car. And then we'll plan how to storm the castle."

They had a lot of strategizing to do if they wanted to reach their target. Ronan had stormed a number of actual castles in his time. Every one had presented unique challenges and nearly impossible odds, and caused him serious bodily harm...and he'd enjoyed every minute of it. And yet he had to admit storming another, even a metaphorical one, sounded like even more fun when she suggested it.

"Let's go." Arkady wrapped her arms around his waist. "I don't know about you, but I ain't got all day."

Smiling to himself, he drove them off into the night.

"It can't be done," Arkady proclaimed, her chin on her fist as she leaned on her kitchen counter and swiped through the photos of Carmody Tower's interior yet again.

"You're right." Ronan drained the last of his coffee and leaned against the counter next to her. "Now that we've gotten that out of the way, how do we do it?"

She rolled her eyes and poured them both another cup of what she'd referred to as "thinking juice." He accepted his refilled mug and tapped it against hers in a mock toast.

"To recap," she said, ticking the items off on her fingers, "to get into Carmody, we have to get past what looks like serious security both in the lobby and underground garage. Not only are there guards, there are cameras everywhere. According to the website, the penthouse floors have a private elevator accessible only from the garage or lobby. The elevator opens directly into those apartments, but each has a second zero-clearance door that's locked unless opened by someone inside the apartment, or a key fob. And as if that wasn't bad enough, the records show there are *four* apartments on the building's top floor, three of which have an adult female resident. Any of them could be our target. So once we get up there, we *still* have to figure out which one's secretly a demon before we shake her down for the names of the people who work for her and send her soul to wherever demons go when they croak. And *then* we have to get out again."

"Demons don't have souls," he said absently. He slid her phone closer and looked through her photos once more. "That's what makes them demons."

"I was under the impression it was their smell." Sipping her coffee, she leaned against his side. "And their barbed genitals."

He grimaced. "Yes, that too."

"Can you imagine? I mean...*barbs?* Why?" When he started to reply, she waved her hand. "No, no, forget I asked. I suppose the answer is obvious."

"Unfortunately, their use is precisely what you're thinking." He reached for Katy's sketch of the stick figure in bed with a shadowy form hovering above. "As unpleasant as the thought may be, it does give me a theory. Look how the shadow is above the sleeping figure. Are you familiar with incubi and succubi?"

"Not *intimately* familiar, at least as far as I know," she said dryly. "But I get the general idea. Are you suggesting our female demon might be a succubus?"

"Or an incubus." He tapped the sketch thoughtfully. "Katy said the shadow sits on her throne and wants to be worshiped. It's a common misconception that a female demon is only a succubus. An incubus is a dominant partner in a sex act. A succubus is a submissive partner. This is true regardless of sex or gender."

"An incubus, huh? Interesting theory." She pursed her lips. "I suppose that fits with our tentative profile. But even if you're right, how does that help us?"

"I'm not sure yet, but the more we know about our adversary, the better." He considered what he knew of this particular class of demons. "If we're dealing with a female incubus, whatever she's posing as, she won't be a nobody. She'll be someone of importance. Incubi thrive on power and control. They can't even *pretend* to be subordinate as part of a ruse. It's just not in their DNA."

"Messed around with a few incubi in your time, huh?"

"Never—not in the way you're thinking," he said with a smile. "I primarily just killed them."

"Given the barbs, probably the safest route to go."

"Poison in her bite *and* on her nails and tail as well," he warned. "So, yes—a quick beheading is the best and safest option."

Arkady skimmed back through the information they had on the residents of Carmody Tower's penthouses. "The woman who lives in 42A is Melody Fullerton. She lists her employment as 'None.' Her husband is apparently an agent."

"Agent as in...?" he prompted.

She typed quickly. "As in an agent for actors and actresses. He must be doing pretty well if they can afford that place on one income."

"I can't see a demon, especially an incubus who wants to be worshiped, living as a housewife, even in a penthouse," Ronan said.

"Me either." She closed that screen and opened the next one. "42B is Abigail Rouse, a sixty-two-year-old retired private school educator and widow. Not exactly the kind of person a demon would jump at the chance to be."

"Agreed."

"Only one adult male in 42C. Steven Apland, sixty-three, divorced three times. President of a chain of banks. Lots of money and authority in that gig." She pulled up his photo on the bank's website and wrinkled her nose. "Hmmm. Not exactly a DILF."

He shook his head. "Female demons can take the form of human males, but incubi are vain. Very unlikely."

"Scratch off 42C. On to 42D." She reviewed the information on its resident. "Now, here's a definite possibility. Dr. Dana McMahon, psychiatrist and executive director of Bright Horizons Mental Health Center. That's pretty powerful. Plus she'd be likely to encounter teenagers and young adults in crisis, giving her the chance to find potential victims."

"Best lead so far," he agreed. "Can we see her picture?"

She located the facility's website and skimmed the doctor's biographical information. "Photo looks ordinary enough, but if they can pass for human, we can't judge a book by its cover—or a doctor by her professional headshot. Education, professional affiliations and awards, past employment...it's all listed here, and it matches up with what's in the database. Seems legit, at least on the surface."

"And it might be," he pointed out. "Who knows how long this demon has been posing as a human in your world? They may have earned these credentials, or taken over the life of someone who earned them. The latter is probably more likely."

After a beat, she said, "In *my* world?"

He cursed himself for the slip. "In the human world, I meant. As opposed to the demon realm."

"Nice save." She studied him, then glanced back at her phone. "Moving on for the moment, do we think it's this Dr. McMahon?"

In her photo, Dr. McMahon wore a white coat over a dark blue suit. She had shoulder-length dark brown hair, brown eyes, and glasses with thick frames, and wore simple jewelry. Her features were strikingly beautiful, but her smile appeared forced—or perhaps his suspicions made it seem that way.

"I can't tell," he said finally. "But that seems like our best bet, don't you agree?"

"Based on our profile, and assuming Katy's right about the location, yes. And now we're back to where we were ten minutes ago. How do we get into her penthouse?"

"Maybe we don't go to the tower. Maybe we go after Dr. McMahon at her place of work."

"The clinic?" She raised her eyebrows. "I like that idea way better. Still tricky, but not nearly as much security."

He glanced at the clock. "I like to hit a target early. It's almost six now. The clinic opens at seven thirty. The director is probably in her office by eight. That gives us two hours to come up with a viable plan."

"Yeah, but I doubt we can just waltz in there and demand to see the executive director."

"Posing as patients might get us in the door, but we wouldn't have much freedom to roam about the place."

"Yeah, I vote against that, just from a practical standpoint." She hummed under her breath. "We need in with credentials. Something that lets us meet McMahon without arousing anyone's suspicion, including hers. *And* we need a way to confirm she's the demon without her knowing we know until we're ready to show our hand."

She had no way to know he was a walking demon detector.

Their encounter with the flying minor demons at Nyx had confirmed that he'd retained enough of his angelic nature to sense the presence of infernal creatures. If he masked his own signature power, a demon shouldn't be able to detect what he was. Arkady was pure human. If she dressed more casually and acted the part, she could pass as nonthreatening—for a little while, anyway.

"I have something that will identify our target," he said.

"A spell?"

"More or less."

"Hmm." She didn't look pleased at his evasiveness. "You gonna let me in on that plan, Ronan? Or are you going to make me get it out of you the hard way?" She perked up. "Oh, *please* say you want to do it the hard way."

He had to grin at her eagerness. "I *was* going to tell you, but when you put it that way, I think I'd rather make you work for it."

"Bastard." But she was smiling. "Fine, keep your damn secret. I'll get it out of you, one way or the other."

He sipped his coffee and considered their options. With so little time for preparation, their plan needed to be simple. Everything he thought of was too complicated. Fortunately, he wasn't the only person thinking about the problem.

"I've got an idea," Arkady announced suddenly. "It's boring as shit, so you're probably going to hate it, and frankly *I* hate it because it's so dull, but I think it'll get us into McMahon's office. That's really all that counts, right?"

He made a rolling gesture. "I am all ears, Miss Woodall."

She described her idea. He rubbed his bristly chin and thought. "You are correct: it is incredibly boring," he said finally. "But it's absolutely a perfect plan. Well done."

"Thank you." She sighed. "Zero points on the fun meter, but between Bella's and Nyx we already racked up enough points for originality tonight, right? Not everything we do has to be a fireworks show."

She appeared so thoroughly dejected by the banality of their plan that he had to set his jaw to keep from laughing. Much as an incubus was physically incapable of posing as a subordinate, Arkady Woodall chafed mightily at any ruse that didn't involve major drama.

"Indeed it does not," he said very seriously. Her shoulders slumped more. Maybe she'd hoped he'd suggest a more exciting plan. He hid his smile and set his mug in the sink. "We should get ready. Unless you're too tired to go into the lion's den one more time."

In reply, she pulled a knife from her boot and threw it past him into the living room. The blade whizzed by his ear, missing him by about an inch, and ended up dead center of the target hanging on the wall opposite the couch.

"I'll take that to mean you're good to go," he said.

She grabbed his ass and kissed him. With her lips against his, she murmured, "Baby, I'm good to go."

ARKADY

D R. D ANA M C M AHON WAS ONLY TOO HAPPY TO WELCOME THEM into her office.

"Joining the Regional Chamber of Commerce would have immediate benefits for your clinic," Arkady said with a smile so bright that it hurt her face. "The economic development is the obvious benefit, but the Chamber also offers marketing and creative services, member-to-member discounts on a variety of products and services, a directory listing on the Chamber website, six to ten networking events per year, the opportunity to sponsor high-profile local events, and of course a plaque and window stickers celebrating your affiliation with us." She took a brochure from her briefcase and pushed it across McMahon's desk. "And that's just the tip of the iceberg."

The brochure, like the idea for their ruse, had come from a recent visit to Looking Glass Investigations by an actual representative of the Chamber, who'd given Alice and Arkady the hard sell on the organization after dropping into their office earlier in the week. They'd heard the rep out and promised to consider joining. Arkady had taken the Chamber materials home to read.

She and Ronan had studied the Chamber website and printed materials, donned business casual clothes, and presented themselves and their homemade credentials to the clinic receptionist at precisely eight that morning. Fifteen minutes later, Dr. McMahon came out to the waiting area to greet them personally and escorted them to her office. Boring or not, the ruse had worked even better than they'd hoped. She made a mental note to keep it in mind for future use.

While Arkady gave McMahon the spiel she'd practiced at home, Ronan had stayed quiet. Whatever spell he was using to confirm McMahon was a demon, it seemed to take a lot of his energy and attention. It was her job to hold McMahon's focus while he did his thing.

Arkady kept talking to the doctor and waited for some signal from Ronan. "As you can see, all those great benefits are just the beginning. We also host weekly and monthly gatherings and seminars, connect business leaders to various advocacy groups, and sponsor ribbon-cutting events for new and existing businesses who are opening or expanding their facilities. I'd list everything we do, but we'd be here all day." She laughed. "I'm sure you're very busy, so those are just the top reasons to join."

McMahon put on a pair of reading glasses and picked up the brochure. "Your enthusiasm is certainly catching, Ms. Whitman." She peered at Arkady over her glasses. "You make it seem like an easy choice."

"Call me Anna," Arkady chirped. If she had to keep smiling much longer, her face might crack. That made her think of Farrell, whose cheeks had split open when he disgorged the demon horde. She banished the mental image and resisted the urge to look impatiently at Ronan. "I'm sure you have questions about the Chamber. Anything I can't answer, I'll find out and get back to you."

"I appreciate that." McMahon skimmed the brochure. "As a medical clinic, our needs are a bit different from most of your members."

"We have quite a few clinics on our roster," Arkady countered. "And yes your needs are different than a retail store or restaurant, but there's still a lot of overlap—not to mention all the ways the Chamber can help your clinic take its success to the next level." She had to fight not to make a face at that last part. It was verbatim what the Chamber rep had said to Alice and herself about their PI business. It was such a corny, clichéd line that she'd have rolled her eyes at herself if it wouldn't have given away their ruse.

The doctor closed the brochure, tapped it on the edge of her desk, and leaned back in her chair. "You know, I'm good friends with Bob Thornton. He's been after me for years to join. I'm surprised he'd send you to see me. We're having lunch on Saturday."

Arkady didn't recall seeing the name Thornton on the Chamber's website. *Could this be a test?* If so, what could have possibly tipped McMahon off that she and Ronan weren't who they claimed to be? *Whatever you're doing, hurry the hell up*, she willed Ronan, and tried not to grit her teeth.

"We didn't intend to step on anyone's toes," she said, and feigned a sheepish smile. "We recently noticed how many local clinics aren't members and decided to prioritize visiting them this month."

"But you *do* know Bob?" McMahon persisted. "VP of Economic Development?"

Yep, it's absolutely a test. Something had tipped McMahon off. Nothing to do but bluff. "I don't know a Bob Thornton," Arkady said firmly. "Are you sure you're thinking of the Regional Chamber? He might be with a different organization."

"We're journalists," Ronan said.

She turned to stare at him. He'd affected the same semi-slouched posture she'd seen in Carly's backyard, with his legs stretched out in front of the expensive leather chair across from Dr. McMahon. And he was smirking.

She'd thought her smirk was good—and it *was*, as it had started numerous fights and been known to push even the most even-keeled people over the edge. But Ronan's was freaking *outstanding*. McMahon's face had already reddened. What the hell was he doing?

"What do you want?" McMahon demanded, rising from her chair. "How dare you misrepresent yourselves to get into my office?"

The more relaxed Ronan seemed, the angrier McMahon got. He'd gone completely off-script at this point. Arkady figured he must be trying to get a rise out of the doctor, but why? To get her to lash out in some way that proved she was a demon? She stared pointedly at him, but he ignored her.

"Don't act like you don't know why we're here, Dr. McMahon," Ronan countered. "We got a tip. A *very* detailed tip."

McMahon blanched. "I—I have no idea what you're talking about. Get out."

Whatever he was up to, he'd apparently hit pay dirt. She figured she might as well go along with it. "We'd like to get your side of the story, Dr. McMahon." She made a show of settling back into her chair, but she was ready in case McMahon decided to go full-on demon. "Better to get out in front of it, you know? Whoever's story comes out first usually wins the day when it's all said and done."

"I have nothing to say to you." McMahon had gone from flushed to pale and back to flushed. "You got in here under false pretenses. Who do you work for? I'll sue."

"Then we'll have to turn over everything we know to the police," Ronan said easily. "Once we finish digging, that is."

"*Digging?* What do you—" McMahon cut herself off. "Get out of my office *right now*."

"Happy to." Ronan rose.

Arkady did the same and picked up her briefcase. She also took back the brochure, since it would have their fingerprints on it and she had no idea what kind of friends McMahon might have.

"Best of luck keeping this under wraps," Ronan added, backing up toward the door.

"I have nothing to hide," McMahon insisted. Her emphatic statement was somewhat undermined by the way her hands trembled at her sides.

Ronan did...something...just then. Power flared, the scent of salty sea air swirled, and for a moment Arkady saw a flash of the same aura she'd seen at Nyx. Then it vanished as quickly as it had appeared, leaving only the smell of the sea.

"We'll see ourselves out," Ronan said, his tone curt. He gestured at the corridor. "After you, Anna."

McMahon came around her desk as they stepped into the hall. As upset as she was, she shut the door quietly after them rather than slam it. *Probably doesn't want to attract anyone's attention*, Arkady reasoned.

And neither did she, so she didn't get in Ronan's face until they'd exited the clinic, walked a block, and gotten into her SUV, which she'd parked on a side street away from the clinic's exterior cameras.

"We had a plan," she snapped as he closed his door. She tossed her briefcase into the back seat and glared at him. "What the hell was all that?"

"We followed the plan," he countered with infuriating calm. "Right up to the point she sniffed you out, and then we needed a new plan."

"She could have just as easily sniffed *you* out, you conceited ape," she shot back. "I did a perfect Chamber rep act. I was so freaking good at it, I talked *myself* into joining. You probably looked shady as shit, Mr. Silent and Broody. Whoever heard of a *broody* Chamber rep?"

His mouth twitched. "Are you interested in whether or not the good doctor is a demon?"

"Obviously she's not, or we'd still be in there instead of getting ourselves thrown out," she said, exasperated.

He eyed her.

Realization dawned. "Oh," she said, and crossed her arms. "Okay, fine, so she won't go looking for us because she thinks we have something on her. As if *you* came up with that idea. It's the oldest trick in the book."

He chuckled. "I never tried to take credit for it, Miss Woodall."

"But you sure as hell enjoyed trying to throw me off my game by suddenly claiming we were reporters." She scowled. "So the doctor might have some skeletons in the closet—maybe even literally—but she's not a demon."

"That's the situation." He glanced down at his polo shirt and khakis. "Given that's the case, I don't know about you, but I'd like to change."

"Respectable businessman is definitely not your vibe," she agreed. She pulled out into traffic and headed for home. "I can't imagine you even use that ruse very often. I'm surprised you had the clothes in your saddlebag." She frowned. "As a matter of fact, I could have sworn you *didn't* have those clothes with you when I went looking for a shirt to wear earlier. All I found were jeans and dirty T-shirts."

"My saddlebags are…unusual."

"Oh, gee whiz, you don't say," she said sarcastically. "I'm going to hazard a guess: they conjure up certain things you need when you need them."

"Certain things," he admitted. "But they don't conjure them. Everything that comes out of them, I've put in them. They can store quite a lot. More than they can hold, in fact."

She had to think about that for a few minutes as she drove. "So they're bigger on the inside?" she said finally. "I've seen a show about something like that."

"Fae objects can come in very handy, as long as the person who has them understands how to use them."

She slid a glance at him. He raised his eyebrows.

"You have fae saddlebags on your Harley," she said, just to hear the words aloud.

"Yes," he said easily, as if that was a perfectly ordinary thing for anyone to have. "Much more expensive than the regular kind, but infinitely more useful."

"How expensive?"

"Very." He smiled. "Thinking about some for yourself?"

"Maybe. I do also have a birthday coming up, in case you're not sure what to get me."

He laughed. She liked his laugh.

"So, the doctor isn't a demon," she said with a sigh a few minutes later as they pulled into her driveway. His Harley was inside the garage to hide it from anyone who might be looking for it. She parked out front and turned off the vehicle. "We might be completely off about the drawing being Carmody Tower. Or maybe it's not the penthouse floor. We need to talk to Katy again."

"She's still asleep," Ronan said to her surprise. "I texted Carly a few minutes ago. She said Katy will be asleep for several more hours. She had no interest in waking her any sooner than that."

"I'm not surprised. I don't think she liked how far Katy pushed herself to give us the answers we've got." Arkady unlocked the front door, led him inside, and tossed her keys on the kitchen counter. "What now? Sit on our hands until Katy wakes up?"

He shut the front door and locked it. "I'm no more a fan of sitting on my hands than you are. Point us in a direction to go."

"All we have right now is Carmody." She draped her blazer over the back of the couch. Under it, she'd worn a blue top, slim but stretchy pants, and dressy-looking boots. All were far from her usual attire, but still ideal for running, kicking, or stomping. Unfortunately, their trip to the clinic had not given her the chance to do any of those things, and now she was antsy. "We still feel pretty sure our demon isn't the bank president or the widow?"

"Pretty sure." He pulled his polo shirt off over his head and tossed it on the back of the couch next to her blazer. "I'm not saying it's impossible, but my instincts say no."

"I'm all about instincts." She'd been in the middle of unzipping her boots, but she abandoned that activity to run her hands up his bare chest.

Alice had mentioned more than once how much she loved Sean's signature scent, which she described as smelling like a forest. It was a big turn-on for her, just as Alice's own scent turned Sean on. Arkady had seen Sean sniff the air in the hallway at Maclin Security even ten or fifteen minutes after Alice had walked past and his eyes turned golden.

Though she'd certainly appreciated various men's scents over the years, Arkady had figured that was more of a shifter thing...until now. Ronan smelled really, *really* good to her. And not just his leather and denim. Even his skin drew her in.

"We've done pretty well following our instincts so far, haven't we?" she asked, pressing a kiss to his sternum so she could taste him again too.

"Yes." He cupped her ass with both hands and lifted her up easily. She wrapped her legs around his hips and kissed him hard. With his hands under her thighs, he returned the kiss with even more demand and ten times the heat.

"What did you do right before we left her office?" she asked when they broke the kiss.

"I flexed." He stared into her eyes, his gaze hot with desire. "One last test, just to be sure."

"And if she'd been a demon, she would have reacted?"

"Yes." He squeezed her. "If she'd been a demon, she would have come at me. She wouldn't have been able to resist. It's instinctual."

She kissed him again because he was so good at it. She supposed that skill, like many others, improved over time. And if she was right about him, he'd had a long, *long* time to get good at it.

She'd had a theory forming for a while. She wasn't sure when the clues had begun to click into place, but somewhere between Farrell's jibe that had cost the vampire his life and Ronan's ability to detect a demon—and vice-versa—certain things had begun to add up. And the more she thought about it, the more sense it made.

Ronan drew back, his brow furrowed. "What's wrong?"

Of course he'd sensed she had something on her mind. Instincts again. Instincts *always*. Hers kept her alive before, during, and after her time in the army and working for the vamps. Then they pushed her to forge not only a friendship but a partnership with Alice.

And then they drew her to this man. And his had drawn him to her.

A ridiculous thought popped into her head and made her chuckle: *I gave head to a fallen angel.* She truly had no idea how to process that fact. Nor did she know how to deal with the knowledge a fallen angel had expertly gotten her off in a vampire sex dungeon.

Another thought: *Wow—he must be* really *fallen.* This time instead of making her laugh, her ridiculous thought turned her on. What it was about him being a fallen angel she found particularly arousing, she wasn't sure, but it absolutely made her want to rip his clothes off.

When she didn't immediately respond to his question, his frown deepened. "Miss Woodall?"

She ran her fingers through his hair and gripped it tightly. "Take me to bed, Ronan."

"I plan to." The way he said it—part promise, part warning—made her shiver with desire. His gaze searched her face. "What were you thinking about just now?"

He knew she'd figured something out. The question was whether to tell him *what* she'd figured out.

She'd had the best of intentions when she chose not to tell him she'd seen his scars, and that hadn't worked out how she'd planned. She didn't know how he'd react to her figuring out his secret, but she was pretty sure he'd take it better now than later. And besides, he needed to be crystal clear she was the looks *and* the brains on this team.

"You're a fallen angel," she said simply. "I like that a lot. Now show me just how fallen you are."

He moved so fast that everything around her blurred. She let out a very uncharacteristic shriek—not in fear, but in pure exhilaration.

She wanted nothing to do with being a dhampir or vampire, or even one of the Court's human enforcers, but she'd always envied how fast vamps could move and wondered what it felt like. Now she knew. And it absolutely fucking *ruled*.

In a blink she and Ronan had made it from the kitchen to her bedroom. He tossed her on the bed, toed off his shoes, crawled up her body until his knees straddled her hips, and ripped her top and bra in half. His eyes blazed with desire and the hint of silver magic she'd seen earlier. Angelic magic. Power thrummed in the air around him.

She didn't fear him at all. Not one bit. But the way he looked at her, as if she was a feast laid out before him, and the thought of him striking terror in the hearts of others, made her grind against him impatiently.

"I *said* show me how fallen you are," she snapped. "Don't make me repeat myself."

He made a rumbly sound deep in his throat and kissed her deeply. "I wouldn't dream of it," he said.

His hot mouth moved down her throat to where his hands cupped her breasts, already aching for his attention. He sucked, nibbled, and flicked her nipples with his tongue until they grew painfully hard.

When his right hand slid down her abdomen and slipped into her pants, she dug her nails into his shoulders. "Yes," she breathed, moving her hips in rhythm with the strokes of his fingers. "Oh, God, *yes*."

His mouth returned to hers and she gasped against his lips, her back arching as she moaned. She was so close to coming...so close...

Without warning, he took his hand from her pants. "What are you doing?" she demanded breathlessly.

He kissed her lightly as he unfastened her belt. "I told you at Nyx I wanted you to come with my mouth on you," he said, his lips against her ear. "I meant what I said. And I want you to scream my name when you do."

She shivered hard and gripped the comforter as he slid her pants down her legs. They joined her torn top and bra on the floor. But when she tried to slide her red lacy thong down her hips, he pushed her hands aside. "Leave that," he commanded. "I like it."

"But—"

He silenced her protest by pushing the thin material of the thong aside and slipping first one and then two fingers into her. She couldn't hold back a ragged cry when the tips of his fingers brushed her most sensitive place. "Ronan," she gasped.

He kissed her and then slid farther down the bed. "Open your legs wider, Miss Woodall."

This time she obeyed him without question. He kissed his way up both her thighs. She could feel him tasting her with his tongue as he went. Then he raised her hips to meet his seeking mouth. He licked her slowly, his gaze locked on hers. "I was right," he murmured. "Ambrosia."

"You imagined how I'd taste?" she asked, breathless.

"From the first moment I saw you at the Pelican."

She had no idea what to say to that...other than she'd imagined how he'd taste too. It had proven impossible not to. And she would have told him so if his mouth hadn't immediately closed on her and sucked gently. Her confession turned into a series of wordless gasping cries.

Oh, Ronan, she thought almost deliriously. *Oh, my fallen angel...*

With her hands twisting in the comforter, she screamed his name and came hard, her hips bucking wildly in his grip. He held her in place, his tongue flicking mercilessly to make her cry out twice more as she gasped and almost sobbed with the intensity of her orgasm. How many times she screamed his name, she wasn't quite sure. She lost track of that along with everything else.

Ronan stayed where he was, stroking her with his tongue until her cries faded. "I like your scream," he said, giving her one last lick to make her shake.

"Enough to make me do it again?" she asked, her chest heaving.

"Absolutely." He slid her thong down her legs and off, but he didn't throw it aside as he'd done with her other clothes. Instead, he stripped off his own pants and rejoined her on the bed, gloriously aroused, her panties in his hand.

She licked her lips in anticipation. "The appetizers have been outstanding, but I'm ready for the main course."

"Give me your hands," he ordered.

She raised them, her wrists crossed. "I have something in that bottom drawer of my nightstand that might work better."

"Oh, no, Miss Woodall. I like this just fine." He tied her wrists with the thong, then pushed them up over her head. "Keep your hands here and don't move them."

His stern voice made her smirk and ask, "Or what?"

He bit her ear. "Or I will be forced to correct you," he said, his lips and breath hot against her skin. "I enjoy domination too, *Mistress*."

She raised her eyebrows. "I can play along for a bit and let you tie my hands, but I'm not easy to dominate."

He chuckled and flicked her right nipple just once with his tongue to make her jerk. "That's why I'm going to enjoy it so much," he told her.

She opened her mouth to retort and found it filled with Ronan's magnificent arousal. "Mmm-mmm-mmmph," she said, her words unintelligible. She tried to move, but he pinned her hands to the bed.

He smiled down at her. "I think you know what to do, Miss Woodall."

Indeed she did. And she did it so well that he lasted less than a minute before he had to stop. Leaving her hands where they were, still tied, he moved between her legs, put her calves on his shoulders, and teased her with gentle strokes and nudges until she was reduced to begging.

When he pushed inside her the first time, her back arched and she moaned. "Ronan."

"My Valkyrie." He leaned down to kiss her throat as he thrust hard again and again. In that position, he stroked against her G-spot almost every time. She screamed, her mouth against his shoulder until he realized what she was doing and raised himself up so she couldn't muffle her cries. "I want to hear you," he said, thrusting harder. "Scream for me."

She couldn't have stopped crying out if she'd wanted to. Earlier, she'd wondered if sex with Ronan would be more than she could handle. *Well, if this is how I go, so be it*, she thought. She felt another orgasm building.

He must have sensed it too because he rolled them both over and steadied her astride him with his hands on her hips. "Ride me," he commanded.

She'd fantasized about doing that since the parking lot at the Pelican. He thrust up hard, moving in tandem with her as she braced her tied hands on his chest and ground herself against him. In moments her breathing turned ragged again. "Come for me," he told her, gripping her hips. "I want to see you come again."

His command and the intensity of his thrusts sent her over the edge. She threw her head back and cried out. He reached between them and stroked her until she screamed his name. The man had no mercy. None at all. She wanted to smack that smug look off his gorgeous face.

Instead, she slid free of him, turned around on his chest, and made him put his mouth to better use while she returned the favor.

And of course, because everything with Ronan was a competition, he used his tongue in a quite different place than she'd expected, eliciting a muffled cry of surprise.

"Can't take it?" he asked from behind her, his tone mocking.

She grazed him lightly with her teeth to make him writhe before she replied. "I can take anything you can dish out," she told him when her mouth was free.

It was, she reflected some hazy time later, maybe not the wisest thing to have said to a man like Ronan, because he took her at her word.

His size presented a real challenge. She liked challenges as a general rule, but even after plenty of prep, at a key moment she found herself covered in sweat and trembling.

With his arm around her waist from behind, he kissed her ear. "You trust me," he said softly.

It wasn't a question, but she nodded. "Yes."

"Then relax. We'll take our time."

She eased back against him and gasped. He stayed still with his arm around her waist, his other hand stroking her gently but purposefully. Everything he did, he did with careful attention to maximizing her pleasure as well as his own. And though it had to take Herculean effort, he didn't so much as twitch until she'd slid all the way back against him and told him she was okay.

She was stunned when the moment he moved, she came with a cry.

"There you go," he murmured, his hands on her hips as he thrust gently. His movements turned her cry into screams of pleasure. She bent over on her knees to make it easier for him, her bound hands gripping the comforter.

As difficult as the process had been, she'd never felt anything as good as how he filled her so completely. She had no doubt it felt every bit as good to him too. His breathing turned ragged almost immediately, and he had to stop every few strokes to stay in control.

"You don't have to hold back," she said, her cheek pressed to the bed as he groaned and slowed his movements again. "Come for me."

"Isn't that my line?" He kissed her back. "I think you have a few more to go."

"I really don't. You've wrung me dry." She tugged her hands free of her panties and ran her fingertips up and down his hard thighs. "Come all over me, baby. I want you to."

He kept stroking in and out of her with infuriating slowness. "I'm sure you don't mean that."

"I'm sure I *do*." She dug her nails into his thighs. "Otherwise, I wouldn't have said so."

His voice sounded a little strained when he said, "Then turn around."

She eased away from him and turned to face him, sitting back on her heels. He stroked himself, his gaze locked on hers. "My Valkyrie," he rasped.

She smiled and licked her lips. "My fallen angel."

He groaned, shuddered, and came. She waited until the first spurts splashed across her face and chest, and then she caught the last few on her tongue.

When he finally fell back, she smiled at him. He was breathing hard, his broad chest rising and falling in a way she found rather hypnotizing. "I enjoyed that immensely, Miss Woodall."

She winked. "I could tell."

A few minutes later, once they'd recovered somewhat, she rose from the bed and tugged on his hand. "Join me in the shower?"

"With pleasure." He followed her into the bathroom and watched as she turned on the spray in the large glass custom shower. "This is a much nicer bathroom than I'd imagined, given the size of your house."

"The bathroom is my one indulgence." She chuckled. "I like having a small house, but I'm a tall gal. I need a great big shower. It especially comes in handy when I want to shower with an oversized bounty hunter."

His eyes sparkled. "I thought you rather approved of my size, Miss Woodall. You said so several times."

"I guess I probably did." She stood under the sprayer and closed her eyes as the water streamed over her head and down her body.

She hadn't heard him approach, but when she wiped the water out of her eyes and stepped out of the spray, he was in front of her. His expression had turned serious. He seemed to be bracing himself. The man who'd claimed to fear almost nothing seemed to fear even now that she might reject him.

"Long, long ago, my name was Remiel," he said. "I've lived among humans as Ronan for nearly six hundred human years."

Arkady had known vampires much older than six hundred years, so it wasn't as difficult for her to process that information as it might have been for most. Six hundred years wasn't even particularly long-lived for a vamp. The real difference was how long he'd existed before that six hundred years.

"Eons," he said.

"Hey." She scowled. "Can you read my mind?"

"No, but I didn't have much trouble figuring out what you were thinking."

She absorbed what he'd said. *Eons. Not centuries or even millennia. Eons. Millions of years.* Compared to her own thirty-some years of existence, it seemed incomprehensible.

"So with me you're robbing the cradle big time," she teased when he seemed to be waiting for a response. "What, can't find any women your own age?"

He didn't return her smile. "I broke angelic law twice. I'm a mortal man now. Not human, but mortal. With a mortal lifespan and everything that comes with it. It's a punishment."

She moved closer to him and rested her hand on his chest. "Is it?"

"Yes." He took her hand and pressed a kiss to her palm. "Or at least it was supposed to be."

"See, now you're getting it. Nobody can diminish us without our permission, and fuck 'em for trying." She glanced down between them. "You know, for a supposedly mortal man, you seem to have remarkable powers of recuperation."

That finally elicited one of his rare real smiles. "What can I say? I've never had much trouble in that department, and lately I've been a bit deprived." He kissed her neck. "Also, how any man could look at you and not get hard, I have no idea."

"Yeah, yeah, no need to flatter me." She rolled her eyes. "I've already invited you to my bed. And my shower."

"Yes, you did." He pinned her against the wall. "So I'm going to make the most of it."

Despite her exhaustion and the hot water, she shivered with anticipation. "Well, if you insist."

15

RONAN

A DEMON LIVED IN CARMODY TOWER.

Katy had confirmed upon waking that Carmody was the building she'd seen while scrying and their target resided on its top floor. But even if he hadn't gotten that confirmation, the moment Ronan and Arkady approached he would have known.

"There's a demon here," he said as Arkady pulled to the side of the wide boulevard that led up Castle Hill to the tower. "And the tower is built on a crossroads."

She frowned and scanned the area. "I see one road going in. It dead-ends at the tower. What do you see that I don't?"

"It's not what I see, but what I sense." He gestured from left to right. "Two roads intersected here long ago before this area was made a park. They're no longer visible but once created, a crossroads is forever. Its power remains."

"So a crossroads deal is a real thing?"

"*Very* real."

"Good to know. Not that I plan on making one." She drummed her fingers restlessly on the steering wheel. "Why would a demon reside at a crossroads?"

"A crossroads is a liminal space—a place that is no place, between places, neither here nor there," he explained when she frowned. "Portals between realms are made more easily in such locations. Spirits often traverse roads that no longer exist and become confused where they intersect. Powerful spirits also sometimes travel between realms at crossroads. Demons feed on those spirits, among other things."

"So a crossroads is a power source, a food source, *and* a convenient location to make a door in case they want to visit other places. That makes Carmody a perfect spot." She studied the tower. "Kinda makes me wonder how many demons might be living here. Just our girl or an army of them?"

He'd been considering that very question since they'd identified Carmody as the demon's probable residence. "Not an army. A concentration of many demons would attract the attention of numerous powerful entities for whom low-level demons are either food or to be destroyed."

"How do you know it hasn't?"

He gave her a bland look. "The tower is still standing, is it not?"

Arkady laughed. "Okay, fair enough." She sobered. "So our number of adversaries is somewhere between one and not an army. I don't like that great big question mark. You got any other secret powers that can help us here?"

The matter-of-fact way she asked caused him to take her hand and press a kiss to her knuckles. He'd seldom interacted with anyone so adaptive and unfazed by anything that came their way. Thanks to only a handful of clues, she'd figured out he was a fallen angel with breathtaking speed and taken the news almost entirely in stride. The only time he'd noticed her thrown off-kilter even a little was when he revealed his true age—and even that hadn't unsettled her much. Possibly the only other people who'd reacted so calmly were Alice and Malcolm, and the Guardian warrior Lucy Stone, who lived in what Alice referred to as the "Broken World." None of them were mundane humans, however, and as such were far more used to interacting with supernatural beings.

"I will be able to tell you more when we get closer to the building." It felt odd to speak so candidly with someone who had no magic of her own. Then again, Arkady had shown no signs of being at a disadvantage, and power did not come from magic alone. "I'm dampening my remaining angelic power so I don't alert them to our proximity, as I did during our meeting with Dr. McMahon, until the final moments."

He saw her wheels turning long before she spoke. "Angels and demons can sense each other?" she asked.

"Always. We are..." Ronan searched for an adequate human word to describe the antagonism between them. The angelic term had no direct translation. "Natural enemies," he finished.

"Gotcha," she said briskly. "So if you walked into the tower lobby flying your angel flag for all to see and sense, whatever demons live there would pop out of the woodwork like earthworms on the sidewalk after it rains?"

"Much like that, yes." He considered her words. "Are you suggesting I do so?"

"Unless you've got a better idea. If McMahon isn't our target, it's got to be one of the other people who live on the top floor, but we're not sure who. And nearest I can tell, reaching the penthouse undetected is going to be something close to impossible. Next best thing is to make this demon come to us—or come *at* us. The more we talk about it, the faster I'm running out of reasons not to just ring the doorbell."

The prospect of charging headlong into a confrontation with demons clearly energized her as much as it did him. The obvious problem was, they would no doubt be outnumbered, and though they both carried mundane weapons and he retained some angelic power, the demons would have numbers on their side. As a fallen archangel, he could have ensured Arkady's survival as well as his own against these demons. As a mortal man, he could not.

He hadn't realized he hadn't done a very good job of keeping those thoughts off his face until Arkady practically leaped over the center console and grabbed a fistful of his shirt, flushed with fury. "*How dare you,*" she snarled, her nose an inch from his own. "How dare you think it's your job to protect me?"

"Is it not?" He met her angry gaze with his own calm one. "When you served in the army, was it not the desire of each person in your unit to protect the lives of the others, even at the cost of their own life?"

"It's not the same and you know it," she shot back.

Clearly this was a sensitive topic for her. As such, he knew he must address it directly and very honestly, or risk losing far more than her confidence in him.

"I think it is." Carefully, he disengaged her hand from his shirt. "Haven't we fought side by side? Haven't you already protected my life with your own?"

She leaned back, her knee on his seat between his thighs, and glared at him. "It's not the same," she repeated stubbornly. "You want to protect me because we're lovers."

"You're reading *my* mind now?" He took her hand and held on when she tried to pull away. "My Valkyrie, I have recognized you as a warrior since I first saw you in the Pelican. I believe I knew you as such even before that, when you spoke to me as I slept in Alice's house. I do not recall your words, but I know in my soul that I heard you speak of battle, honor, and sacrifice. To have you as my lover is a great honor. To fight at your side is an even greater one. So when I speak of protecting your life, I do so as a brother in arms *and* your lover. The latter does not preclude the former."

Arkady stared at him for a long time, her eyes narrowed. "Did you practice that speech on the way over here?" she asked finally.

"No." When she continued to eye him, he relented. "Some of it," he admitted. "I rehearsed the part about hearing what you said to me while I lay sleeping. I did want to tell you that."

"Why?"

"I'm not sure. Perhaps it's part of what drew me to you, despite my belief that pleasure and longing are just as much a part of my punishment as pain and mortality."

She flinched at his words. "It's as bad as that, huh?"

"It was meant to be, I think." He stroked her cheek with the back of his hand. "But I may have looked at my situation the wrong way."

"Being mortal or human isn't the punishment some people or beings might think it is. It's got a lot going for it, really." She cupped his face with both hands and kissed him. She tasted of coffee and the cinnamon raisin bagel she'd eaten before they left her house. Quick breakfasts and little kisses were a few of the simple joys of mortal life he'd begun to appreciate.

"And if I'm any judge of this sort of thing," she added, "you're enjoying the hell out of the pleasure part."

"That I am." He raised his eyebrows. "As are you, as the fingernail and bite marks in my back and other places can attest."

"Mmm." She licked her lips and eyed him in a way that reminded him of a raptor studying its prey. "You *are* a delicious hunk of a man. And I think there are a few places I haven't gotten to taste yet."

"Likewise." He cleared his throat. "However, before we become too distracted, we should return to our original conversation. If you believe our best course of action is to ring the doorbell, as you called it, I'm inclined to agree."

"Glad to hear you're on board with my plan. Fly that angel flag. I'm ready to see what we can do against this particular enemy." She returned to her own seat, shifted gears, and headed toward Carmody's enormous porte cochère. "But I'm warning you: if you start acting like some googly-eyed man-child or go all *Hulk smash* trying to keep me from getting hurt because we're getting it on and not because we're on the same team, I will shoot you."

His mouth twitched, but he held back a chuckle and nodded gravely because she seemed dead serious. "Understood."

As they approached the tower, he lowered the shields that hid his angelic power. Doing so made him uneasy. Even archangels rarely deliberately antagonized demons other than in purposeful combat. From the earliest eons of the universe, both angelic and infernal beings had recognized the futility of endless warfare and the myriad ways that balance was necessary to sustain existence. No angelic law forbade it, so he had no reason to expect reprisals from Michael, but he couldn't help but feel as though he was casting a stone into a vast body of water without a clear sense of how large the ripples might be or how far they might reach.

He could have tried to summon a vision to guide his decisions, but he hadn't done so voluntarily for centuries and had no intention of doing so now. The fleeting thought did, however, conjure the memory of the vision he'd glimpsed in the Pelican's parking lot of himself trapped in a cage as Arkady fell with a knife in her heart. The penthouse of a very modern glass-and-steel skyscraper seemed an unlikely place to find a subterranean lair made of bare rock, and Alice's survival had proven his visions were not the inevitable events he'd once believed them to be. Still, he couldn't dismiss the vision...or shake the growing uneasiness in his gut.

By the time Arkady parked under the porte cochère, his angelic power was no longer hidden in any way. No one waited for them or came out of the building, however. Even the valet stand was abandoned.

"Try a flex." Arkady shut off the vehicle, pocketed the keys, and got out. "Maybe they're out of range of passive energy."

"They are not out of range." He exited the car as well and stood facing the building's large doors. The tinted glass prevented him from seeing into the lobby, but he sensed it was deserted. In the middle of the day, he would have expected *some* people in the lobby—residents and employees going about their daily business. "They know we're here. The lobby's empty."

"Empty's just as bad as full. Maybe worse." She came around the car to stand beside him and gave him her hunter's smile. The sword he'd given her for this confrontation rested in its scabbard on her back. The sight of the hilt on her shoulder somehow made her even more desirable to him. "You ever get the feeling you're about to walk into a trap?" she joked.

He returned her grin with one of his own and adjusted his own sword and scabbard so the hilt rested comfortably against his upper back, ready for a quick draw. "All the time."

"Has it ever stopped you from going in?"

"Not yet."

"Me either." She cracked her knuckles. "And today doesn't feel like the day to break tradition."

They crossed the tiled area under the porte cochère and entered the lobby. The photos they'd seen online did not do the six-story atrium justice, but at least they'd been able to see the layout before arriving. A large reception and security desk spanned the wall directly opposite the main entrance. To the left was a coffee shop and several boutiques. A bar and restaurant took up the area to the right of the desk. All were ominously dark and shuttered. And as Ronan had already surmised, the entire area was devoid of people—human, demon, or otherwise.

"Is it just me," Arkady mused, "or is this all the demon version of a big flex?"

He mirrored her posture, weight on the balls of his feet and hands at his side, ready for an attack. "It is absolutely a flex."

His belief that they were being watched was confirmed when all the TV monitors in the lobby suddenly flared to life. Each one showed the same smiling young woman with long dark hair, high cheekbones, and striking green eyes, sitting on a sofa in front of windows that overlooked the city to the south. "Hello, darlings," she said, her voice coming from all directions via the monitors. "We meet again."

Her hair color had changed, but Ronan knew her face and voice. Judging by Arkady's muttered curse, she'd recognized the woman at the same moment he did.

"Bunny, you sneaky bitch." Arkady put her hands on her hips. "Or should I call you Melody?"

"Call me whichever you prefer. Neither are my true name, which of course you've figured out, lovely Arkady." Bunny's smile widened. "And you've brought me the delectable Ronan. Rumors of your triumphs have reached me even in this provincial world. How disappointing to finally meet you in the flesh, only to find you've been stripped of your glory and power. It's hardly worth my time to kill you."

"I was going to say the same thing to you," he said easily. "But maybe that's not the way this has to go."

In another none-too-subtle flex, all the monitors shut off except the screen behind the security desk. On it, Bunny raised an elegantly shaped eyebrow. "I don't see this ending any other way than with you two in my stomach, but I'm willing to entertain other possibilities. Why don't you come up so we can meet properly? The penthouse elevator is on your left. I'm sure you know my apartment number already."

"Oh come on, Bun-Bun, we're not getting on an elevator in this demon shithole," Arkady snapped. "If you know who we are, you know we're not new to this game." She made a wry face and hooked her thumb at Ronan. "He's *seriously* not new to it."

Bunny rested her chin on her fist in an exaggerated thinking pose. "Oh dear, that means we're at an impasse. I'm up here and you're down there. We'll never settle things this way."

"We could just wait until the next time you want to slum at Bella's," Arkady pointed out. "Sooner or later you'll have to come down to get your fix of being worshiped. I don't mind biding my time. Anticipation makes everything better."

"I've had my fill of Bella's for now. And how many more lost little waifs will fall into my web while you wait?" Bunny chuckled. "For every one you think you save, ten more disappear. But yes, please do just wait for your chance to catch me by surprise."

"Yeah, right." Arkady snorted. "You are so full of shit. If your organization was that big, you'd never have gone undetected for so long. You're all talk. What my CO in the army used to call *big hat, no cattle*."

Bunny's eyes flared red. "You know nothing, little human. Nothing about me *or* your pathetic lover."

"Sticks and stones, Bun-Bun." Arkady made a show of rolling her eyes. "You're just jealous that I'm getting some and you're stuck in your little apartment humping a cactus or whatever you demon bitches do to get off."

Ronan could guess her motivations for antagonizing Bunny. Angry people—even angry demons—made mistakes. If they could bait her into revealing more about the trafficking ring, that would help them dismantle it. So far Arkady seemed to be doing an excellent job of pushing Bunny's buttons. His Valkyrie's hobby of being extraordinarily aggravating had its practical uses.

Bunny chuckled. "I may have to revise my opinion of you, Arkady. You're actually rather entertaining. Under different circumstances, we might have gotten along quite well." She tapped her chin. "Perhaps, as your companion suggested, this might go another way. We must meet and discuss our situation. Would you both care to join me in the lobby bar for a drink?"

She'd intended the suggestion to seem spontaneous, but to Ronan it was anything but. Then again, he figured the bar was no safer or more dangerous than anything else in this building. "The bar," he agreed. "Shall we say five minutes?"

"Oh, do give me ten minutes to get ready." Bunny smoothed her hair. "A lady likes to look her best, you know."

"What's that got to do with you?" Arkady asked.

Bunny clucked her tongue in disapproval. "How rude you are. I suppose it's not surprising given what sorry excuses for parents you had. All those years of beatings and starvation. A shame they couldn't have beaten some manners into you as well."

At no point since they'd met had Ronan seen Arkady knocked back a step, until this moment. Her head snapped back as if Bunny had landed a physical punch. And she couldn't manage a reply, not even one of her trademark *fuck you*'s. He could almost taste her pain.

If Bunny—or whatever her real name was—had been within reach at that moment, he would have ripped her apart limb from limb for that alone.

"Down in two shakes, darlings," Bunny said. The monitor went black.

Less than a second later, one of Arkady's blades shattered its screen dead center, right where Bunny's forehead had been. Her chest heaved.

"Miss Woodall," he said.

"Don't." She stalked to the monitor, reclaimed her knife, and headed for the darkened bar. He followed silently, flexing his fingers and imagining how satisfying it would feel to use them to crush Bunny's throat.

Just before they entered the bar, his skin prickled. He touched Arkady's shoulder and bent his head to murmur in her ear. "Low-level demons inside. About a dozen of them."

"Is that all there are in the building?" she asked, her voice tight.

"I believe so."

"Two against twelve. I like our odds." She shoved the metal gate of the bar's entrance aside and started to go in.

He halted her with a hand on her arm. "Calm and focus," he said, his mouth pressed to her ear. "We are smarter and better prepared than she thinks. She can't beat us unless we let her."

She took a deep breath, exhaled, and looked up at him. "When this is over, I'm going Harley shopping, and then you're going to help me get some of those cool saddlebags you've got."

He took advantage of her closeness to kiss her lightly. "Deal," he murmured against her lips.

Inside, they found the dozen low-level demons he'd sensed lined up in front of the bar. All had removed their clothing and reverted to their natural forms. As far as he knew, Arkady had never seen any infernal creatures other than the horde they'd dispatched at Nyx.

Presumably to make Bunny think she'd succeeded in rattling her, Arkady didn't hide her disgust at the demons' red leathery skin, vertically slitted pupils, glowing red eyes, and thick raised scars that covered their bodies almost from horns to hooves. She cringed at the sight of their aroused, barbed genitals and made a show of keeping Ronan between herself and them. He might have been fooled by her acting if he hadn't known better.

"All in a row, like a Rockettes kick-line from Hell," she muttered in his ear.

He didn't know what that meant. He'd have to ask her to explain later.

The demons chittered and hissed at them, showing their jagged teeth. Unlike Arkady, Ronan had no reason to show fear or revulsion, and these low-level creatures deserved a reminder that they weren't shit, as Arkady would have phrased it. He didn't want to waste power putting them in their place. Instead, he braced himself and flexed his wings as much as the bindings would allow. The pop of sound and angelic magic sent the demons scurrying for the darkest corners of the bar. He smiled with satisfaction.

"Ha. Take that, you stinky little shits." Arkady glanced around, hands on her hips. "Who do I have to shank to get a drink around here? Ugh, never mind. Whatever demons drink probably sucks anyway—or it's poisoned. Or both."

The back of Ronan's neck prickled. Bunny's voice came from the darkness on the far side of the bar. "I believe this establishment has some very fine tequilas. None poisoned, as far as I am aware."

Arkady palmed a blade and spun it in her hand. "Oh, gee, in that case pour me a double."

Chuckling, Bunny emerged from the shadows. She'd gone back to being a redhead and wore a slinky, semi-transparent green dress that emphasized her lack of undergarments in every possible way. Given her human form was as much a costume as her hair and clothing, Ronan found the sight of her body highly unappealing. Judging by Arkady's wrinkled nose, she felt the same way.

Bunny went behind the bar, poured herself a glass of whiskey, and leaned against the counter directly across from Ronan and Arkady. "What a meanie you are, Ronan. Scaring my little ones so badly, and without provocation." She sipped her drink and smiled. "No more manners than your bedmate. At least she has good reason for her conduct. I expected better of an archangel—even one so disgraced."

"Have you nothing but petty insults for weapons?" Ronan asked. "Frankly, I'm bored with you."

"Bored? Of me?" She laughed. "Not possible."

He scoffed. "I've never met an incubus *less* interesting."

"You both found me interesting enough at Bella's." Bunny came around the end of the bar nearest them and posed with her elbow resting on its top. "You were hard for me, and your woman grew wet from my touches. Do you deny it?"

He laughed. "I wouldn't take either of those things so much to heart. It wasn't you we were lusting over. We'd been fantasizing about fucking each other from the moment we met—so much so that we've indulged ourselves how many times in the past twelve hours?" He would not normally use such language to describe the intimacy between himself and Arkady, but their purpose was to antagonize their adversary into reacting without thinking.

And of course Arkady understood and played along "Four." She smiled. "How many times have you gotten some today, Bun-Bun? Pretty sure the answer is none. Some *incubus* you are." She put air quotes around the word. "You couldn't get laid if you were the only woman on the menu at a Nevada cathouse."

Bunny's eyes blazed red. She slipped the straps of her dress over her shoulders and let the shimmery fabric fall to the floor, leaving her nude. She caressed her ample breasts and cupped them proudly, as if expecting her audience to fall to their knees in reverence. "I am Atonoskelis, worshiped by legions of demons and men. You would fight each other to the death for the privilege of having me."

"No thanks," Ronan said. "Not if you were the last piece of tail on the planet."

"And speaking of tails," Arkady added, "where's yours? I bet it's stumpy, like one of those little yappy dogs."

Whether on purpose or not, with that jibe she'd finally found a nerve. In Ronan's experience, upper-caste demons took great pride in three things: using their power to grind others underfoot, the golden tattoos that covered their bodies in demon form, and the length, strength, and attractiveness of their tails. Few other insults could have elicited such an instantaneous and near-crazed reaction.

Bunny—Atonoskelis—let out a piercing scream that caused both Ronan and Arkady to almost double over in agony. Never before had a demon's cry caused him pain, much less stunned him for the few precious moments that might spell doom for them both.

In a paroxysm of rage, she launched herself straight at Arkady, changing form in midair with a pulse of sulfurous infernal magic, poisonous claws and fangs extended. Her wings unfurled like sails. Her tail whipped through the air, its barbed tip aimed at Arkady's heart.

Arkady was still disoriented by Atonoskelis's scream and wouldn't be able to react in time to avoid the deadly blow. Ronan pulled his fighting sword in what might have been his fastest draw in recent memory. Certainly the fastest since his mortal life began. His swing missed Atonoskelis's tail by less than an inch.

With no time to think, he used his momentum to put his body between that deadly barb and its intended target.

"No," Arkady said.

Atonoskelis's poison-tipped barb impaled him clear through his right shoulder. The pain was instantaneous and nearly whited out his vision. That pain was quickly replaced by almost mind-numbing agony as she lashed her tail again and flung him with all her might. His body weight and the force of her tail snapping like a whip ripped the barb free. He sailed halfway across the bar and crashed into a thick support column with enough force to break what felt like all the ribs on his right side.

As he hit the floor, Arkady shouted something unintelligible and threw the knife she'd palmed earlier. It was on target for the demon's heart, but the air movement caused by her wings pushed it off-course. The blade ended up buried hilt-deep in Atonoskelis's belly.

The demon pulled the knife out and licked her own blood from its blade with her forked tongue. "You missed," she said with a sibilant hiss.

Through a haze of pain, Ronan felt poison and paralysis spreading from his shoulder through his body faster than he could have believed possible. He was losing blood quickly as well. If he hadn't utilized one of the emergency transfusion kits he kept in his saddlebag, he would already be unconscious. Once that poison reached his heart, he would likely die.

Atonoskelis dove straight at Arkady again, moving so fast Arkady barely had time to draw her own sword before Atonoskelis collided with her and knocked it from her hand. As it clattered to the floor, Atonoskelis picked Arkady up and carried her through the air.

Arkady tried to stab Atonoskelis with her backup knife, but the demon broke her arm with one vicious twist. Arkady screamed as her blade fell from her grasp. "*Ronan!*"

He made a split-second decision and used every bit of healing magic he had in his body to heal his wounds and rid himself of the poison. That would leave none for either Arkady or himself later, but if he didn't do this now, there would be no later for either of them.

Days, even hours, earlier, he had looked upon his mortal life with despair. Killing scumbags had seemed the only thing worth doing to pass the time while he served his sentence. Now his survival—and hers —meant everything to him.

I want more time, he thought savagely as his healing magic fought the poison and his injuries to keep his mortal body alive.

Was Michael watching him now, waiting for him to die and face another trial? Or waiting for him to draw his celestial sword to save

Arkady and seal his own fate? The thought filled him with rage, and the rage got him on his feet.

He staggered against the blood-splattered column he'd struck earlier. Atonoskelis, with Arkady dangling from her grip, flew toward the wall opposite the bar. The mural painted there crackled with demonic power that scoured his skin. A portal.

He grabbed Atonoskelis's tail as she passed. His hands were slippery with his own blood, but he hung on with every ounce of strength he had as she slammed him into tables and chairs, trying to knock him off.

Arkady, her face white with pain, reached for him with her good arm. He grabbed her hand just as his grip on Atonoskelis's tail finally slipped.

Hand-in-hand, they plunged through the portal. Arkady's scream was the last thing Ronan heard before they spiraled away into the darkness.

16

ARKADY

THE DEMON REALM SMELLED LIKE ASS. LIKE AN *ASS'S* ASS. THE SMELL was worse than the torture, and the torture was pretty damn bad.

Arkady landed on her knees, spat out blood, and gave Atonoskelis her middle finger as best she could given her right arm was broken. "Almost felt that one, Bun-Bun. But keep working on it. You'll get good at this someday."

Atonoskelis hissed and stalked back and forth, her hooves clacking on the stone floor. The two smaller demons guarding Ronan's cage howled with glee.

Arkady stole a glance at the cage on the other side of the room. Ronan still hadn't regained consciousness as far as she could tell. He could be playing possum, waiting for an opportunity to catch their captors by surprise, but she didn't think that was the case. That shoulder wound and getting thrown across the bar like a rag doll had seriously done a number on him. On top of that, Ronan had said a demon's tail barb was poisonous. He had healing magic, but maybe not enough to survive this. Eons of existence, only to end up locked in a ten-by-ten cage he probably could have vaporized with the flick of a finger before. *Fucking demons*, she thought.

Before the past day, she'd figured vampires were the worst. Come to find out, they had competition in that category. At least vamps couldn't drag someone through a portal to another realm where the oceans were filled with lava and everything smelled like the puddles that formed under dumpsters on a hot summer day.

Wake up, Ronan, she willed as Atonoskelis drew back one of her legs to kick her in the ribs again. *I can't take much more of this.*

She rolled away from Atonoskelis's hoof, but that put her close to the wall and reduced her room to maneuver. The demon's next kick connected with her side. She hit the wall, her jaw clenched so she didn't cry out. The demon guards cackled and danced and mimicked her facial expression, much to each other's merriment.

Atonoskelis towered over her. Her tail swished back and forth almost like a cat's. Ronan's bloody handprint was still visible about midway down its length. Arkady felt torn between relief he was here and guilt that she'd held onto him and pulled him through the portal. She had no doubt he'd intended to go through with her, but now he might die in that blasted cage. Somehow, she had to make sure he didn't. He deserved better than that.

"Scream, little human." Atonoskelis smiled down at her. "The tougher you act, the worse I'll make it for you."

Arkady hated avoiding looking up because not making eye contact made her feel cowardly, but from that angle if she wasn't careful she'd get another eyeful of Atonoskelis's barbed genitals. She'd already had enough of that sight to last several lifetimes.

"It's not an act," she managed to say, her good arm wrapped protectively around her ribs. "I really am this bad-ass."

She braced herself for another kick, but instead Atonoskelis chuckled. "I really do think I like you. Are you being brave to impress your lover? I wouldn't bother, darling. One way or the other, he's going to die in that cage. The question is, which one of you will I kill first, while the other one watches?" She leaned down and caressed Arkady's cheek with the back of her clawed hand. Her skin felt rough and hot, like a lizard's. "Will he lose the will to live if he watches you die?" she mused. "He fought so hard to follow you here, hoping to save you. He was a broken man before you gave him a reason to fight. Without you, why would he want to live?"

Arkady snorted even though it hurt. "He and I slept together. That doesn't mean we're each other's only reason to live. He followed *you* here, you moron. He wants to kill you. So do I."

Atonoskelis's harsh atonal laugh made Arkady's hair stand on end. "I'm sure you do, but neither of you have any weapons, and I have no intention of dying just to please you." She tilted her head. "But perhaps you could both die to please me...or pleasing me."

"Hard pass." Arkady sat up, her back against the wall, and cradled her broken arm in her lap. "Honestly, you're just not my type."

"Darling, I'm *everyone's* type." Atonoskelis stepped back. Sulfuric magic swirled around her, hiding her body from sight for a few seconds. When it dissipated, she was back in her human form, complete with red hair.

"Still no." Arkady got to her feet using the wall for support. "You can dress yourself up however you want, but a demon skank by any other name is still a demon skank."

"You are making two key mistakes," Atonoskelis said, posing with one hand on her hip. "The first is thinking I care whether my partners are voluntary participants in our activities."

Arkady's eyes narrowed. "Yeah, that figures. And the second thing?"

"That it's you I intend to kill first." Hips swaying, the demon sauntered toward the cage. "Perhaps you are less of a *bad-ass* than you believe. Let's find out."

As she walked, Atonoskelis turned into a kind of black mist. The mist drifted through the bars of the cage to hover above Ronan's unmoving body. Only her mouth was visible in the cloud, smiling and full of jagged teeth.

Arkady jerked. Katy's drawings. A black mist with a single line, floating above a sleeping figure. She'd thought the sketches were creepy, but the reality was so much worse.

And then, as if the cloud wasn't bad enough, it turned into an almost-perfect imitation of her own naked body. She went cold all over.

"Ronan, I want you," Atonoskelis called in Arkady's voice. She drifted down until she was straddling his hips in a grotesque parody of

Arkady and Ronan's earlier lovemaking. The sight made Arkady's stomach rebel. "Rooooo-nan..."

Finally, his eyes opened. He blinked slowly, clearly disoriented and unable to focus very well. "My Valkyrie," he rasped and reached for Atonoskelis.

Limping badly, Arkady ran toward the cage. "Ronan, don't! She's the demon!"

Atonoskelis hissed at her, then turned back to her prey. "My Ronan," she cooed. "I will make you glad to be alive."

Desperate to break the demon's hold over Ronan, Arkady toed off her boot and threw it as hard as she could. It hit the bars of the cage and bounced off. Atonoskelis laughed, her voice a stomach-churning mix of her own and Arkady's.

To Arkady's shock, Ronan took advantage of the distraction and stuck his fist straight into Atonoskelis's chest. With a scream of pain and rage, she turned back to mist, flew out of the cage, and crossed the room to its far side before reverting to her red-skinned demon form. She doubled over in obvious pain, clutching her abdomen with her clawed hands.

"I ordered you both to search him!" Atonoskelis shrieked at the demons who cowered beside the cage.

"We did, my lady!" the more scarred of the two wailed. They groveled even lower, their claws scrabbling against the stone. "We did, I swear!"

Ronan got to his feet using the bars of the cage for support. In his hand, he held an amulet Arkady hadn't seen before. "Where'd you have that stashed?" she asked, clutching her side.

"You don't want to know," Ronan rasped. He looked terrible, his face drawn and pale. It was the way he looked at her, though, that really rattled her. She saw fear in his eyes...and guilt. She recognized that look. He knew something she didn't, and she didn't like that one little bit. What the hell had he kept from her and why?

With a screech, Atonoskelis flew to the cage and fell on the demon guards. Their screams and pleas for mercy went ignored. Blood and leathery flesh splattered everything in the room as she ripped them to shreds.

"A knife." Ronan reached through the bars for Arkady while Atonoskelis was occupied. "She'll kill you."

The way he said it—not as a danger, but as a certainty—caused her to go still. Before they'd left her house for Carmody Tower, she'd done a quick online search for his angelic name and skimmed what little information was available. Most of it was speculation, but one thing that had stuck in her mind because several sites mentioned it was that Remiel, also called the Thunder of God, supposedly had the gift of foresight. Suddenly Ronan's fear and guilt made sense.

"Bastard," she breathed. She took a step back. They stared at each other. "I called you an honest man," she added bitterly. "And you kept this from me."

He offered no defense of himself, probably because there wasn't one. Instead, he gripped the bars of the cage and tried to pull them apart. "Release me, Atonoskelis," he demanded. Though still weak, his voice had that imperious tone she'd heard him use on the vamps. "I will fight for our freedom. A human is no worthy combatant for a powerful demon."

Angered by both his tone and words, Arkady inhaled sharply. He returned her glare with one of his own. "Look at yourself," he said coldly. "She has already beaten you. You live only because she is toying with you. What can you do against such an adversary, without even a knife to defend yourself? You are not an opponent. You are *prey*. You'll go down with a knife in your heart, dead, just like Alice."

She frowned. *Dead, just like Alice...?* To her knowledge, Alice had never been stabbed in the heart, by a knife or anything else. What the hell did Ronan mean?

Atonoskelis laughed. "This is all so wonderful, darlings." She was covered in dark blood and bits of flesh. There wasn't enough left of the demon guards to fill a cup. What she hadn't eaten, she'd flung around the room. "Moments ago, you were lovers. Now you hate him."

"I don't hate him." Arkady didn't look at Ronan. "I don't feel anything for him at all."

Atonoskelis's forked tongue flicked out. "Such anger. It tastes like honey." She picked up two knives from the puddle of blood at her feet.

They were Arkady's own knives, confiscated by the guards when they'd arrived through the portal.

She held them out to Arkady with a mocking smile. "Choose a weapon, little human. The pathetic fallen angel has made a fair point. You're no worthy adversary against my claws and poison, but knife against knife, perhaps you will have a chance."

Not much of one, Arkady thought grimly. Ronan's comment about her dying from a knife wound had obviously given Atonoskelis the idea. Against any human, Arkady liked her chances in a knife fight, but the demon bitch was still larger, faster, and far less hindered by injury. And if Atonoskelis really meant what she said about not fighting with her claws, teeth, or tail, Arkady would eat Ronan's motorcycle boots.

Ronan had to have an ulterior motive for suggesting they fight with knives. He clearly couldn't tell Arkady what it was, so she would have to figure it out.

Maybe the clue was in his strange statement. *You'll go down with a knife in your heart, dead, just like Alice.*

Dead, just like Alice—who wasn't dead at all. Suddenly, it all made sense. Arkady had to bite the inside of her cheek to keep from laughing. *Son of a bitch fallen angel.* He'd remembered.

She chose the larger of the two knives that Atonoskelis offered her. "I'm not much of an adversary with a broken arm and cracked ribs, either," she said, fumbling to hold the knife though she was almost as good with her left hand as her right when it came to wielding a blade. "You want a good fight, give me that healing spell I had in my pocket and let's make it less lopsided. Otherwise you might as well just shish-kabob me with that fancy tail and be done with it."

"Oh, very well." Atonoskelis glanced through the remains of her guards and pointed. "There. Use it."

Arkady took the crystal containing one of Malcolm's mid-range healing spells and retreated to the far corner of the room before she invoked it. The damn thing hurt almost as bad as when Atonoskelis broke her arm in the first place. She clenched her jaw as the pulses of Malcolm's familiar earth magic healed her arm and what felt like three or four cracked ribs, plus assorted minor injuries. It seemed to take forever, and when the last of the magic rolled through her, she had to take deep breaths to get through the nausea.

Atonoskelis didn't give her much time to recover. "Get up," the demon said impatiently, her hooves clacking on the stone floor as she paced. "Get up, or I'll kill you where you lie."

"Oh, eat a dick." Arkady said it before she realized Atonoskelis probably did that quite literally with some regularity. With a groan, she rolled to her hands and knees and then staggered to her feet. "Give me a minute, okay? Healing spells suck. I think I'm going to throw up."

"If you vomit, I will make you eat it," Atonoskelis snapped. "Pick up your knife."

"What's the hurry? You got somewhere to be?" She toed off her other boot, peeled off her socks so she could fight barefoot, and flexed her right arm experimentally. Her elbow felt stiff. Not surprising, but disappointing. She'd hoped for full range of movement. She hadn't really expected Atonoskelis to let her use the spell at all. Maybe the demon really did want a good fight. *Fair enough*, she thought. If there was one thing Arkady Rose Woodall could do, it was fight for survival. She'd been doing that as long as she could remember.

Atonoskelis attacked first with three quick slashes aimed at Arkady's midsection. She seemed decent enough with a blade for someone whose primary weapons were claws and a tail, Arkady decided as she jumped back just in time to avoid being gutted. And she did seem to be sticking to what she'd said about only fighting with a knife, at least for the moment.

She spun, slashed with her own knife, and scored a deep cut across Atonoskelis's left shoulder that made the demon howl. "First blood to me," she said as they circled each other. "Still time to tap out if you want to. I won't tell."

With a hiss, Atonoskelis attacked again, this time aiming for Arkady's right arm. The knife sliced through her sleeve and left a shallow cut that stung and trickled blood. Arkady feigned serious injury, gripping it with her left hand and crying out as she rubbed it to smear the blood around and make the wound appear worse than it was.

She didn't spare Ronan a glance, but out of the corner of her eye she saw him still trying in vain to bend the bars of the cage. Just the fact he was alive after being wounded and poisoned was remarkable. He was stubborn—she had to give him that. Hopefully stubborn enough to find a way out of that cage.

"Mmm...delicious." Atonoskelis licked Arkady's blood off the edge of her knife. "Still time to tap out if you want to," she added, mocking Arkady's earlier words.

"It's just a flesh wound." Arkady made a show of gritting her teeth and let Atonoskelis get a good look at her bloody hand. "I've had worse paper cuts."

They traded threats, insults, and minor injuries for several minutes. Arkady pretended her wounds were far more debilitating than they really were, hoping to catch her opponent off guard, but Atonoskelis proved to be a skilled fighter and didn't give her any openings. They were closer to an even match than she'd prefer—and that was without factoring in her teeth, claws, and tail.

And then, without warning, everything went to hell.

The ground and everything around them rumbled and shook violently in a sudden earthquake. Thrown off balance when the floor heaved, Arkady stumbled. Atonoskelis pounced, jabbing her knife deeply into Arkady's upper back near her left shoulder blade.

Despite the pain, Arkady managed to hang onto her own knife, but she couldn't avoid Atonoskelis's brutal kick. She hit the wall hard and crumpled to the floor, dazed.

"No!" Ronan shouted, furiously pulling at the bars of his cage. "This isn't how it happens!"

So he *had* foreseen her death at some point. *Nice of him to tell me so,* she thought grimly.

Arkady coughed up blood. "Maybe not, but this is how it's happening," she said. Best to not waste her remaining breaths calling him names. Atonoskelis was approaching, and she had the look of a demon who intended to finish things off. "If you get back home and I don't, tell Alice I did this on purpose to get out of wearing a bridesmaid dress."

What Ronan thought of that statement, Arkady had no idea. With a hiss, Atonoskelis hauled her to her feet. Her knees wouldn't hold her up, so the demon pinned her against the wall with a clawed hand fisted in her shirt.

"Strange that after all you've been through and seen, you end up dying here," Atonoskelis said, grinning. "Any last words, my sweetness?"

Through the ringing in her ears, Arkady heard Ronan inhale sharply. Maybe it was that hated nickname, which she supposed Henry Farrell might have learned from Atonoskelis in the first place. Or maybe it was the thought of watching her die from inside a cage. At that moment, she didn't really care.

There was only one way out of this mess and it was going to require the biggest gamble of her entire crazy life. At least if this turned out to be last call, she'd had a good, long, wild ride.

She spat out some blood, wiped her mouth with the back of her hand, and forced herself to stand up straight so she could look Atonoskelis in the eye. "Just the ones I figured would be my last," she said. "Which are, fuck you."

With a smile, Atonoskelis drove Arkady's own knife right through her heart.

17

RONAN

ARKADY WOODALL, THE FIRST WOMAN RONAN WOULD HAVE DIED for in all his long existence, was dead before she hit the floor.

He couldn't breathe. For a moment, he thought somehow he'd taken that fatal blow in her stead. He even looked down at his own chest, half expecting—half *hoping*—to see the hilt of a knife protruding from his sternum, but there was nothing there. The knife was buried in Arkady's heart where Atonoskelis had left it. Her death had simply sucked the air from his lungs.

What if he'd been wrong about Arkady's knife? How could he go back to Alice and Malcolm and tell them she was dead? Alice would demand to know why they hadn't called on her for help. All he would be able to tell her was that he and Arkady had wanted to go into Carmody Tower alone to take on something that was out of their league, just to see if they could beat it. Alice would tell him that was a worthless excuse and she would be right.

Atonoskelis left Arkady's lifeless body where it had fallen with the hilt of the knife still sticking out of her chest, but she took the knife Arkady had used in their fight and came to his cage. He trembled with the force of his rage and grief.

"Was that as good for you as it was for me?" Atonoskelis purred.

She licked some of Arkady's blood off her palm. "Oh, there is nothing as delicious as the blood of someone you've killed. I look forward to roasting and eating her flesh. It's an honor I give only my best adversaries. Everyone else I consume raw, of course. A much more expedient method of feeding, as I'm sure you'll agree."

His stomach rebelled at the thought, but he swallowed hard and met her mocking gaze with his own cold one. "She was right—you *are* pathetic."

"I see one of us standing and one of us dead." Atonoskelis chuckled. "If one of us is pathetic, it is your lover. Your *former* lover, who is now my future meal."

"You know why you're pathetic?" he continued as if she hadn't spoken. "You crave worship and power and yet you have none. All you have is the illusion of it."

Her slitted eyes flashed. "I am worshiped in any form I take and wherever I go, wingless little man."

"I don't think so. Your demon minions are so incompetent and fear you so little that they didn't even check me for hidden weapons. You poor, pitiful, hoofed creature." He brandished the amulet, which caused her to take a step back. "In the human world, you're reduced to employing humans to kidnap and traffic the weak and vulnerable."

"In the human world, I'm a savior of the weak," she said, preening. "They believe I am like a god."

"You've never saved anyone in your entire existence," he retorted. "Why lie about that to me?"

"As Melody Fullerton, I run an online message board," she snapped. "Young humans cry out for help. *Save me*, they wail in the night. The ones who will be missed, I send to safety. The ones who will not be missed, they are never to be found again. I am their god too, but a god of cruelty and doom." She smiled and caressed her hips. "And to the men at Bella's, I am a goddess."

"You're deluded. Those men you think look at you with such admiration look the same way at every other woman there."

"My lovers are legion," she hissed. "More men and women have writhed beneath me and called my name in their release than your puny mind can comprehend."

"They may call out a name, but it isn't yours." He snorted. "You seduce humans by posing as their lovers, because if you came to them as yourself they wouldn't touch you. Arkady had you figured out right from the beginning. You are to be pitied, not worshiped or feared."

Enraged, Atonoskelis whipped her tail at him. With the bars in the way he had time to dodge. She tried to stab him with her knife, but he blocked her arm.

"You know it's true," he said as she glared at him. "Somewhere in this realm there's a demon lord who owns you, isn't there? A prince, perhaps, or a duke, or a general at the end of whose chain you crawl. Maybe you have more freedom than most, Atonoskelis, but you and I both know you don't rule either in my world *or* your own." He stepped up to the bars, putting himself well within her reach. "You. *Serve.*"

She lunged for him with a screech that reminded him of the tiny winged demons at Nyx. He grabbed her wrists with all his strength.

"You will kneel before me!" She struggled to free herself. "*Fear me!*"

"Not a chance," Arkady said from behind her. Her voice was rough and raspy, but the sound was as sweet to Ronan's ears as celestial bells.

With a grunt of effort, she drove her knife into the side of Atonoskelis's belly with both hands and sliced upward. The blade carved through the demon's thick leathery skin and opened a gaping wound from her lower abdomen to her ribs. The demon screamed in surprise and agony, her wrists still trapped in Ronan's iron grip. Foul dark blood, guts, and organs spilled out. Her shrieks turned to gurgles.

"Surprise, bitch," Arkady said into the demon's ear. "Never turn your back on a Valkyrie—not even a dead one."

Ronan took Arkady's tactical knife from Atonoskelis's claws and used it to cut through her chest. He tossed the knife away, punched his hand through her ribs, and pulled out her heart.

Atonoskelis stared at her heart and then at him, her expression somewhere between fury and utter disbelief. Her mouth moved, but nothing came out but blood.

Centuries had passed since he'd last held a demon's heart in his hand. The organ smelled like dead, rotting things and felt like a concentrated form of all the evil in the world. He crushed the heart in his fist and dropped it.

With its source of life extinguished, Atonoskelis's corpse shriveled. They let go of her body and it crumpled to the floor next to the remains of her heart.

Breathing hard, her shirt soaked with blood—Atonoskelis's and her own—Arkady wiped her spelled knife on her pant leg, returned it to the sheath on her belt, and stared at Ronan.

"I owe you the ass-kicking of a lifetime," she said.

He couldn't argue with that. "I deserve it."

"Well, way to suck the joy out of it." She put her hands on her hips. "I ought to leave you in there to rot, you hypocrite. You jumped on me for trying to spare your feelings by not telling you I'd seen your scars, and *this whole fucking time*—"

"I have no defense." He pressed himself against the bars to get as close to her as he could. "I don't expect forgiveness. If I thought it would help, I would grovel."

"You're right—it won't help." Her expression remained cold and angry. "But you could try it anyway."

He took a gamble and reached through the bars for her hand. She didn't pull away, but she didn't curl her bloody fingers around his. Her skin felt cooler than normal—because, albeit for only a few minutes, she'd been dead.

"I am sorry," he said. "I saw the vision in the parking lot at the Pelican. I've tried not to experience visions for a very long time because I'm unable to prevent them from coming true. I had a vision of Alice's death not long after we met, but she survived. So I hoped it would happen with you." More quietly, he added, "And perhaps I feared that if I described what I'd seen to you, I would speak it into existence."

"So you went the route of keeping it to yourself and hoping it didn't happen. And after I told you not to be a dick." She raised her eyebrows. "Apparently, living for eons doesn't make you exempt from making shitty decisions."

"Apparently not."

"Well, at least we agree on that." She pulled her hand from his and crouched in the messy remains of the demon guards. "Grrrrr-*oss*," she grumbled, poking around in the slurry of flesh and blood. "So...knife in the heart, dead, just like Alice. You remembered what I told you at Nyx about my spelled knife. Not bad for a half-dead asshole." She picked up a large key and rose. "I never thought I'd end up using it like that, but I guess nobody really knows when they might need to die and be resurrected. Did you see that in your vision?"

He shook his head. "I only saw you stabbed in the heart."

"So you figured out a way to let the vision come true...but not in the way it seemed." She unlocked the cage door, but when he reached to push it open, she held it closed. "I'm still pissed at you. Any more visions you need to tell me about?"

"No."

"That had better be the truth." She studied him, eyes narrowed. "If you get any more visions of me, will you tell me?"

That question gave him hope that he hadn't damaged their relationship beyond repair. "Yes. No more secrets between us."

"Whoa. Slow your roll." She opened the cage door. "I'm not asking you to give up all your secrets, and I'm not offering you all of mine. Just don't keep anything back that involves me or people I care about. Sound fair?"

"Sounds more than fair." He stepped out of the cage. "May I kiss you?"

"Ew, seriously?" She looked down at herself. "I'm covered with blood. *Again*."

He smiled slightly. "Do I look like I care?"

Only when she returned his smile did the heaviness in his heart lift. "You remember when I said blood isn't sexy?" she asked wryly.

"I do. Is this one of the exceptions?"

"Are you joking?" She wrinkled her nose. "Demon blood smells like dumpster juice. It is the least sexy thing on the planet."

"On *our* planet, perhaps. Not on this one."

In the distance, they could hear a horde of demons howling, and the noise seemed to be getting closer.

"Speaking of which...how the hell are we going to get home?" she asked. "We'd better figure something out quick. That sounds like more demons than even *I* want to take on."

"That makes two of us. Do you know where the portal is where we arrived?"

She shook her head. "Another room, but I have no idea where. I was sick and dizzy. Everything was a blur until she dragged me in here. Are we screwed?"

"Possibly not." He gestured at the ceiling, where a faint black circle was just visible. "I believe that's a portal above us."

"Where does it come out in our world?"

"I don't know, but wherever it is, it'll be better than staying here."

"Damn it, I was really hoping you'd say Bali." She made a face. "How do we get through it, though? I'm assuming a demon portal requires a demon to operate, and at the moment, we're fresh out of demons. Whole ones, anyway."

"We might not need a whole one." He reclaimed his sword from where the demons had tossed it next to the cage and then picked up Atonoskelis's crushed heart. "There's probably enough demon magic left in this to get us through and out the other side."

"Probably?"

"Probably." He nodded in the direction of the demons' howls. "As opposed to *definitely*, which is how likely we are to die very unpleasantly if we're found."

"Point taken." She joined him under the portal. "We don't fly, though, and that ceiling's about fifteen feet up. Unlike the elevator at Nyx, you can't just give me a boost and then pull yourself through. How do we get up there?"

The howling demons sounded like they were approaching fast. Their time was about to run out. He figured they had one chance, and it was even more of a long shot than trying to use Atonoskelis's heart to get them through the portal.

"We take a leap of faith." Ronan switched the heart to his left hand and held out his right arm. "My wings are bound, but I may have just enough strength to lift us."

"I'm not much on leaps of faith, but sometimes that's all you've got left." She nestled herself against his side and let him wrap his arm around her waist. "Good thing I have faith in you, O Great and Mighty Asshole."

If she had faith in him, he'd be damned if he'd let her down.

He held her tightly against his side, raised the bloody, dripping heart above his head, and braced himself. "Whatever you do, don't let go of me, Miss Woodall."

"I don't plan to," she said.

With a flutter of his aching, bound wings, he jumped.

* ❦ ❦❦ ❦❦ ❦ ❦❦ ❦❦

They landed on black satin sheets that smelled of perfume and demon.

"I used to think satin sheets were kinda sexy," Arkady mumbled from somewhere on Ronan's right. "Never, ever again."

With a groan, he managed to roll onto his back and look up blearily. The enormous mirror on the ceiling showed they'd landed in the middle of a custom bed roughly the size of Arkady's living room. In the mirror, he saw a circle that crackled with power and magic. The portal.

He still had Atonoskelis's heart in his hand. He tossed it over the side of the bed and turned to Arkady. She lay where she'd landed, face down, her arms spread. The stab wound in her upper back had soaked her shirt with blood.

His own shirt wasn't in much better shape, but he tore it off and pressed it to the wound. She jerked and sucked in air through her teeth. "Jackass, warn me when you're going to do something like that. That hurts."

"Why didn't this heal?" he demanded.

"My knife was spelled to bring me back and it did, but it's still a damn knife. And the spell doesn't heal all wounds—just the one that killed me." She took a shuddering breath. "Alice told me dying hurts, but coming back hurts worse. I wish I hadn't just found out it's true."

"I wish neither of you knew that." He rested his head on the bed so he could look into her eyes. "Tell me how to help you."

"All I need is a healing spell and I'll be fine. This stab wound isn't going to kill me." She caressed his face with her bloody hand. "Thanks for getting us home." She looked past him and her eyes widened. "Oh, shit."

"What?"

"What do you mean, *what?*" She rose up on her elbows. "Ronan, it's night!"

He went to the floor-to-ceiling windows that overlooked the city. The night-time view of the skyline was beautiful for several reasons—not the least of which was that they'd made it back to Arkady's world more or less in one piece.

Our world, he reminded himself. *This is my world now too.*

She crawled to the side of the bed and stumbled across the plush carpet to him. "It was daytime when we left. How long have we been missing?"

He used a remote on the nightstand to turn on the television. "About thirty-six hours," he said when the screen displayed the date and time. At her incredulous expression, he explained, "Time often passes differently in other realms. We're very lucky to not come back twenty years in the future."

She gaped. "Are you serious?"

"Completely." He tossed the remote on the bed. "I expect she constructed her portals to travel between realms without much loss of time."

"So this is Casa Demon." She looked around. "It's got a damn good view, I'll give her that. But how do we keep more demons from coming here looking for us when they find Atonoskelis's body?"

He drew his sword and scratched the tip across the portal's edge. The magic crackled violently and then faded as the spellwork disintegrated. "That takes care of that one," he said. "We'll do the same to the one downstairs as we leave."

"We're not leaving until we figure out how she was running this trafficking ring and who's involved in it beside Mora and Farrell." She scrubbed her face with her hands. "We didn't find out anything about it, though. Damn it."

He returned his sword to his scabbard on his back. "While you were...unconscious, she told me as Melody she ran an online message board where teenagers ask for help. She saved the ones that she thought would be missed and funneled the rest into her trafficking ring. She called herself a savior of the weak."

"Oh, that's vile." She scowled. "Savior of the weak, my ass. What bullshit." She stormed out of the bedroom.

He followed her to a spacious office, where she eyed the laptop on the desk. "Online message board, huh?" she mused. "Odds are this has information on it we can use."

"It's equally likely to be secured and will be wiped if you attempt to access it," he pointed out.

"Luckily, I know someone who can help with that." She dug her phone from her pocket. The screen was cracked, but it still worked. She made a call on speakerphone. The phone rang three times, and then a familiar voice answered.

"Arkady, where the hell are you?" Alice snapped. Despite the hour, she sounded fully awake—and fully furious. "Do you have any idea how worried we've all been? Are you all right?"

"I'm fine, more or less," Arkady assured her. "At the moment, I need help from our black-hat friend. Do you have a number I can use to reach her?"

Alice sputtered. "You disappear for an entire day, then call me out of the blue at three in the morning to ask for a phone number without bothering to explain where you've been?"

"Sorry." Arkady winced and flexed her injured arm. "It's a super long story."

Bedding rustled and Sean spoke in the background. "Arkady, do you need backup?" he asked. "Where are you?"

"I'm good," she said, glancing at Ronan. "I have *backup*." Ronan's mouth quirked.

"Who?" Alice demanded. "Malcolm's here with us. Who have you got with you? This Johnny that Malcolm mentioned?"

Ronan didn't want Arkady to have to lie or refuse to answer, so before she could reply, he spoke. "I'm here with her, Alice."

For several long moments, the only response was a quiet growl from Sean. "Ronan?" Alice asked finally, her voice thick with emotion. "Is that you?"

Despite what Carly had said about Alice's worry over his disappearance, he wasn't at all prepared for either her joy and relief at his voice or the depth of his own feelings.

When Alice said his name, he experienced a strange combination of happiness and terrible guilt. She meant far more to him than he'd realized.

Weeks earlier, he'd left her home because he thought he might break under the weight of his burdens, and he hadn't wanted to be anywhere near her when that happened. Only now did he realize the folly of his choice. Out of love, she and her pack had offered him shelter, comfort, and healing, and he had left that behind to crawl into a hole and feel sorry for himself.

Arkady's assessment of him had been correct. He *was* an ungrateful shit.

"Yes, it's me," Ronan said around an unexpected lump in his throat. For once, he didn't care that everyone listening could hear the emotion in his voice. "Miss Woodall and I have been working on the trafficking case. We have some minor injuries—"

"But nothing a little healing magic won't fix," Arkady interjected before he could give away any details. She probably didn't want to worry Alice any more than they already had. She slipped her hand into his back jeans pocket and gave his ass a little squeeze. "Are Regan and Mireille okay?"

"Yes." Alice sounded far less angry now. "While you two were MIA, we got Regan into an in-patient treatment program. I had a long talk with Mireille and she told her father where to find this ex-boyfriend. Odds are he won't be bothering her again."

At Ronan's quiet sigh of relief, Arkady gave his ass another squeeze. "We're very glad to hear that. And the car out at the Pelican?"

"My garden has been well fed, and the car is now a rusty pancake at a salvage yard," Alice told them. "And now that I've answered all *your* questions, I would like to know *where the hell you've both been.*"

"I'm sorry for disappearing," Arkady said. "I promise to explain, but seriously, we need that phone number before our evidence of this trafficking ring goes poof."

"Fine." Alice gave them the number. "Let it ring twice and then end the call. She'll call you right back. And if you're not at my house in an hour with a damn good explanation, I will set Malcolm loose on you both. He's itching to take a chunk out of both your asses."

"He'll have to get in line," Sean said in the background, a growly edge to his voice. "Disappearing acts are only appreciated on a magician's stage. That goes for both of you."

"Understood." Arkady hesitated, then added, "Thanks, guys. It'll be good to see you."

"You too," Alice said warmly. "Both of you."

Once she'd ended the call, Arkady rose on her tiptoes and gave Ronan a quick kiss. "You'd better practice your groveling before we get to their house," she warned. "Alice deserves to give you a piece of her mind, and her forgiveness will come a hell of a lot easier than Sean's."

"I would imagine so. An alpha werewolf doesn't take kindly to anyone hurting his mate, either physically or emotionally. Speaking of which..." Ronan caught Arkady's hand before she had a chance to call the number Alice had given them. "What did you mean about getting out of wearing a bridesmaid dress?"

"Believe it or not, Alice and Sean got engaged. Big beautiful ring and everything. The whole pack's acting like a bunch of puppies." At his stunned expression, she smirked. "See what you miss when you run away to mope? I hope they make you the flower girl."

He kissed her blood-matted hair. "I'm told I look quite fetching in white tulle."

"Mmm, I bet you do." She gave his ass one final squeeze, then picked up her phone. "Let's call Cyro, hacker extraordinaire, to get everything off this laptop. And then let's get the ever-loving hell out of here."

18

ARKADY

"I COULD GET USED TO THIS," ARKADY SAID.

They lay together in her bed, sweaty and satisfied. Or at least as satisfied as Ronan could apparently get. The man had superhuman recuperative abilities—so much so that she hadn't had a decent night's sleep since they'd made it back from the demon realm. He'd been deprived of companionship for a century during his imprisonment, he'd told her. She'd started to think he intended to make up for it all in a single week. Not that she minded, of course. Even Malcolm's teasing about how tired she looked each morning couldn't dampen her mood.

What *did* dampen it, however, was that Ronan didn't reply.

"Ronan." She craned her neck to look at him. He stared at the ceiling, his expression distant. She nudged him with her elbow. "This is the part where you say *Me too*."

He leaned down and kissed her brow. "I apologize, Miss Woodall. I was lost in thought."

"About what?"

"The information from the laptop and what this federal agent you mentioned will do with it."

She might have guessed his mind had drifted back to their case. It hadn't been far from her thoughts either. "We'll get an update as soon as Supervisory Special Agent Trent Lake has one to give us. With everything Cyro got off the laptop, the feds will be able to get everyone involved. You know these things take time. They won't want to move before they know all the players."

"I know." He ran his fingertips down her side and over the curve of her hip, raising goosebumps over her entire body. "I'm accustomed to taking care of business myself. It's difficult handing the responsibility over to someone else."

"I know, Big Bad Bounty Hunter." She entwined their fingers and marveled at how much larger his hand was than her own. "And if it was anyone else but Lake in charge of the investigation, I'd feel pretty restless too. You don't know him, but I hope it means something that both Alice and I have faith in him."

"It makes all the difference. Neither you nor Alice trust easily, and I'm sure that goes double for federal agents." He rested his chin on her head. "I would prefer to execute all members of the trafficking ring one by one."

"Me too. We'll have to be content with the justice they get from the courts. Luckily, federal sentencing guidelines for traffickers are tough, and with the evidence we gave Lake, everyone involved is likely to spend a very long time in prison. They'll have a tough time of it." She caressed his bristly cheek. "So given that's the case, let's get back to more pleasant topics."

He raised his eyebrows. "Such as?"

"Such as how much I like having you in my bed."

"Just in your bed?"

She chuckled. "And in my everything else."

"Glad to hear it." He let go of her hand and stroked her hip. "Because I very much enjoy being in your everything else every chance I get."

"I noticed." She rested her hand on his to still its movements because his touch was distracting and she had something very serious to say. "We're very much in lust. That's good enough for me for the time being, but I've seen you go all googly-eyed when you thought I wasn't looking."

"You have seen no such thing." His expression turned indignant. "I have never once appeared *googly-eyed*, Miss Woodall."

"Okay, if you say so." She patted his hand and gave him one of her best, most aggravating smirks. "You're catching feelings, my fallen angel. Don't try and deny it. A woman can sense these things."

"I have caught feelings," he agreed. "I would give my life to save yours. I have not said that to any woman in all my eons of existence."

He said it so matter-of-factly that it could only be the truth. And for one of the very few times in her adult life, Arkady Woodall was stunned into silence.

"You may call this lust, or love, or anything you like. I accept your terms, whatever they may be." He cupped her face with his hand. "I have an entire mortal life to live, my Valkyrie, and I want to spend this part of it with you, in your bed and in your everything else."

"Is this because I saved your bacon in the demon realm?" she demanded. "Because I'm all for a good *quid pro quo*, but—"

He rolled her on top of him and held her in place when she squirmed. "I'm fairly certain I saved *your* bacon, Miss Woodall. The plan with the spelled knife was mine, was it not?"

She sucked in a breath. "You conceited—the knife was *my* plan! I had that blade spelled more than a month ago!"

"But did you think to use it in the fight before I suggested it?" he persisted.

"I might have, in another minute." Her eyes narrowed. "What's your point?"

"My point is, we work well together." He caressed the curves of her ass, making it difficult to stay focused on being angry at him. "And we do other things very well together as well. I suggest we continue to do both, as often as possible. Starting now."

"Starting—?" Her eyes widened at the sensation of him growing hard between them. "Ronan, I know you're good, but I have nothing left. I couldn't come again if my life depended on it."

"I don't think that's true." His eyes gleamed. "I'm far better than good, and you *will* come again. And again, and again, and again. I won't stop until I keep that promise."

He wouldn't stop, she thought with a shiver. "My stubborn fallen angel," she said aloud.

"Yours, for as long as you'll have me." His grin turned more than a little wicked. "Now, ride me, my Valkyrie. We only have three hours until the sun comes up and I don't plan to waste them sleeping."

Sleep? Who needs it anyway? she thought wryly. *Looks like Malcolm will get to give me shit for dragging myself into the office again today.*

She smiled down at him. "Well, if you insist."

Thank you for reading! Did you enjoy? Please add your review because nothing helps an author more and encourages readers to take a chance on a book than a review.

And now, explore more urban fantasy with BAD GIRLS DRINK BLOOD by City Owl Author, S.L. Choi. Turn the page for a sneak peek!

You can also sign up for the City Owl Press newsletter to receive notice of all book releases!

SNEAK PEEK OF BAD GIRLS DRINK BLOOD

BY S.L. CHOI

I'd been nursing my drink for the past hour, along with my pride. I didn't want to face my sisters. I didn't want to tell them I'd screwed up.

The morning sun broke through stained-glass windows high on the far wall of the shotgun-style front room. It illuminated the rich mahogany bar top and the pale red layer of melted ice atop the disgusting virgin Bloody Mary I'd made the mistake of ordering.

"I don't smell nos blood." A hand large enough to crack a watermelon like an egg slid in front of me and tapped a chipped fingernail on my glass.

"Too early for that stuff." He didn't need to know I was allergic. That type of info would ruin my rep. "Tomato juice and plenty of vodka."

"Yous should go straight vodka. Don't mess with that vegetable stuff."

"Fruit."

"What?"

"Never mind." I swung around on the well-worn saddle of my stool and faced the ogre. Rip, a regular fixture at the bar, had a remarkably expressive face for something that resembled an unfinished block of gray sculpting clay. Broad as a refrigerator and somewhere close to seven feet tall, he dwarfed my already short stature. Both of his ever-roaming—and more than a little creepy—chameleon-like eyes landed on me.

"Lane Callaghan." He pinched the lapels of my jacket to straighten it. The shifting sides revealed a shoulder sheath holding a push dagger under each arm, and he tweaked one with a thick finger. "What's a bad girl like yous doing in a nice bar like this?"

Despite playing into the corny cliché, I snatched his finger and bent it back, stopping before it reached the point of pain. "Never touch a girl's hardware unless you're prepared to lose a finger." I tempered the action with a wink. Though, I meant it. Don't touch my blades.

"No touch. Gots it." He threw his hands in the air. Such a drama queen.

From the front of the bar voices rose, furniture clattered on the hardwood floors, and a bottle shattered. The only one to react was Teddy, the bartender, bar owner, and resident eye candy, who appeared from behind the bar and easily vaulted over the counter before the fighters could cause any damage to his establishment.

A nice bar, indeed. Nice was relative in Interlands, but the ogre did run a bookie business from the booth he rented here, so he was biased. To be fair, Teddy kept the place in surprisingly good shape, considering the locals and some of their shady side businesses. Myself included.

Cleanliness was not a typical werewolf trait, not that I'd ever seen Teddy go furry. Not in the seven years I'd known him, but it was obvious in the way he moved, the way he easily cowed other wolves—and just about anyone else, really.

I hitched my elbows on the bar behind me and leaned against it. "What's up, Rip?"

He rolled his thick shoulders and did a quick side-to-side look, as if there might actually be someone in here who didn't know why he'd approached me.

"Yous lookin' for work?"

My nostrils flared with a slow, deep breath. The crisp grapefruit scent of whatever cleaner Teddy used to keep a bar full of humans, fae, and other degenerates suspiciously clean invaded my senses. If I said yes, my sisters would be pissed. I was already on a job, but I'd screwed it up, and we were less than a month away from having our electricity cut off, so why not?

"You know, being propositioned for work in a bar would offend most women." I tugged my ponytail forward and began twisting the deep auburn strands into a fat braid. A red so deep it was nearly black, but not the black-on-black of a true blood fae.

The ogre's full belly laugh sounded like stones rattling inside a bass drum. His gut was about the size of one, too. "Most don't get paid to beats up folks and take their money."

"True." My business card might say private investigator, but as my failed attempt to tail someone solo proved this morning, I should stick with being the muscle of my sibling trio, even if my sisters insisted otherwise. "All right. Who is it, and what's the timetable?"

"Lotta whos. Grounders. A pack of them."

I barked a laugh. "You want me to shake down a bunch of overgrown hamsters?"

The trenches carved into the big guy's forehead deepened. "Yous don't know much about them, do you?"

"Enough. Doesn't matter. I'll swipe the Easter Bunny's carrots, so long as you're paying. Here." I pulled the palm-sized pad emblazoned with the business name, YML Investigations, from my jacket pocket and handed it to Rip. "Details. Names, descriptions, their usual haunts. You know the drill."

The pad disappeared into Rip's massive mitt. He paused. His thick lips pressed into a tight line. "Yous don't underestimate these guys. Theys not so easy."

"Hey, I'm the big bad blood fae, remember?" Blood fae enough. "That's why you hire me. Let me worry about me."

Rip reached across the counter, grabbed a pen, and began scribbling the info. "Yous still on that other job?"

My turn to frown. Although, I shouldn't be surprised. Information kept him in the bookie game. "How'd you know about that?"

"Word gets 'round. I gots money on you bringing her in by end of tomorrow." He paused his scribbling to look me in the eye, which took getting used to. His protruding, conical-shaped eye sockets swiveled in all directions. "Yous gonna deliver?"

"Geez. Is there anything you don't run bets on?"

"Nope." His broad grin revealed two cracked teeth and a whole lot of pride. "Yous company is popular. YML makes me good money. Stupid tourists bet against yous. House wins."

"Why didn't I know about this? As the L in YML, I should have. I could've been double dipping, doing the jobs and betting all along." And paying bills on time.

Rip returned my pad. "Didn't seem ethical."

"Riiight. Because you're all about ethics. Put me down for a grand. I'll have your money by three."

One conical eye remained on me while the other rotated to the clock above the bar. His hairless brow shot skyward. "Almost noon. Yous telling me yous wrap this up in three hours?"

"Yup. I got this. Odds?"

His puffy lips pulled wide in a slow grin. "No bet. Yous bring my money in three hours or less, yous keep half."

"Let me guess, if I'm late I don't get paid?"

Rip tapped his bulbous nose, smiled, and pushed his way through the crowd toward his booth in the far corner. A brass plaque embossed with his name hung on the wall above the back bench.

Hot damn, half of what the grounders owed. They better owe a lot. It'd been a slow year for YML Investigations. Good for me and the more physical jobs—money collection, intimidation, even a little bit of protection. Those jobs were fun, for me, but didn't pay nearly enough to cover our bills. Unfortunately, it wasn't easy to drum up investigative business in a town of degenerates and criminals that didn't want to be investigated. The job I'd bombed this morning was meant to be our big payday.

I returned the pad to my pocket, but it caught on a bar napkin I'd shoved in there. Not from this bar, but to the bar in the fae-friendly casino I'd trailed my mark to this morning. Notes were never good. The one scrawled on the napkin was no exception. I tugged it free and fit the pad into place. Instead of replacing the napkin, I smoothed it on the bar top and stared down at the spindly black script.

Better luck next time, hybrid.

Fury roared through me. My ears burned and scalp tingled.

"What the hell is that?"

I spun with a snarl. My fangs elongated instantly, painfully.

Teddy's tall, lean frame bent over my shoulder as he read the napkin. My body thrummed with the surge of unspent adrenaline and possibly the intimate proximity. I flexed my fingers, curled them, flexed again.

"It's nothing." I snatched the napkin and jammed it into my jacket pocket. I'd deal with how exactly that woman knew I was a hybrid later. That was a secret for me and my sisters, and I aimed to keep it that way.

There was only one hybrid, and I was the unlucky genetic winner. It wasn't for lack of fae mixing, that was something they did often and copiously, but offspring were always of one race. It kept their magic powerful, and if fae worshiped anything, it was power. My existence wasn't an exalted position.

"But—"

"It's nothing," I stressed, my gaze steady on his. I meant business.

"Okay, okay." He tipped his forehead toward my face. "You should holster those things before you hurt someone besides yourself."

Crap, not again. All at once my lip became a persistent throb, reminding me of the pain from my fangs punching out. I dragged a finger along the edge of my mouth. It came away sticky, warm, and wet. When startled, I had zero control of the things. It was embarrassing.

Teddy tucked a clean napkin into my palm and pulled me close to whisper, "You shouldn't be wasting blood when you refuse to drink it."

His hot breath warmed my neck and tickled my ear. The heady mixture of woods, earth, and vanilla—Teddy's distinct scent—filled my nostrils, made me dizzy. Something melted and puddled in my core. My gaze fastened on the way my dark red hair danced with his bourbon-brown strands. The way they both brushed against the hard line of muscle leading from his neck to his shoulder.

Damn it.

That delicious scent shouldn't be so strong. My olfactory sense was the same as any other fae, unless I'd smelled their blood. Then again, with the amount of brawls Teddy broke up in this joint, he was bound to have bled at some point.

I stepped away and scowled in a desperate attempt to hide my reaction. "And you should mind your own business." What was wrong with me lately? I'd known the guy for years, but recently Teddy seemed more flirt than friend. I felt disgustingly girly when he got near.

"Whatever you say, sweet fangs." He chucked a knuckle under my chin, letting it linger long enough to turn the gesture from playful to intimate.

I rubbed my chin on my shoulder. This was Teddy. He couldn't possibly be flirting. He'd known me since I roared into Interlands at fifteen with way more balls and bravado than sense. More importantly, I wasn't his type—empty headed and easy.

He swaggered toward the end of the bar, and some mysterious magnetic force pulled my appreciative gaze to the way he filled out his denim. My view disappeared as he stepped behind the counter. When I looked up, Teddy watched me with a knowing grin. I bared my fangs. He laughed.

I growled under my breath and turned to leave as he circled the bar and headed for the spot across the counter from me.

"Why take these jobs, Lane? They're bad. You're so much more than this."

Teddy's earnest words stopped me, and I looked back. His bottomless black gaze gripped mine.

My chest tightened. Teddy didn't know how misplaced his faith in me was. I grabbed a freshly filled tumbler full of amber liquid from the bar.

"Hey!" The owner of the drink turned, opened his mouth to say more, and laid eyes on me. I raised my brows in a dare. The guy wisely spun to face the bar and tapped the counter, ordering a new drink for himself.

"Because I'm really, really good at it. Besides, haven't you heard?" I slammed my confiscated drink. The taste of gasoline chasing cinnamon scorched a path down my throat. My nostrils burned and eyes watered. I shoved down the sensation and flashed a smile filled with a whole lot of fang. "I'm a bad girl."

With that mic drop moment, I turned away from the bar prepared to swagger my sweet ass out the door and instead came nose to leather-clad chest. I stumbled back and focused on the crest pinned to the left pectoral area of the moon fae who wore it. A silver moon, intersecting a gold sun, with a tree rising in front of both—the Royal Fae Guard insignia. Or since that was more breath wasted on fae who didn't deserve it, the RFG.

"Duskmere," I said and straightened.

"Malaney Callaghan, there is no bad. There is no good. There simply is."

What was with the self-help, infomercial crap? "Don't waste your philosophy lessons here. I don't give a damn what anyone thinks of me."

His silver eyes tightened. Duskmere was all hard angles and sharp lines, just like his personality. Narrow face, slashing cheekbones, the elongated points to his ears, even the way his lips compressed into a razor's edge. His spiky, close-cropped silver hair didn't dare have a strand out of place. He nodded to an occupied booth near the door and headed that way, not waiting to see if I followed.

I blew an angry breath from my nose and stomped after the moon fae.

Duskmere stared down the patrons in the booth. Judging by the two empty pitchers on the table, the trio were deep in their cups but not so far gone to miss the lethal energy emanating from the moon fae. They quickly scooted from the benches. I grabbed a half empty mug from one of the former booth occupants as he passed. He glanced at me and kept moving.

With a sigh, I slid onto the still-warm seat and waited for Duskmere to settle across from me.

He set his elbows on the tabletop, leaned forward, and wasted no time getting down to business. "Once you have captured the banshee, Etta'wy, you will bring her to us."

I barked a laugh. "I'll do no such thing."

"You will."

"Uh, no, I won't." I held out a fist and flipped up the index finger. "First, you're RFG, so by use of the royal 'us,' you mean the sun fae. There is no scenario where I help them."

He opened his mouth to respond, but I continued and popped a second finger.

"Second, Etta'wy is a job. Someone hired my sisters and me. That someone is paying us to bring her in, so they're the one we'll be delivering her to." I held up another finger. "Third, since you didn't seem to hear me the first time, I will never help the sun fae."

"I am aware you were hired by the banshee's husband. He has agreed to allow for delivery to us in his stead. We will pay your fee."

"Nope." I slapped my palms down on the tabletop and pushed to my feet. "I'd say sorry you wasted your time, but I'm not. See ya around."

Duskmere surged from the booth and grabbed my elbow. He leaned close, voice going low. "The sun stones have been stolen."

"So? Get some more."

"You misheard," Duskmere said. "The sun stones have been stolen. The stones. The source. There will be no more shards."

A slush of ice coursed through my veins, and my nostrils flared on a sharp inhale. I met his pounded steel gaze.

"The banshee was involved. It is imperative we question her. The stones must be found."

I didn't know Duskmere well, but he'd always been a stoic, by-the-books prick who never showed emotion. The desperation, the intensity of his plea punched me in the gut.

"That, I am sorry for, but I'm not the one you should be asking for help." I swallowed and turned to focus on the door. Escape. "Good luck."

"There are many things said about you, but petty was not among them." I sneered at his insult, and Duskmere's grip tightened. "You issue a death sentence with your refusal."

"Doubtful. This is a sun fae problem we're talking about. They're resilient. They don't need me."

"Sun fae problems affect all fae." He tilted his head. "You're fae."

Something bitter and vile twisted inside of me. I clenched my fists on my thighs.

"I think the word you're looking for is abomination. Monster is a popular choice. Or you could be trying for something fancy like mistake of nature. I've heard them all."

"Perhaps there is something wrong with my hearing." Duskmere's voice came at me soft and sly. "I thought you said you do not care what anyone thinks of you."

My stomach clenched. I looked up and let him see everything in my mismatched eyes—one black, one violet. Eyes which forever set me apart. All the rage, all the pain, the black hole of sadness I would never escape no matter how much I lied and told myself I didn't care.

"Trust me, even if the sun fae did need me, they wouldn't want my help. They would rather die than accept anything from the likes of me. Who's the petty ones in this situation? Good luck, Duskmere," I said again, and this time I meant it. I could at least give him that.

The moon fae's hand dropped from my elbow. Ignoring the way his gaze went dull, I turned away and headed for the exit. Time was ticking. Getting hijacked by Duskmere had eaten up twenty minutes of my deadline with Rip.

With every step I took toward the doors, away from Duskmere, fae problems slid from my conscience.

Outside, the stale afternoon air filled my lungs. I slipped on my sunglasses and smiled. This was going to be easy money.

My feet hit the cobbled sidewalk that ran along the front of the bar as the door swished open behind me and heavy footsteps followed onto the wood porch. "Hold up, sweet fangs."

I froze, a snake of anticipation coiling around my spine, pulling it taught. If I didn't shake this reaction I'd been having to Teddy, I'd have to move my place of business. He was less eye candy these days and more serious distraction.

Warm fingers gripped my elbow. They glided to my hand, engulfing it, and he tugged me around to face him. "That moon fae giving you trouble?"

He didn't drop my hand and heat bloomed up my arm from his touch. I licked my lips. "Nothing I can't handle."

Teddy's head dipped closer to mine, and the smile that curved his lips was nothing short of criminal. The mouth-watering scent of musky forest and sweet vanilla teased the knots from my back that the encounter with Duskmere created. Anticipation left my spine to settle in my chest, pressure shortening my breath. His lips brushed my ear, and goosebumps skittered across my neck, tickling my scalp.

"I know," he said and chuckled. The soft laughter fluttered my hair, and my lips parted at the airy caress. Still gripping my hand, he straightened. "But I'm here for you if you ever need me. You know that, right?"

Damn, it was hot out here, or was that just my proximity to this male? Nothing rattled me, except a nice ass and devilish dark eyes, apparently. Seven years I'd known Teddy, and suddenly my hormones decided to have a party and issue him an invitation.

"I heard the job Rip is sending you on." Teddy released my hand at last and leaned against a porch post. "He wasn't wrong. There's more to those guys than size indicates. You want back up? Zee's here and it's slow, I can take a break."

"Thanks, but I've been doing this for a while. I think I know what I'm doing." I ran a hand over the hairs escaped from my loose braid, tucking several behind my still-tingling ears.

"I have no doubt that you do. Just offering a helping hand. Remember, grounders are really sensitive about their fur." He winked and strolled back into the bar.

"What the hell does that mean?" I shouted at the swinging door and rubbed at the suspicious vacancy the evaporated pressure left in my chest.

Don't stop now. Keep reading with your copy of BAD GIRLS DRINK BLOOD by City Owl Author, S.L. Choi.

Don't miss more urban fantasy with BAD GIRLS DRINK BLOOD by City Owl Author, S.L. Choi.

Jessica Moore only has five days to catch a killer.

Thanks to a goblin's curse, Jessica gets a magical high from humanity's suffering. While the guilt of thriving on misery could bury a girl, she atones by using her power to hunt the bad guys—until one of them frames her for his crimes.

In desperation, Jessica seeks refuge with the one person she trusts—a satyr named Lucen. Like every member of his paranormal race, Lucen uses his lusty magic to control Boston's human population, and Jessica isn't immune to his power.

But the murder victims belong to a rival race, and when they discover Lucen is harboring Jessica, dodging the cops becomes the least of her problems.

With time running out, Jessica faces a danger every bit as serious as the brewing magical war—succumbing to Lucen's seductive power. Will their tenuous relationship survive, or will more misery prevail?

Please sign up for the City Owl Press newsletter for chances to win special subscriber-only contests and giveaways as well as receiving information on upcoming releases and special excerpts.

All reviews are **welcome** and **appreciated**. Please consider leaving one on your favorite social media and book buying sites.

For books in the world of romance and speculative fiction that embody Innovation, Creativity, and Affordability, check out City Owl Press at www.cityowlpress.com.

ACKNOWLEDGMENTS

In 2022, in just a few short months, I lost two women who meant the world to me: my mother Shirley and my "second mom" Jacque, who was the mother of my best friend Stacey. To say these losses upended my world would be an understatement. Even now, months later, I'm still processing my grief. Above all else, however, I am so very grateful to both my mom and Jacque for everything they did for me throughout my life to shape the person I've become and support my dream of becoming an author. Thank you both for everything, from the bottom of my heart.

As always, I am supremely thankful for my lovely and brilliant editor Heather at City Owl Press, who in addition to her usual editorial duties also pinch-hits as a part-time therapist and cheerleader, and even a hangover nurse when her author has a bit too much...ahem, *fun* at the writer retreat. Many thanks also to the Dynamic Duo of Tina and Yelena at City Owl for all they do getting our books into the hands of the readers who want them.

It's no secret I adore Felicity Munroe, audiobook narrator extraordinaire. She doesn't just read or even narrate my Alice Worth books—she brings all the characters to life! From danger addict Alice to snarky Malcolm and sexy Sean and all the rest, they come to life thanks to Felicity's incredible talent and acting. Every day I count all my lucky stars that she narrates my books. I hope I didn't use up all my good karma scoring her as my narrator, but if I did, I'm fine with it. Thank you for being your awesome self, Felicity!

Super-duper thanks to my part-time PA and author wrangler Joie. I'm a hot mess but she's doing her darnedest to help me keep it all together. Please be aware that all mistakes, dropped balls, snafus, and disasters are of my own making and should not be attributed to Joie, who no doubt did her best to prevent them.

Speaking of author wrangling and part-time therapist duties, many thanks to my long-suffering friend and alpha reader Dr. Marie Guthrie, who does all that and more. Thanks as well to my trusty squad of beta readers, including Luna Joya, Shannon Butler, Stacey Kelley, Dr. Adrienne Foreman, Carla Ruehl, and Dr. Robert James. Carla also deserves extra-special thanks for continuing to provide background information and insights on witchcraft and magickal practice.

All my love to my sister Susan Michelle Edmonds, my brother-in-law Josh, my niece and nephew Lexi-Lou and Madden, my sisters-in-law Jenn and Amy, and my cousins Antoinette and Felicia. We're a strange family, but we're a lot of fun.

And finally, and most importantly, I'm forever and ever grateful for the love and support of my hubby Bill, who's been through a lot with me and for some reason seems to want to stick around. You're my favorite traveling companion, my love. Let's see the rest of the world together.

ABOUT THE AUTHOR

LISA EDMONDS was born and raised in Kansas, and studied English and forensic criminology at Wichita State University. After acquiring her Bachelor's and Master's degrees, she considered a career in law enforcement as a behavioral analyst before earning a Ph.D. in English from Texas A&M University. She is currently an associate professor of English at a college in Texas and teaches both writing and literature courses. When not in the classroom, she shares a quiet country home with  her husband Bill D'Amico and their cats, and enjoys writing, reading, traveling, spoiling her nephew, and singing karaoke.

Want an exclusive look at the playlists for the Alice Worth novels? Check out her website: www.lisaedmonds.com

And be sure to find Lisa Edmonds across social media.

f facebook.com/Edmonds411

X x.com/Edmonds411

instagram.com/edmonds411

ABOUT THE PUBLISHER

City Owl Press is a cutting edge indie publishing company, bringing the world of romance and speculative fiction to discerning readers.

Escape Your World. Get Lost in Ours!

www.cityowlpress.com

facebook.com/CityOwlPress

x.com/cityowlpress

instagram.com/cityowlbooks

pinterest.com/cityowlpress

tiktok.com/@cityowlpress